Thieves' Honor

A Novel By
David Combs

ISBN-13: 978-1-7350034-2-9

DEDICATION

To Sarah, Emma, and Libby

CHAPTER ONE

The young woman fell back towards the great picture window as blood gushed through her fingers from the tear in her throat. She slipped in the widening, crimson pool at her feet, and crashed to the floor. Her free hand trembled as she tried in vain to pull herself to her knees with the corner of the nearby ancient desk, but her legs buckled again. As her sight dimmed, she attempted to focus on something, anything, to keep herself conscious. Her failing vision fell upon the hellish red glow of the eyes that watched her from the far corner of the room.

"Why?" she asked. Her voice was nothing more than a hoarse croak. She shivered uncontrollably and could see her shallow breaths in the chilled air as her attacker casually approached. "Why me?"

Cold, hissing laughter floated out of the darkness. "Do not flatter yourself, my child. There is nothing at all special about you. You are simply one more piece, one more pawn in a far grander scheme. Soon, everyone in the great port city of Tarnath shall kneel, and call me master."

The girl felt the brush of an icy finger caress her cheek to wipe away her tears, although she saw nothing reach towards her. She recoiled from the touch just the same though and collapsed in the bright light of the pale moon that still hung low in the early evening sky. The shadowy figure drew closer, knelt beside her, and pulled her into his arms just as he had done earlier. He savored toying with her, relished the thrill of a predator stalking prey. She looked again into the gleaming red of his eyes, becoming lost in their swirling depths. As she spiraled into darkness, the pain of two tiny needles stabbed into the flesh of her neck. She scratched at her attacker, but she was far too weak, and he was far too strong.

The shadowy form soon dropped her lifeless body to the floor. Standing to his full height he basked in the glow of the moon as the woman's warm blood rushed through his veins. The moonlight stretched forth, like pale fingers caressing an unsuspecting victim, over the lavish furnishings he had brought with him. These personal belongings predated many of the mightiest cities in Belynna, and some were even older than the fallen Thelvenin Empire of the elves.

He knew that the moonlight signaled the start of the real action in the city of Tarnath. Although empty to the naked eye, he saw the alleys full of common thieves, derelicts, and other lost souls of the night doing whatever they must in order to survive another day. The Lords' Council called them a "blight on the face of a magnificent city".

He called them prey.

He opened the heavy window with a casual push and leaned forward to smell the night air. The scent of potential victims teased his heightened senses. His eyes gleamed with their blood-red light. "Soon, I will have everything ready to set into motion. Then Tarnath will belong to me." A chilling laugh like a hissing wind echoed through the dark alley below.

A gentleman walking by pulled his cloak tight against himself when a sudden icy gust blew through the streets as if something had soared overhead at a terrific speed. Yet, all that he saw was an open empty window above him. He wondered for just a moment what a thief might find if he were to go inside that house, but a sudden shiver raced down his spine. He quickened his steps and dismissed the thought from his mind.

The moonlight watched over the room, keeping a silent vigil over the corpse of the young girl. Her body was the only evidence of the danger that awaited the city.

The hunt had begun.

*   *   *

The grappling hook sailed through the night air and caught the balcony rail on the first throw. The darkness came alive as a cloaked figure raced up the rope with the skill of a spider on a silken thread. As his wiry, athletic frame landed without a whisper of sound on the ledge, Galen Thale pulled the hood away from his curly blond hair and produced a thin wire from the back of his glove. A sparkle filled his blue eyes as he examined the lock on the balcony door. In seconds, the lock was picked with a practiced ease that suggested that Galen was far older than his mere eighteen summers.

Among the thieves of Tarnath, Galen Thale was unanimously regarded as a reckless, daring, and unbelievably foolish rogue. He was an inspiration to the new recruits and an irritation to the guild masters. The fact that he had never once been caught, however, had earned him a certain measure of leniency. He had never been so much as suspected for some of the most lucrative heists of his thieving career. His purpose here tonight was more daring than any other caper he had ever pulled off and would earn him the undisputed reputation as the greatest thief in the entire city. Tonight, the prized and fabled jewel collection of Lord Adolphinus Merkalan, Finance Minister of the City Governance, would be his.

It had taken Galen three weeks of eavesdropping, bribing, and casing the manor, but he had finally learned where in this magnificent estate the legendary jewels were kept. More importantly, he knew that the entire Merkalan household had left the city three days past for an extended tour of the Eastern Realms. Galen couldn't understand any man's desire to travel across the blasted wasteland of the Fire Plains rather than sailing west across the Dharvastian Sea, but the nobleman's travel arrangements held but one real significance to him. Lord Merkalan flaunted his fortune at every opportunity, so he had taken nearly all of his household guards, servants, and retainers with him. His glorious treasures were left safeguarded by only a few remaining soldiers who had not been included in the nobleman's entourage.

As Galen crept carefully along the hallway's plush carpeting, he figured that his only real concern this night was running afoul of the "Dockside Slayer" who had terrorized the dock ward these past few weeks and had caused more of the "low life scum" to disappear without a trace. The city watch was completely baffled, without so much as a single clue about who might be responsible for these disappearances.

Galen pushed such thoughts out of his head. He wasn't afraid. The young thief was the self-proclaimed master of the shadows in Tarnath. If anyone invaded the dark places that he called home, then Galen was prepared to rudely throw the offender out.

The young burglar padded softly down the hallway, ignoring the doorways that lined the long corridor. The gallery he sought was located all the way down at the far end of this hall. The rooms around him were merely bedrooms and private chambers for Merkalan and his family, all of which were now conveniently empty. Although they doubtlessly held stores of wealth in their own right, such baubles would pale in comparison to what he was here for.

The thief paused at the top of a great marble staircase that split the hallway. He listened to the bored and sleepy voices of a few of the remaining guards that drifted up to him from below. The soldiers had no reason to suspect that an intruder was about and certainly expected no trouble tonight. With any luck, thought Galen, I'll be long gone with the jewels before they even think to patrol this wing.

He quickly crept past the stairs towards the entrance to the Grand Gallery but stopped about fifteen feet away from the archway. Galen studied the wall to wall rug that covered the wood floor before him. As he gingerly lifted the corner, his trained eyes caught the telltale outline of a pressure plate concealed in the planks. It was a good and effective trap, he mused, but one that was only likely to catch a novice. Galen pressed himself tightly against the wall edging his way past the device.

A careful examination of the gem-studded arch yielded the next line of Merkalan's defenses. A thin wire ran across the portal at ankle height. Galen followed the wire to a cleverly concealed trigger mechanism for three dart traps whose missiles would fire out of hollow false gems on the archway's side. The thief smiled as he cut the wire with a razor-sharp dagger. It was truly a wonder that the gems had remained in Merkalan's possession this long, he thought.

Galen sucked in his breath at the sight of the treasures before him as he entered the chamber. Sculptures from the renowned dwarven stoneworkers of the Southern Reach sat on pedestals of the finest marble. Gemstone eyes stared eternally from solidly fixed gold and platinum settings. Paintings in gilded frames by some of the greatest artists ever to hold a brush adorned the walls. Masterful portraits appeared so lifelike that one could almost believe someone else stood in the room beside them. Colorful landscapes were so vibrant that you could almost smell honeysuckle in bloom. Any one of these works could have made a thief wealthy beyond his imagination, and allow him to live out the rest of his days in comfort.

Galen Thale wanted none of it.

He moved quickly and quietly to the rear wall of the chamber. The young cutpurse had learned that the secret door to Merkalan's vault was hidden here. The entire wall was one massive mural depicting the greatest battles in Belynna's history. Armies marched around burning cities in the eastern lands. Another panel showed the siege of nearby Shorassos, where the surrounded city found victory after feigning surrender to the Warlords of Daltivar. Centuries of history fanned out before Galen, but his focus was elsewhere.

The thief soon found the nearly invisible crease of the door, concealed within a scene of an elven knight bearing a gleaming sword driving back some shadowy horror into the depths of a cave. Galen suddenly shivered and found himself drawn to the image. He thought for one moment that he could actually feel the hatred that burned from within the evil creature's glowing red eyes.

He smiled in spite of himself. Still young enough to enjoy children's bedtime tales of heroes and monsters, yet skilled enough to break into the home of one of Tarnath's leading citizens. Galen's smile widened as he located a pressure stone on the floor. One final survey of the panel assured him that there were no traps to be found, so he stepped lightly on the trigger. Soundlessly, the door to the jewel vault of the Merkalan's opened for him.

If the treasures of the gallery had impressed Galen, he was even more so by the appearance of the vault. The jewels rested on fine satin pillows inside a case of clear crystal. The rogue stared in awe of rubies the size of apples, diamonds the size of goose eggs, and emeralds easily as large as his fist. Taking a deep breath, he whispered a prayer to the patron god of cutpurses then pulled a glasscutter from one of his many pouches. He set the blade against the case and ran it over the crystal with a faint squeak.

The surface didn't even show a scratch.

He tried again, believing that perhaps he hadn't applied enough pressure to the instrument. Galen winced at the resounding squeal his tool made, and he spared a glance over his shoulder to make certain that he was still alone. As he examined the case his jaw dropped open when he saw that, as before, no mark had been made.

Galen ran his hand through his hair in frustration. "Guess we'll just have to do this the hard way," he muttered. He drew his sword, closed his eyes, and then slammed the hilt of his weapon down on the case as hard as he could. A spider web of cracks shot across the crystal, but still, the case held. He heard distant shouts of alarm from somewhere downstairs and knew that his time was running short.

He was sweating now. Once again, he slammed his sword onto the case. This time the heavy crystal seemed to shimmer for a moment and quivered from the blow. Purely on instinct, Galen ducked. He rolled away just as the jewel case exploded, sending knife-like shards out in every direction.

Galen quickly dusted himself off, wincing at the few minor cuts he had suffered. Long slivers of crystal stood out from the walls where they had embedded themselves like a volley of arrows. With a sigh, the thief realized how fortunate he was that he hadn't been slashed to ribbons. Time was precious now, and he knew that he had only moments before the house soldiers arrived. With caution abandoned, he grabbed a monstrous diamond from the pillow and stuffed it into a sack. He barely noticed the faint puff of yellow dust and the faint smell of rotten eggs that rose up from the disturbed pillow. Instantly, he realized his new danger, for sulfur was always a prime ingredient in fire magic. He turned to run, praying that he could escape before the protective magic was released.

His world exploded in a blast of heat and flame, which hurled him across the main gallery, and slammed him against the far wall. The very air scorched his lungs as the inferno raged around him. He tried to stand as he gasped for air, but he hurt too badly to pull himself up. The ringing in his ears, however, did not muffle the stamping sound of booted feet closing in around him.

As he finally pushed himself to his hands and knees, a steel-tipped boot caught him solidly in the ribs, rolling the thief against a hard marble pedestal. The sculpture upon it crashed to the ground and shattered. When he looked up, Galen Thale saw a guard with the arms of the Merkalan family proudly emblazoned on his breast pointing a loaded crossbow at his face.

*   *   *

Lightning flashed from the young wizard's fingertips as the electric bolt tore through the ranks of the giant, brutish, yellow-skinned humanoids. Those beasts that survived scampered for the cover of the forest intent on seeking out less dangerous prey for their supper. The smoke on the battlefield shimmered, and the forest glade returned once again to the dining hall of Lord Tantros Kandlemeer. Servants ran to fill wine glasses and empty plates while the dinner guests' eyes were riveted on the robed man who stood at the end of the long table.

He stood with his hands raised into the air. Motes of light twinkled like tiny stars around his gloved fingertips. Aside from the effects of age, he was identical to the wizard in the illusion. The thick, brown hair now showed the slightest hint of gray at the temples. The smooth face bore a few more creases. He regarded his audience with his glittering eyes, one green and the other brown, that showed more wisdom than had those of the illusory mage. His build was unusual for a student of magic, as his well-defined frame pressed against the fabric of his sky blue robe.

The mage lowered his consciousness from the first level of magical power, returning to the "real" world. The lure of higher levels and increasingly greater power always sang to him when he worked his castings, but he knew too well the dangers that could lie within. Finally, after a dramatic pause, he spoke with a strong and captivating voice that drew in everyone in the large banquet chamber.

"In desperation, I showered the bloodthirsty kargs with bolts of lightning. The farmers were spared from future attacks, and prosper in that valley to this day." The wizard bowed deeply to the sudden burst of applause the audience gave him. He then looked to the far end of the table where, in a massive chair, sat the even more massive nobleman, Tantros Kandlemeer. The fat man pulled himself from his seat and regarded the wizard silently. Then, he let out a great, booming laugh, and clapped the fellow seated beside him on the back with enough force to cause his guest's beard to flop into his soup.

"Did ye see the way the beasties ran?" Kandlemeer clapped his meaty hands together. "Tyrell Amalcheal," he said as he addressed the wizard, "as always, you have proven yourself to be as great a showman as you are a sorcerer. Sit down, my friend, and let us continue the feast, yes?" The man snapped his fingers at the musicians who struck up a merry dancing tune.

Tyrell smiled graciously, although he knew he was in no way 'friend' to Kandlemeer. He was nothing more than another servant. Rather than toting trays of meat or flagons of ale though, he was the pet wizard hired only to amuse the haughty aristocracy at gatherings such as this. He sighed. At least he was paid well enough for his efforts.

The mage moved gracefully to his seat between two gentlemen of Tarnath. Pompous, self-serving fools would be more accurate, he thought to himself. He forced a smile to the man on his left. The silly little fop had been so deep in his cups all night that a ladder couldn't rescue him. The young dandy, some petty duke or another, had pestered him all evening long with tiresome question after question regarding magic, adventures, the general state of the city, and who among the serving maids was the most attractive. Tyrell had actually complimented himself on his remarkable sense of self-control. He had so far restrained himself from tugging the fool's ridiculous cap down over his head and tying it closed with a piece of the man's own silken cape. *I swear,* he mused as he sipped his wine, *if he tugs at my sleeve once more I am going to recommend to his lordship that he venture to the docks, and take a lengthy stroll off of one of the shorter piers.*

Tyrell felt a sharp tug at his sleeve.

He turned slowly with his teeth clenched in what he hoped resembled a smile and faced the young lord. The man nearly tottered off of his chair as he struggled to focus on the wizard with his glassy eyes.

"Nice show," he said. It came out more like 'Nisshhh shhow'. "Do you really expect anybody to believe it? I mean, if yer such a great magishun, why are you workin' a dinner party. You could just magic up all the money you want." The young duke belched loudly in his face, and the stench of potent spirits caused the wizard's mismatched eyes to water.

The mage grimaced at the blunt question. The truth was that Tyrell was a far better storyteller than sorcerer. He looked down at the leather gloves he always wore and thought about the one and only time that he had opened himself to the level of magic required to throw bolts of lightning from his fingers. All too clearly, the memories of the flames, exploding chemicals, the smell of burning flesh, and the screams of the dying filled his mind. He clenched his fists unconsciously, envisioning in his mind's eye the network of crisscrossed burn scars that covered his hands. Since that horrible day, he had contented himself only with lesser magic and illusions rather than risk drawing on a power that he couldn't control.

Tyrell glared at the young noble and tried to carefully word his response so that he wouldn't have to admit his shame to the likes of this audience. *I swear,* he mused to himself for the dozenth time tonight, *that* meeting one of Alhambra's demonic minions would be more pleasant than working as a nobleman's pet wizard. At least the demon would have the courtesy to eventually rip him apart.

"Frankly," said the wizard, "I found adventuring to be a bit too dangerous for the money. Too much risk for too little reward. I was making only slightly more than when I was living on the streets, so I decided to turn my talents to something more profitable." He whirled around suddenly to the man on his other side, hoping to strike up a conversation before the little fop could continue his drunken tirade. His other neighbor, however, was so engrossed in his dinner that he was face down in his plate. An echoing snore bubbled its way through the congealed gravy on the serving dish.

There was another tug on his sleeve. Tyrell slowly turned, frustration and rage boiling beneath his glare. "What," he snapped.

"Yer too court-like to have lived in the streets." The duke hiccupped and wobbled, but to Tyrell's chagrin, he just wouldn't pass out. If I were a real wizard, he thought, I'd turn this little toad into something nice and quiet, like a rock.

"I grew up in the streets of Daltivar and learned sleight of hand tricks to keep myself fed. I was fortunate enough to have caught the attention of a wizard who was so impressed with my aptitude that he offered me an apprenticeship. I learned enough to start adventuring, but shortly left my company, and began to work for nobility. That's my story, here I am, and if you'll be so good as to excuse me, I think I see someone more important than you that I want to talk to." The wizard jumped from his seat and pushed his way through the assemblage towards the far end of the table. Tyrell swore a silent oath to Taradon, the patron deity of wizards. Even speaking to Lord Kandlemeer wasn't as annoying as listening to that little twit. Hells, he thought. I could be gnawed upon by a toothless dragon, and wouldn't feel so annoyed. Tyrell couldn't help but smile in spite of himself.

The wizard hoped to pass by the chair of his employer unnoticed, but fortune apparently still had some bone to pick with him this night. "Tyrell," called the fat nobleman, "you should've just heard the tale told by this good, worthy gentleman." Kandlemeer slapped his neighbor again on the shoulder, sloshing wine all over his immense tunic. The wizard sympathized with the gentleman beside his employer. From the expression of pain on his face, Tyrell assumed that Kandlemeer had given him so many good-natured slaps to the back that the man wouldn't have the use of his arm for days.

Tyrell bowed. "Lord Kandlemeer, you've given an . . . unforgettable party as always, but I believe that I shall now re-." The mage was suddenly interrupted by a tugging at his sleeve. Please, gods, he begged, don't let it be a drunken, petty noble who can barely hold on to his wine cup. He slowly turned around.

It was a drunken, petty noble who promptly spilled the contents of his wine cup on Tyrell's boots. "Show me a trick. I don't think you can fool me," said the swaying lordling. He pulled a ring bearing the crest of some noble house, presumably his own, from his belt pouch. "Make this disappear."

Kandlemeer roared with a belly shaking laugh, and slapped the table so hard that plates leaped into guests' laps. "Yes, Tyrell, my friend, please amaze us with one last trick at Lord Tessarin's request. One final stunt before ye leave us for the evening." A crowd had begun to form around the wizard.

Tyrell smiled weakly and bowed to his patron. He took the ring from Tessarin, studying it carefully. "I'd rather make you disappear, you little fiend," he muttered.

"Speak up so we can hear you, lad," bellowed Kandlemeer.

Tyrell cleared his throat. "I will now make this disappear, if you know what I mean," he said. He elbowed the young duke in the ribs, making sure to add just a little extra force just for his own satisfaction. Tyrell smiled, and with a dramatic wave of his hands, he palmed the ring, tucking it into his sash, and out of the audience's sight. It was a very simple trick, but Tyrell figured that this drunken crowd would be none the wiser.

He nearly laughed out loud at the gasps of genuine amazement when he opened his empty hands. Tessarin's jaw dropped to his chest as he looked back and forth for his missing ring. The crowd pressed close, jostling Tyrell roughly as they strained to see.

"Bring it back now," yelled Tessarin. "That's my family's signet ring." The duke looked as though he were about to burst into tears. The crowd laughed at Tessarin's outburst.

"Of course, Lord Tessarin," said Tyrell. He waved his hands again, reaching into his sash with a casual pass. This night couldn't possibly get any worse, the mage thought.

He was wrong.

Tessarin's ring was gone. Tyrell quickly patted his waist to see if the ring had shifted, and then searched on the floor in case it had fallen out, but he saw no trace of the missing bauble.

"Is something wrong, Tyrell?" asked Kandlemeer in a low voice.

"Of course not, my lord," replied the wizard. He forced a smile. "I'm only building up dramatic suspense." The audience laughed again, but Tyrell was sweating now. Someone had to have stolen the ring from him when the crowd jostled him. These dinner parties were notorious gatherings for pickpockets. He studied the press of people, but couldn't begin to guess who the thief might have been. He had to do something.

"Where's my damn ring," growled Tessarin, who was suddenly

more sober than he had been all night long.

"My lord," said Tyrell slowly, "I beg your pardon, but your ring is no longer where I placed it. I don't know if I dropped it, or if it was stolen from me, but I fear I no longer know its whereabouts." Tyrell shrugged and looked to Kandlemeer for help.

Before the wizard could say anything else, Tessarin punched Tyrell squarely in the face, knocking him into the waiting arms of one of Lord Kandlemeer's house guards. Before the wizard could protest, the armored man clubbed him in the back of the head with a mailed fist, and Tyrell plunged into darkness.

*   *   *

Coins clattered onto the table. "I'll raise you forty royals," said the red-bearded warrior, "and I suggest you get out while you can, friend. I may be from a barbarian tribe, but Nestor Canaith is civilized enough to know when he's got someone beaten so badly that he offers them mercy." Clad in rugged leather armor, and bulging with battle-hardened muscles, the hulking Nestor looked at the King's Cycle he held in his hands, the second best outcome in the game of Tharot. The young gambler across from him had played a charmed game all evening, but Nestor couldn't lose this hand. More importantly, the money he would win would more than pay his debt to the church of Kuriathor, the god of chance.

Nestor's hand touched the pouch of shattered crystal that hung from his waist. The god of fortune had certainly abandoned him after he had accepted the task of carrying a precious sculpture from the dockyard to the church. It was bad enough that he had dropped the fragile treasure, but to have dropped it right at the feet of the church Patriarch was even worse. He still didn't understand why he had to carry the pieces around with him until he could compensate the church though. 'Luck will provide' indeed. He sighed.

The barbarian's opponent studied his cards and then threw his money into the center of the table. "Let's see what you've got."

Nestor smiled as he laid out his hand. "Looks like this round is mine, Count Remen." The barbarian started to rake the money to him when his opponent put down his cards.

"I don't think so, Redbeard." Nestor's smile melted when he saw the natural King's Blade, the highest hand in the game. "Guess your luck just wasn't here tonight, my friend." The count laughed as he drew the money to him. The nobleman pulled out a leather pouch, shoveling his winnings into it.

Nestor was in shock. What in Alhambra's Hells was he supposed to do now? He winced in defeat as Remen left the table with the jingling pouch full of coins in his hand. The warrior slammed back the rest of his drink, and let the liquor burn his throat as he pondered what to do next. Suddenly, his break came.

A large, drunken patron rose from his chair just as Count Remen passed by, and knocked the nobleman to the ground. Remen's money pouch landed a few feet from Nestor. Quickly, the barbarian scooped up the Count's pouch, tucking it away while he replaced it with his own pouch of broken crystal. He approached Remen, who had been helped to his feet by the offending man.

"You should be more careful about throwing your money around, my lord," said Nestor. He gave the pouch an appreciative jingle. "Not all men are as fortunate as you are." The count nodded his thanks and collected his hat as Nestor dashed out the door. He prayed that he would be long gone before his dupe was discovered. Fortune, however, hadn't finished toying with the barbarian.

Nestor was barely ten strides from the tavern door when the cries of "Stop, thief" came from within. Remen barreled out of the door, hurling the pouch of crystal at Nestor's head. The warrior easily ducked the clumsy missile but was unable to dodge Remen's blow to his stomach. Nestor staggered back, and the Count followed up with a solid punch to the side of the barbarian's head. Nestor fell to the ground, but grabbed his attacker's boot, and jerked Remen's feet from under him. The nobleman crashed to the cobbles beside Nestor.

Canaith sprang to his feet again. He tasted blood and dirt on his lips. Remen was up just as quickly and stared boldly at the bigger, stronger man. "Give me back my money, thief. I am not without mercy, and I will let pass this entire incident. Otherwise, you'll hang for this." As the Count shook his fist at the warrior, a card fell from the cuff of his sleeve. Remen stared in stunned silence as the card floated to the ground.

"You cheated me," growled Nestor. "The money is mine by right."

"I don't see it that way. You should have found a way to out cheat me." The Count threw a wide punch, which Nestor easily ducked. The warrior brought his knee into the nobleman's stomach and then fired a crushing blow across the man's jaw. Remen staggered, but when Nestor closed in for a follow-up attack, the aristocrat's knee came up powerfully into the barbarian's groin. "I don't play fair in any sport, friend," he purred into the crouching barbarian's ear. Remen moved to the side of the road, tearing a loose rock from the cobblestone street. "You should learn to admit when you've lost."

"A lesson for us both," snarled Nestor. A dagger flashed in the barbarian's hand and whipped across the distance separating the men. The hilt blasted Remen's nose into a bloody smear. Nestor charged forward, landing another powerful blow that sent the nobleman to the ground once again. The aristocrat's head slammed against the cobbles, and he lay motionless. The barbarian quickly checked to see that the man was still breathing, retrieved his weapon, and turned to run. The last thing he needed now was for any spectators from the tavern to join in.

Nestor spun around to leave the scene, only to find six city guards with swords drawn blocking his path at the end of the street. Fortune, it seemed, had yet to play its last card.

"I don't suppose you'd allow me a head start before you give chase?" he asked. Wordlessly, the soldiers surrounded the warrior and fastened shackles around his wrists. Knowing that resisting arrest would only get him in a worse predicament, Nestor accepted his capture stoically.

Suddenly, a scream broke the relative silence of the night.

The watch sergeant swore. "Take this one in quickly," he said as he jerked his thumb at Nestor. "I'd hoped for a quiet evening, but looks like we've got another Dockside Slaying to deal with tonight."

*   *   *

The shadowy figure closed the windows with no more sound than he made when he stalked his prey. A thin smile creased his face when he licked away the last drops of blood from his lips. All of his plans were proceeding flawlessly. Not that centuries of diligent planning could have any other result, he mused. He thought briefly of his victims from tonight's revels. It was a pity that the last one had been so noisy. He was forced to rush his kill before people came to investigate.

The shadow indifferently noticed that the girl's corpse had been removed as he went into the dark corner near the fireplace, and opened a secret panel there. He descended the stairs that went deep into the bowels of the city, arriving at last to his daily resting place. With the strength of ten men, he moved aside the stone lid of the sarcophagus and crawled inside. Yes, he thought to himself, my plans are proceeding exactly as I had hoped. Soon this wretched city would kneel to him.

"And the best part is just beginning."

CHAPTER TWO

Tyrell awoke with his head resting against a slimy, stone wall. A tiny window in a stout door provided just enough light for him to see that he was in a cell. The close cubicle reeked of human waste, sweat, and blood. A painful rasp of breath from the far corner of the cell drew his attention to the dim outline of a young man curled up on the filthy floor.

"Where are we?" Tyrell asked. The man across the room slowly rolled his head around to face him but was wracked by agonized coughing. The wizard saw dried blood and fresh burns all over his newfound companion. The coughing fit finally passed, allowing the younger man to slowly draw in a breath.

"We are currently enjoying the hospitality of the city dungeons," he croaked. Tyrell crept closer to better see his cellmate. Sweat ran down the man's face as he clenched his teeth in anguish. He held one hand to his ribs while a trickle of blood ran from the corner of his mouth. Even in the low light of the cell, Tyrell could see it was the bright, pink blood of a punctured lung.

"Did they torture you?" asked Tyrell. He tried to pull the young man's hands away from his wounded side, but the mage's cellmate jerked away from him. The pain of the sudden movement nearly caused him to pass out.

"Got kicked in the ribs before I was brought here. The guards weren't exactly gentle or attentive to my injuries on the way to this place.

At least I stopped coughing up blood a little while ago, so there is that. Shame I probably won't be around long enough to join you at the gallows though. Be sure to give my warmest regards to the hangman, and tell him I'm sorry I couldn't attend." He started to chuckle, but the laugh turned into a retching cough.

"Let me see if I can ease your pain," said the wizard. He pushed the younger man's hands away from his side and saw the ugly purple bruise through the tear in his shirt. Tyrell closed his eyes, letting himself fall into the embrace of the magic around him. Carefully, he channeled the energy into the body of his cellmate. As he directed the healing of the shattered rib, the mage felt rather than heard his companion's breathing ease. Tyrell released his hold on the realm of magic, feeling the familiar wave of exhaustion settle over him that came from pushing his skill to the limits of safety. He closed his eyes, stretching out along the cell floor.

The other man rubbed his side, surprised to find that it hardly ached now. Even most of his burns had faded. "Thanks," he said. "I guess now instead of dying in a pool of my own blood, I can have my neck stretched."

"No one ever said there was a good way to die," said Tyrell. He opened his eyes and studied the other man's face. "You seem rather young to be in here. What did you do to attract the hangman's notice?"

"Same thing you did."

A chill ran up Tyrell's spine. "What do you mean?"

"Stealing from an aristocrat is a capital offense. Don't worry though. At least you'll have some company at the gallows pole now."

"I don't suppose anyone would believe me if I said I was innocent, would they?"

"You don't say? Well, there's a twist. We should dash straight up to the Lord Magistrate's office. I'm sure he'll jump to correct this mistake."

The thief snorted. "Forget it, friend. This is a court of law we're dealing with. Whatever made you think they were interested in justice?" He sighed. "All they care about is giving an entertaining public execution from time to time."

"With us as the main attraction."

"Now featuring the notorious Galen Thale, and the ever amazing-" The thief paused, and looked at the mage with his eyebrows raised. He stretched his hand out in mock introduction.

"Tyrell Amalcheal, wizard and soon to be corpse, apparently." He grabbed Galen's hand, shaking it firmly.

"Oh, come on," said Galen with a laugh. "Did you want to live forever?"

"Well, I was somewhat taken with the idea."

"Not me. I think immortality would get boring after awhile. I mean, you can only steal so much treasure, and chase so many barmaids before it becomes a dull routine. Then it starts to seem too much like work." Galen laughed again, and Tyrell found the thief's mirth infectious. Two condemned men laughing in the jail cell must seem insane, the wizard thought, and he laughed harder.

The door suddenly burst open, and soldiers threw a hulking, red-bearded barbarian into the cell. The door slammed shut with a loud bang. "Bastards," roared the barbarian as he hammered his meaty fist against the door with enough force to rattle the planks. "Don't think for a moment that this is finished!" Finally, the newcomer turned and glared at the other men.

"What are you scum staring at?"

"Fellow scum," replied Galen.

"I'm an innocent man, you gutter trash."

"Another one?" Galen grinned at Tyrell. "So, the criminals truly are running the courts. Never saw a jail so full of innocent men. What is this city coming to?"

"Easy, friend." said the wizard. He hoped that the burly warrior didn't hear Galen's comments. "We're-"

"Nestor Canaith is no friend to beggars and thieves."

"Beggars and thieves?" asked Galen incredulously. "We prefer to be known as the League for the Betterment of the Poverty Stricken. As you can see, when our membership is made public, we are treated rather rudely. Seems those with all the money are intent on keeping it for themselves."

Nestor moved with surprising speed for a man of his size. He hauled Galen to his feet, slamming the young thief against the stone wall. Galen's teeth rattled from the jarring impact. "Don't mock me, boy. No one treats me as a fool. No one living, anyway."

"Well, if the boot fits," Galen quipped. He squeezed his eyes shut as Nestor's fist drew back to pound the thief into the wall of the cell. A slender, but strong, hand firmly grabbed the barbarian's wrist. Nestor turned his head and locked stares with the mismatched eyes of the mage.

"You started this quarrel, Redbeard," said Tyrell. "We've all had a rough night, and tomorrow isn't looking any better."

"You may not last even that long," growled the big man. He dropped Galen to the floor and shoved Tyrell back. "Come along then, and take your share if you think you can stand it."

Tyrell whispered some words in the strange language of magic that caused his eyes to glow with illusory flames. Nestor, superstitious as the barbarian people were inclined to be, gasped, and reflexively stepped back from the mage. He tripped over Galen who had crawled behind the distracted barbarian. Nestor wind milled his arms in an attempt to keep his balance, but Tyrell charged forward, driving his shoulder into the warrior's stomach. They both crashed into the wall beyond.

Nestor, however, was a warrior born and bred and he recovered quickly. His stomach was nearly as hard as the stone wall at his back, and easily absorbed the wizard's blow. He grabbed a handful of Tyrell's hair, yanked the man's head back, and slammed his fist into the wizard's throat. The mage fell to his knees, gasping as he struggled to draw breath.

Nestor whirled around, facing off with the young rogue. "Time for yours now, boy!"

Galen had nimbly regained his feet after he had tripped the warrior but now faced the enraged barbarian alone. He knew that he would only get pulverized in a contest of strength against the barbarian, but the thief hoped his speed and agility would keep him out of reach long enough for Tyrell to recover. Only together did they stand a chance of subduing their furious cellmate.

The barbarian launched a barrage of attacks at him, but the nimble young burglar was always a step ahead of each punch. He sidestepped, dodged, and scampered all around the tiny cell. Nestor began to get frustrated but refused to let up. He feigned an attack, as he swung high with his left hand while he readied his right for the real strike. Galen was less trained in the art of fighting and completely missed the ruse. He leaned right into the path of the real punch and staggered as his jaw exploded with pain.

Nestor grabbed the boy by his shirt and kneed the young man in the groin. Then he threw the thief against the wall again. He smiled with satisfaction as Galen's head cracked against the stone, and the younger man's air whooshed from his lungs. The warrior chuckled as he raised his fist. All of the frustration from this night flowed through him. All of his rage channeled into one punch that would pound the younger man's head into the next cell. With a howl of triumph, Nestor let his fist fly.

Galen ducked.

The howl of triumph changed into a howl of pain as the barbarian's hand thudded against the rock wall with a crunch of bone. Galen tried to dive past him, but Nestor brought his good hand down out of pure instinct, clubbing the back of the thief's head. Galen was knocked into the filth and grime on the cell floor. His newly healed ribs screamed out again as Nestor kicked him for good measure.

"You're not finished with me yet, Redbeard," called Tyrell's voice from across the cell. Nestor turned to see the mage standing near the back wall with his arms casually folded across his chest. "If you're through playing around, perhaps you'd like to tackle a foe more your speed."

"I only need one hand for the likes of a dandy like you," snarled the warrior. Tyrell smiled. Nestor fell into a fighting crouch, watching the mage's body language for telltale signs of a dodge. The wizard gave no such indications as he simply stood with arms crossed, and waited for the barbarian to attack. Nestor roared, propelling himself forward into a diving tackle with his powerful legs.

The attack carried him through the illusory wizard, and headfirst into the wall beyond. Nestor crumpled to the floor. He felt as though all of the miners of the Marble Hills hammered away inside of his skull. The room spun and twisted as the warrior tried to correct his vision. His blood roared in his ears with more noise than the great Tieron Falls.

"Trust a barbarian to lead with his head," said Tyrell, as he knelt down beside Galen to check on the thief. Suddenly the cell door burst open as jailers wielding stout clubs filled the tiny cell. "Nice of you gentlemen to arrive," the mage said dryly. One of the guards shrugged as his fellows grabbed Nestor, and hoisted him up.

"Best betting action we've had down here in a long time. I lost ten silvers on the barbarian. What was that little trick you did?"

"Image shift. Made myself appear to be where I wasn't."

"Nice touch," said the guard.

"Thanks." Galen groaned as the mage helped him to sit up. "Are you okay?"

"I'll survive."

"Only until tomorrow," slurred the barbarian as he shook his head to clear it. Nestor was standing but leaned heavily on the door frame. His eyes were glassy, and he was probably seeing double. "As for you, wizard," he spat, "pray that the hangman takes you before I get another chance to play. I won't prove nearly as friendly as he will." A guard shoved Nestor out of the room, and into the hallway beyond. A second jailer helped Galen to his feet and eventually led the young thief out of the cell. The door slammed shut, plunging the chamber into dismal gloom once again.

As the boom of the closed door echoed in the tiny room, Tyrell couldn't help but wonder if the closing of his crypt door would sound any different.

*   *   *

Tyrell opened his eyes as he rolled over in a vain attempt to find a more comfortable position on the cold and slimy stone floor. His entire body ached from tossing and turning on the filthy cobbles. He swallowed what spittle he had to try to slake his thirst only to wince from the leftover bruising from Nestor's punch. He thought briefly about the fate of the other two men. He imagined he would be seeing them soon enough at the gallows. A pity, he thought. I never want to see that red-bearded son of a bitch ever again, even if he is swinging from the end of a rope.

The mage wondered how much time he had left. Would they give him a last meal, or did the city consider that to be a wasted expense on a condemned man? Suddenly, a key rattled in the lock and broke his daydreaming. Tyrell shielded his eyes as a lantern hood was thrown open, and light assaulted the darkness. A large blur blocked the doorway.

"On your feet, Amalcheal," said a gruff voice. Meaty fingers dug into the wizard's arm. Tyrell was pulled to his feet and dragged out of the cell. The torchlight revealed the soldier as a large man, once heavily muscled but now thickening in the middle. The man's close-cropped white hair was slick with sweat, and his stubbly face was creased with lines that hinted to years of duty that bore heavily on this man's shoulders.

A captain's insignia adorned the man's sleeve. The uniform itself looked as though it was the same one that the man had been issued for his first day of duty. Threadbare as it may have been, and straining at the buttons, the soldier's clothing was meticulously clean and implied that this was a man who took his responsibility seriously.

"Is it time already?"

"There seems to have been a slight change of plans," said the Captain. He roughly shoved Tyrell down the hallway, paying no mind that he occasionally bounced the wizard off of the walls. "All I know is that some of the higher-ups aren't pleased about circumstances at all. Someone's orders have spoiled this morning's fun so you get to stay alive for another day. Now shut up, and move."

He led Tyrell up the stone stairs that led from the dungeon to a thick iron door. His escort pounded on the dull metal which was quickly opened by a young soldier who promptly snapped to attention. The mage was ushered down a series of twisting corridors, and then finally outside.

The wizard was surprised to see that it was early evening. Rain fell heavily and obscured vision to just a few dozen feet. The officer half led, half dragged Tyrell through the downpour to a finely polished black coach that waited near the building.

"Get in," growled the officer.

"Where are we going?"

"Just get in. This business would have been over if you three hadn't caused such a fuss last night. We had to move you all one at a time so you wouldn't kill each other along the way. I ought to be out hunting down the Dockside Slayer, but instead, I get to babysit three scoundrels who should've been stretched this morning."

The reference to the investigation was not lost on the wizard. "You are Captain Knarya, I presume." The fat officer just nodded as the coach started rolling. Weary eyes coolly regarded the mage, and Tyrell suspected that this was but one of many long nights that the Captain had recently endured. Knarya's reputation was spotless. He was a man beyond bribery and was well regarded by the aristocracy whom Tyrell associated with. Despite his predicament, the wizard couldn't help but respect the soldier.

"The others are already at our destination?" Tyrell asked as he sank back into the soft cushions of the carriage. The elegance of the vehicle made it obvious that his liberator was someone of means, but it bore no crests to identify to whom it belonged. Tyrell figured that his benefactor was a newcomer to the city.

Knarya nodded again. "We had to rearrange the watch schedule to accommodate this foolishness," he growled. He pulled a flask from his a pocket and took a quick sip. "I had to leave a few of my men with your friends just to make sure that they didn't destroy his lordship's home. If you ask me, they should've just hung the lot of you, and been done with it all. Would have saved everybody a lot of time and trouble, and the City Watch could be attending to more important matters." He took another drink from the flask, then sank into a moody silence.

Tyrell listened to the carriage wheels grate along the streets, studying the fronts of the houses as they rolled by. As the faces of each edifice gradually increased in opulence, he realized that they were moving into what was known as the Jewel Quarter. The ornate gates of homes he had performed in for Tarnath's elite scrolled by the window. It was this section of the city that Tyrell had made his living for some time.

Who would want me out of prison, he thought. And why? Surely not Kandlemeer. He had to have been disgraced by the fact that such a crime had allegedly been committed by one of his own servants. The nobleman had likely confiscated all of Tyrell's possessions as a breach of contract and settlement for Lord Tessarin.

Furthermore, what roles do Galen Thale and Nestor Canaith play in all of this? Someone was going to a lot of trouble to make sure that all three men were brought together for this clandestine meeting. Tyrell shuddered despite himself.

The carriage finally rolled to a stop before a large townhouse that the mage recognized as a temporary estate leased out to visiting nobility. So very unlikely then that my liberator is a native of Tarnath, he mused. Tyrell tried to recall if he had ever entertained any foreign dignitaries well enough to have such a person save his life. None came to mind.

The carriage door opened, and Tyrell was dragged out by two soaked city guards. The soldiers shoved the mage roughly up the stairs to the main door. One man held the mage by the arm while the other pounded loudly on the portal with his fist. The door swung open revealing yet another guard who escorted Tyrell and Knarya into a grand hallway. On either side of the broad chamber, a massive staircase wound up the back wall. Archways beneath the risers on the side walls opened into lavishly decorated chambers, while the rear wall held access doors that provided the house servants to quickly see to a host's needs.

Tyrell was at a loss for what he was expected to do so he waited while Captain Knarya finished giving orders to his soldiers. "Keep two men inside the doors of the foyer, and tell the rest to get back to their watches. I don't imagine that these idiots will cause any more trouble." He turned back to the wizard. "As for us, we wait right here until we are called for, although that shouldn't take long. Ah, here she comes now." Tyrell turned and saw a beautiful, young woman emerge from the archway to his left. Long, coppery curls fell around her shoulders. A modest, yet complimentary gown of deep blue hugged a statuesque frame. Her deep blue eyes twinkled merrily as she approached the wizard.

"You must be the last of them," she said with a welcoming smile. Her voice was musical and alluring.

Tyrell almost felt hypnotized by her beauty. He bowed low before her. "Tyrell Amalcheal, at your ser-." Knarya cuffed the wizard on the back of the head and scowled.

"She knows too well who you are, thief. You're here for business, not pleasure." The officer fired off an angry glare to the two chuckling soldiers who stood at the doorway. "And the two of you may now resume the rest of your post on the other side of those doors. Maybe the rain washing over your heads will clear out some of those vile thoughts." The soldiers saluted dutifully and went to their new assignments.

"I would ask on behalf of the lord of the manor, Captain, that you treat his guests with courtesy and respect. He would take it as a personal affront if this man were to be injured in his home, and I can assure you that he is not the sort of man you wish to offend." She looked to Tyrell. "In fact, I understand that is something of the reason he has asked for you tonight." Knarya mumbled a quick apology and bowed to the lady.

"Thank you for your consideration, Lady...." Tyrell looked at her blankly, which caused her to laugh, and grace him again with her warm smile.

"Lorelei. Lorelei Riadyn, but I am not the Lady of this manor. I must admit that I am merely a servant for His Lordship. Your formality is kind but unnecessary." She looked him over quickly. "You don't appear to be as banged up as the other two were, but a sip of this should ease you a bit." She offered him a small glass with a blue-green liquid. Tyrell recognized the healing elixir immediately and gratefully drank it down. He could feel his aches and pains fade in the potion's restorative warmth.

"I assumed a woman of such grace and elegance to be the lady of the estate. Your master is gracious indeed to provide so well for his servants." He nodded his head in gratitude.

Lorelei took Tyrell by the arm, leading him through the archway into a massive dining room. A long table was filled with dishes and delicacies that made the hungry wizard's mouth water. At one end of the table, Nestor and Galen sat and glared at one another. When Lorelei led the mage in, Galen got to his feet and bowed to her. He winked to Tyrell.

The wizard almost laughed. The three of them were likely living on borrowed time, yet the young thief was trying to impress their hostess. Tyrell allowed Galen to pull out the girl's chair, and he shook hands with the younger man. Nestor simply scowled at the wizard who, as luck would have it, was seated right beside him.

"All right," said Knarya. "Here's the last of them, so let's eat." The officer rubbed his meaty palms together as he tried to decide what to sample first.

"Anxious to get away from barracks food, Captain?" asked Lorelei as she spread a cloth napkin over her lap.

"Actually, Lady, I'm anxious only to quit playing nursemaid to this pack of rogues so that I may get on with my other duties."

"Protecting innocent pantries," quipped Galen. The thief ignored the officer's glare and looked at the wizard. "Nice to see you again, Tyrell. How are you feeling?"

"Better than I have a right to, I suppose. At least I'm still alive." He glanced over at Nestor who was busily tearing at a piece of roast.

"For the moment, wizard. Our game hasn't finished," said the warrior without looking away from his meal.

The mage ignored the threat. "What of our host, lady?" asked Tyrell. "Should we not wait for his arrival, or won't he be joining us?"

"My lord will join us soon. He regrets that he had some other arrangements concerning the release of the three of you that demanded his immediate attention. He sends his apologies but insists that you relax and enjoy his hospitality. To be honest, even I don't see him that much. I arrive in the early evenings, take a tray to his study, chat with him, and then do some cleaning around the house. I feel somewhat guilty over how well he cares for me considering the truly small amount of work that I do for him. However, to a girl who grew up in the streets, and earned her bread by doing whatever chores she could find within the friendlier taverns, I consider myself very lucky."

"Your master is the lucky one to have made such a fine choice," said Tyrell as he raised his glass to her.

"Here, here," added Galen. He smiled as Lorelei blushed, and lowered her eyes.

"My, isn't this cozy," growled Nestor. "Can we dispense with the courtesies, and get down to why we were all brought here? I have some unfinished business I'd like to take care of." The warrior glared at Tyrell while he pointedly twirled a carving knife through his fingers.

"Don't presume that I'm content to allow you to bully me all evening, Canaith. I assure you I'm not in the mood."

"Well, perhaps I am."

"By the way, how's your head?" asked Tyrell in a not so subtle reminder of the outcome of their last fight.

"Besides thick, of course," added Galen. Too late, the young thief realized that he had provoked a situation that was quickly becoming explosive. Nestor stood, kicking his chair away as he appeared ready to leap over the table to get to the cutpurse. Knarya's eyes darted back and forth to the men, realizing that his own men were too far away and out of earshot to help if needed. The captain had seen enough barroom brawls to know that all Hell was about to break loose, and there wasn't a damn thing that he could do to stop it.

Nestor narrowed his eyes at Galen. "I've considered letting you live, boy. Watch your wagging tongue before I change my mind."

"Don't worry. I'll die of old age long before your mind catches up to the idea of changing."

"You scrawny whelp! You're putting yourself in the wizard's boots. His days are already numbered."

Knarya grabbed Lorelei's arm. "Lady, run to the door immediately and tell the guards there to summon whatever reinforcements are close at hand then get their backsides here as quickly as possible. We're going to need some help very soon. Go now, lass." The captain gave the young woman a gentle push towards the doorway. Knarya's hand trembled as his sword rasped from its scabbard. He didn't know if he felt grateful or insulted as the three arguing men completely ignored him. Lorelei jumped from her seat and rushed out of the room.

"Take the chip off of your shoulder, Canaith," said Tyrell.

"Why don't you knock it off?"

"I command you to stop this at once," bellowed Knarya, but the men paid him no heed. Knarya's years as an experienced soldier readily spotted the subtle shift in weight in the stances of the trio, as they all pitched slightly forward onto the balls of their feet ready to fight. They merely waited for someone to make the first move.

"I'd rather knock off the ugly lump on top of your neck!"

"The only good use for a wizard is as a decoration on the business end of a sword."

"And bullheaded barbarians are only good for karg bait!"

Wizard and warrior suddenly lunged as one. They grappled with each other as Galen dashed around the end of the table. As Nestor pulled back to punch the mage, the thief jumped onto his arm, swinging the off-balance barbarian halfway around. Nestor shoved the thief aside but the delay gave Tyrell the first blow. He slugged the warrior hard across the jaw and knocked him back. Galen tried to throw the big warrior to the floor, but his world exploded in pain as Knarya dropped his sword hilt on the thief's head. The rogue collapsed to the floor unconscious.

Nestor charged back at Tyrell. He tackled the mage, launching them both across the massive table sending plates and crockery crashing to the hardwood floor. Knarya scrambled around the end of the table and grabbed the warrior's tunic. In vain, he tried to pull the two men apart, but his strength was nothing compared to the two battle enraged brawlers. He lifted his sword to bring it down on either one of them but some strange compulsion stayed his hand. A sort of fog fell over the watch captain's senses, and he stood dumbfounded and motionless beside the two combatants.

Nestor's furious instincts spied Knarya standing close at hand with sword drawn. He whipped his elbow backward and blasted the watchman's nose into a bloody spray across the soldier's cheek. Knarya tumbled to the floor. Tyrell took advantage of the reprieve to shove Nestor back and rolled away from the warrior. As he scrambled away Tyrell lashed out with his foot. His solid kick launched the barbarian across the floor.

Nestor slumped on the smooth wood, pressing his hand to the side of his head. Blood matted his hair where the wizard's boot had sliced his scalp. He rolled to the side quickly to distance himself from any follow-up attack. The big warrior snatched up Knarya's sword and leveled the deadly point at Tyrell as the two men both regained their feet.

"Time to finish this game, mage." Nestor lunged, but suddenly found his feet tangled up. Again, he crashed to the floor, and the captain's sword clattered across the wood. Galen, now conscious, jumped to his feet and flashed a quick grin to the wizard.

Nestor wasn't done yet. He grabbed Tyrell's ankles and jerked the mage's feet out from under him. As the wizard's head crashed against the base of the wall, the barbarian rolled to a crouch, whirled around, and blocked Galen's punch purely on instinct. He grabbed the young thief, hoisted him high into the air, and slammed him onto the table with such force that it split in two. Galen writhed in pain among the broken boards, while Nestor caught his breath. The barbarian looked around quickly to make sure no one was sneaking up on him. Knarya still lay on the floor where Nestor had dropped him, but Tyrell had disappeared. The warrior dashed into the hallway, but it was empty.

"Chicken-hearted dandy," he muttered as he went back into the dining room. "He should have known better than to mess with a real warrior." As he stepped back across the threshold, he saw too late from the corner of his eye the chair that Tyrell swung at him. With no chance to dodge, the chair slammed into Nestor's face and knocked him flat on his back into the great foyer.

"Thick headed bastard," said Tyrell as he dropped the splintered chair. "When are you going to learn to quit leading with your face?"

Nestor slowly pushed away from the floor and shook his head. He glared at the mage, his lips curling back in a furious snarl. Each man tensed and waited for the next attack. Slowly they circled each other with masks of hatred on their faces.

"That will be quite enough, gentlemen," bellowed a commanding voice from the top of the grand stairway. The two combatants looked up to see a powerfully built man leaning against the stair rail casually regarding the spectacle. Just then the front door opened as Lorelei rushed in with half a dozen city guards.

She bowed low. "I'm sorry my lord, but it took time to round up Captain Knarya's reinforcements. The heavy rains made treacherous footing." The young woman shivered as water matted down her coppery tresses. Her once fine dress was now heavy with rain and mud, and it clung to her like a second skin.

"That's quite alright, Lorelei," he said. The newcomer was a middle-aged man with long black hair tied into a ponytail. He studied each man with dark eyes that sat perched over a hawk-like nose. He ran his strong fingers over his clean-shaven square jaw, and then rested his hand on the hilt of a jewel-encrusted rapier. The fine black velvet cloak, white silk tunic, fine blue trousers, and highly polished black leather boots left no doubts that this was the lord of the manor.

The nobleman walked gracefully down the long stairway, wordlessly pushed past the two men, and entered the dining room. His keen eyes surveyed the damaged and destroyed furnishings. The corner of his mouth turned up when he saw the unconscious watch captain. Galen had pulled himself into a chair and held his lower back.

"Well, you'll cost me a small fortune in repairs, but you've also proven to me that you have all of the necessary skills that I require. Lorelei," he said to the girl, "see that the kitchen staff cleans this mess up including the puddles that are ruining my foyer floors. Ask for Captain Knarya's men to carry him into my study, and then see too that these soldiers receive some hot food and drink. Get yourself changed into something warm and dry as well." He turned, and carefully regarded each of the battered prisoners.

"Gentlemen, and I do use the term with caution, I order you once and once only to set aside whatever petty differences you have between yourselves. For what I require, the three of you shall have to work with the utmost cooperation if you have any expectation of survival.

"My name is Kellen Ambrose, and I have a job for you."

CHAPTER THREE

Ambrose walked to the chamber across the hallway, and silently beckoned for the three men to follow. "What's this all about?" asked Nestor. Ambrose stopped and sighed.

"All of your questions will be answered if you will just indulge me for a few minutes." The nobleman entered a grand library, then lit a few candles. Nestor, Galen, and Tyrell followed, each sitting down in large, uncomfortable wooden chairs. The City Watch soldiers dropped the unconscious watch captain onto a small couch and then scurried off.

"Now, gentlemen, as you've probably figured out by now, you are currently alive only because of me."

"Are you expecting some kind of reward," growled Nestor. The barbarian ignored the scowl Tyrell shot at him.

"Oh, don't worry, Canaith. I shall be rewarded by you, but not in any way you might imagine. You see, I have need of men of your diverse abilities to help me stop a menace that not only currently threatens the city, but one that I personally have been chasing from one end of this land to the other for the better part of my adult life."

"What sort of menace?" asked Tyrell.

"The murderous kind. Specifically, I refer to the same fiend who has been killing people in the city for several weeks now."

"You mean the Dockside Slayer, then," said the mage. At the very mention of the name, Knarya stirred uneasily on the couch.

"Well, that would certainly be a relief to those of us who work late nights," said Galen. "I know I'll feel much safer when the Guards are the only ones I have to worry about trying to sneak up on me."

Ambrose smiled sadly and rubbed his brow. "I wish, my young friend, that this task was as mundane as your flippancy would make it appear."

Tyrell rose from his chair, slowly pacing before the fireplace. "Why us? Don't mistake me, for I am truly grateful to be free of that cell, but why don't you simply take your information to the city authorities? Help them hunt down this man?"

"Because they would think I was a raving lunatic."

"Why?"

"It isn't a man committing these heinous crimes. The Dockside Slayer is an ancient and horribly powerful vampire. Years ago, this fiend murdered my father and drove my mother to an early grave. I have hunted this demon for what feels like ages, but he always manages to elude my revenge." Ambrose's eyes grew sad and distant.

A heavy silence fell over the room until Nestor broke the quiet with a derisive snort. "A vampire? Gods above, perhaps we can start the by looking under the beds at the orphanage? I won't waste my time listening to ghost stories or any other such foolishness." The warrior rose and marched towards the doorway.

"Just a moment, Canaith. One small detail escapes you."

The barbarian whirled on the nobleman. "And that is?"

"You are still a condemned man. The three of you aren't even supposed to be here. Unless you agree to help me, you'll all be swinging from the gallows by morning." Ambrose sat down behind a large, intricately carved desk, and let his words sink in. "The reason I chose you was not simply because of your talents, but also because you have no choice in the matter. You may assist me, or die."

Nestor glared at the nobleman, but, to his credit, Kellen never flinched from the barbarian's fierce scowl. Slowly, the barbarian returned to his chair, slowly lowering himself back into it. Tyrell stared thoughtfully into the fireplace and ran his hands through his hair. Galen's eyes surveyed the room as if he were appraising everything near him.

"Now that I have your attention," continued Ambrose, "let me tell you what I know. This creature calls itself Darian. This is not his real name, but rather what he has been called ever since my father's association with him. As I said, he is ancient and powerful, old long before my father ever entered into business with him. In life, he was a fearsome warrior, and his strength is even greater in death. I myself have seen him bend steel bars, and crush stone with his bare hands. His eyes glow like embers in the shadows.

"My chase began many years ago in a tiny barony that no longer exists. Darian came to my father as a trade partner, proposing trade contracts from all the far-off exciting ports that piqued my father's greed. One day, my father caught on that his partner was stealing money and merchandise from their trade caravans. When my father confronted him, this thief proceeded to grow fangs and plucked my father from the floor by his throat. Then he hurled him out of a third-story window to his death. Darian turned to attack my mother as well, but the house guards arrived before he could harm her. The beast then left through the same window he had thrown my father from. The fright and sorrow were too much for my mother to bear. She spent her remaining days clutching her bed sheets and jumping in terror at every flickering shadow. Consequently, she followed my father to the grave within a fortnight.

"I took it upon myself to hunt this monster down, and personally avenge my parents' deaths. I've chased him from one end of this continent and back again, but he always manages to keep one step ahead of me. I've never been able to recruit help since no one would believe my story. Now, however, I have you. Together, the four of us will trap Darian, and destroy him once and for all." Kellen looked at each man for a reaction.

"You've never answered my question," said Tyrell. "Why us? I mean, besides the fact that we have no choice. We've never worked together. We don't know what to expect from one another. Why do you think we can succeed?"

"Each of you possesses a talent to counter one of Darian's attributes. You, Nestor Canaith, are the foil for the beast's strength. For centuries, he has honed his fighting skills, which when backed by his superhuman power, makes him a very formidable warrior. I need someone that can be just as dangerous.

"You, Tyrell Amalcheal, are a counter to his magic. His arcane prowess has also developed through centuries of devoted study. What Darian can't accomplish through brute strength, he can achieve through his fell spellcraft. You will also be able to locate his traps and thwart any magical surprises.

"Which brings me lastly to you, Galen Thale. Like Darian, you are a denizen of the night. Your group will need a master of stealth and cunning. He will attack with darkness and surprise. Someone with your experience in the shadows will better protect your companions by seeing this soulless bastard coming."

Nestor made a low growl in his throat. "Where will you be while we're jumping at shadows? I don't suppose you'll be standing shoulder to shoulder with us as we try to drive a stake through him, will you?"

"My greatest contribution is information. I have resources and spy networks across the many lands that Darian and I have both traveled. I shall be able to provide our efforts with counsel and insights that should hopefully keep us one step ahead of the fiend's next moves. Do not concern yourselves with how. Simply accept what I tell you as the truth, and know that you will have my resources at your disposal to see you properly equipped and informed. Know, however, that I will be present when the final blow is delivered."

"Sounds wonderful," muttered the warrior. "We do all of the dirty work, face all of the danger while you sit in the background, and take credit for avenging your family."

"Think of it in those terms if you wish, but the truth tells a different story. I will use my time to gather information to assist us against him. Knowledge is indeed power, and the better informed we are, the better prepared we shall be when we face him. It is imperative to your survival. If that reasoning still doesn't satisfy you, Canaith, then let me simply remind you that you have no choice in the matter, and we will call this discussion closed." Kellen smiled.

Galen jerked his thumb at the still unconscious Captain Knarya. "What about the city guard? It won't be overlooked that three condemned men have suddenly vanished from their cells, especially if they see us roaming the streets looking for your fanged fiend. Sounds like we'll be doing a lot of looking over our shoulders."

"The city watch will do as I ask, with the proper persuasion, of course."

"Going to refuse to attend their annual gala, are you," said Nestor.

Ambrose chuckled. "Nothing so scandalous as that, Canaith. Rest assured that you will have only the vampire's minions to contend with."

"I'll sleep easier knowing that," replied the barbarian dryly.

"So what do we do first?" asked Tyrell.

"A group of Darian's henchmen is traveling now to Tarnath from Daltivar. If you leave tomorrow, you should meet them along the road through the Karghome Fen. These men carry with them a list of the locations of Darian's lairs within Tarnath. I want you to kill these men, and then bring the list to me. I will then set myself to destroying these hideouts."

"I'm not an assassin," said Tyrell. "I don't care what Darian is, or what he's done. You are speaking of murdering men in cold blood. I have a problem with that."

"Even when these men worship a vampire as their deity? Men who bring innocent women and children to their dark god so that he won't go hungry for the night? These men are every bit as foul as the beast that they serve."

"You'll have to excuse him, Lord Ambrose," said Nestor. "These delicate types have neither the taste for blood nor the thirst for justice like some men."

"Or perhaps I just have enough sense not to do anything else that could get my miserable neck stretched, you jackass! We were about to be executed for thievery. Do you think they will do less with charges of murder leveled against us," yelled the wizard. Nestor came out of his seat, prepared to leap at Tyrell again.

"Enough," roared Kellen. "If you two want to kill each other, that is fine, but at least wait until Darian is no longer a threat. After that, you may send each other to Alhambra's waiting arms. Tyrell, you must believe me when I say that these men deserve to die." Kellen's voice softened. "Enough innocent people have died by their hands, let alone their dark master's. They must all be stopped. All of them."

Tyrell looked at Kellen for a long, quiet moment. "I will bring you the list of lairs, but I will find a way to do it with as little bloodshed as possible." he spat.

"As you will, then," said Kellen. "I respect your sense of morality, but understand that no quarter shall be given to you by these servants of evil."

"Should fighting prove to be the only way out, then no quarter shall be given by me either." The mage sighed. "So how will we recognize these vampire cultists?"

"They will be wearing red sashes that symbolize the blood of the victims they bring to Darian. They are a knighthood of sorts, although a sinister one, so they will know how to use their weapons well. They are fierce and well trained so that they can defend their dark master."

"So we just hack up any red sash wearing, armor-plated, bloodthirsty maniacs? They shouldn't be too hard to spot," said the barbarian.

"Even for you," muttered Tyrell. Nestor shot him a dirty look.

"Gentlemen, compared to the time I've spent hunting Darian and his minions, I would expect your involvement to be brief. Now, if there are no further questions, I'll have Lorelei show you to your chambers. In the morning you will begin your quest to help me avenge my family."

"This just keeps getting worse all the time," muttered the barbarian.

Ambrose pulled a cord near the fireplace, and Lorelei soon appeared in the doorway. The young woman had changed from her waterlogged gown into a soft white night robe with fur trimming. Galen leaped from his chair, following on her heels like a fawning puppy.

"Won't you gentlemen please follow me upstairs?" she asked. Her smile remained warm and hospitable despite the fright she had already suffered tonight. She turned and led the way up the stairs. Galen chatted with her, and her laughter echoed in the grand hallway.

"Seems our young ally has found something he enjoys about this mess," whispered Nestor to Tyrell. "Shame he probably won't survive long enough to enjoy the rewards of our labor."

"Would you try to show some sort of hope for us all about this mess, Canaith," whispered Tyrell.

"All I'm saying is that if the hangman doesn't get us, this vampire chase probably will. The walking dead? Please! You're an intelligent man. Isn't our best option to leave town tomorrow, and then ride as far away from Tarnath as fast as we can?"

"I hope you remain this cheerful for the entire trip. Necromancy is seldom practiced magic but it is rumored that there are dark powers that can bring the dead back to the living world. You shouldn't be so quick to scoff."

"Here are your chambers, gentlemen," said Lorelei. She waved her hand to three open doors along a short hallway at the top of the stairs. "Should you require anything during the night, you may ring for one of the house staff." Each man peered into his respective room. The chambers were each lavishly decorated and furnished with a luxurious feather bed, ornately carved chests, and gold fixtures all around the room. Tyrell smiled to himself as he wondered how much of the room's adornments would leave in Galen's pockets come morning.

"Thank you, lady," replied the mage as he entered his room. Nestor and Galen each went to their indicated chambers, and closed their doors. Tyrell threw the lock on his own door and sat down on the bed. His head ached from all of the night's events. How did I get myself into this, he thought? "More importantly," he asked himself softly as he blew out the candles, "how do I get myself out?"

*   *   *

Shattering glass woke Tyrell from his sleep. A hoarse cry and a thumping noise from somewhere downstairs soon followed. Tyrell ran into the hall, just in time to see Nestor already dashing down the stairs with a huge sword in hand. Galen's door was open, but the thief was nowhere to be found. Noises of battle echoed up the stairs, and another crash boomed from Kellen's study. Tyrell raced down the stairs and through the doorway to the study. He gaped in horror at the sight before him.

Ambrose fought desperately against four attackers, while Nestor took on three more just inside the door. The smell of death and musty earth filled the room, and Tyrell noticed that the opponents showed little reaction to pain, even when one was impaled by Kellen's sword. The mage had never actually seen a zombie before, but as he had told the warrior just a short time ago, he had heard enough tales of evil necromancers and their grisly servants to recognize the horrors they now faced.

Nestor hacked through one of the undead monsters, shearing off the thing's limbs. His backhand swing tore away half of his foe's face. Though it might not feel its wounds, the zombie proved less effective when it couldn't see its prey, and it didn't have arms to swing at them. The barbarian saw Tyrell standing motionless in the doorway.

"What the hell are you waiting for? Get in the fight!" Nestor took a mighty swing, but felt his blade snag on bone. He yanked on his sword but it was stuck fast. A second zombie bashed him in the side of the head and knocked him off balance. The barbarian lost his grip on his weapon as he struggled to stay on his feet. Meanwhile, Kellen was backed up against the chamber's rear wall. His vicious cuts could do little more than hold his attackers at bay.

Tyrell knew he had to act fast or all of his new allies would be overwhelmed by the tireless undead. His eyes swept across the littered room for any sort of weapon when an idea suddenly sprang to his mind. He closed his eyes and reached his awareness into the realms of magic. He felt the warming lull persistent in even the lowest realm of power, as magical energy flooded into his being.

Nestor groaned as another solid punch hammered into him. "Help us, for gods' sake!"

Kellen's huge desk began to tremble.

"Do something, dammit," cried Ambrose. The nobleman kicked a zombie's feet out from under it, then spun his way to help defend Nestor from another of the beasts. "We can't hold the back forever!"

The desk rocked back and forth. Sweat beads ran down Tyrell's brow as he fought to bend the magic to his will. The arcane power assaulted the desk, burning Tyrell's mind as it tried to resist his will. He felt as if his head was about to split open.

Nestor lashed out, his punch knocking the jaw of one attacker completely off of the rotting thing's face. "Join in anytime, wizard," he snarled in anger and disgust. The sounds of battle were suddenly overcome by a terrible, cracking noise from Kellen's desk.

Abruptly, shards of wood exploded like a thousand arrows, ripping the zombies into a gory, tattered mess that sloughed to the floor. Ambrose and Nestor dove for cover as the deadly slivers buried themselves into the walls and other pieces of furniture. A cry of pain came from the darkened corner near Kellen, and Galen spilled out of the shadows with a twelve-inch splinter through his arm.

"Did you have to wait so damn long," growled Nestor when the hail was over.

"Sorry. That desk was a lot stronger than it looked. What was it, ironwood?"

"Thelvenin oak," replied Ambrose as he jerked the splinter from Galen's arm. The thief howled.

"Just as strong," replied the mage with a nod.

Nestor whirled on the thief. "And what in Alhambra's Hells were you doing skulking around in the dark while we were getting our skulls bashed in? As if tonight hasn't been bad enough, now we've got allies who won't join the fighting." He threw his hands in the air and went to look for his dropped blade.

"I was about to backstab one of them, but then Tyrell made toothpicks out of the desk. You need to work on your aim, by the way."

"Enough," said Ambrose. The nobleman knelt down to examine one of the decaying corpses.

"So how long have you been getting midnight visitors?" asked Tyrell?

"Darian has never acted so boldly before. It can only mean that somehow he knows that I've recruited help, but it also suggests that he is scared." He sighed. "That puts us all in even more dire circumstances than before. Don't be surprised if he begins hounding you every step of the way now. You must remain alert at all times."

"Great," said Galen. He lifted his wounded arm. "We'd hate for this to seem easy."

"Or sane," added Nestor.

"My friends, all I can say is that you must now be even more careful. You absolutely must be able to work together without hesitation or hostility. If you can't do this, then we'll all die.

"Prepare yourselves, gentlemen. You leave at dawn."

CHAPTER FOUR

A cold rain fell as the men rode out of the city gates the next morning, which did nothing to improve their already short tempers. The arrival of dawn had come without diminishing the horrors of the previous night. Breakfast was served by a quiet servant whose only comment was that Lord Ambrose had left earlier on business, but that all of the gear and supplies that the three of them would need for their trip was already prepared.

Their departure was completely without fanfare. Rolling thunder set the tone in their minds that the trio ventured into exile as punishment for their crimes. None of them felt like heroes who now risked their lives in an attempt to save the city from a ravaging monster.

Nestor grumbled all morning while Galen continued to taunt and bait him, which only made the barbarian's foul mood even worse. They were barely an hour away from the city walls when their shaky alliance had nearly fallen apart. An ill-timed quip from Galen regarding Nestor's mother being overly friendly to a horse had Tyrell barreling between the dodging young man and the warrior's drawn steel, ready to cleave the young thief's skull.

"Look at us," he screamed as he shoved the barbarian away from Galen. The young thief lay on the ground where the warrior had backhanded him off of his mount. "Darian won't have to face us. We'll have killed each other long before he gets his chance." Tyrell studied his companions. "You're naive and reckless," he snarled to Galen. "And you," he growled to the barbarian, "your explosive temper gives you about as much subtlety as a charging bull." The mage shook his head. "And then there's me," he muttered as he thought of his own shortcomings. His eyes dropped to the gloves that covered his scarred hands. Screams from the ghosts of his past echoed in his mind. "What chance do we possibly have?"

"Ambrose thinks we can do it," said Galen softly. Tyrell was startled for he didn't realize that he had spoken his thoughts. Galen smiled at him. "Don't count us out until we're all dead."

The next few days were not much better. Tempers flared time and time again, and it was only through blind luck that no brawls erupted between them. No one trusted anyone else enough to stand guard alone so they were forced to double their watches.

One morning, Tyrell awoke to a rough shake. Galen knelt beside him, and the wizard immediately knew something was wrong from the thief's grim expression.

"Nestor's gone," Galen said.

"What do you mean gone? Where did he go? Maybe he just went for a piss?"

"I don't think so. His stuff is gone. He was here one minute, and not the next. I was out scouting around, and when I got back to camp, he had disappeared. No tracks anywhere."

"Maybe we should turn back, and tell Kellen about the damn double-crosser. Ambrose could set Knarya's men after him."

"Or he might just send us to the gallows instead for wasting his time. Not to mention that it would undoubtedly cost us our window to confront Darian's minions. We need to get that list of lairs."

"Dammit! Nestor said at Kellen's house that we should all just ride off once we were away from town. We were supposed to go into the fen today, and start our preparations against the cultists."

"Let's go ahead with the plan then," said the rogue. "We just won't go as deep into the swamp as intended. Give us a chance to spend more time fortifying a good spot. There's only one road they'll use, and if we set the ambush site properly then we will even the odds. We won't get another chance like this one, Tyrell. If they get any closer to Tarnath, Darian could warn them about us."

"If he hasn't already." Tyrell nodded. "You're right though. It's now or never. To hell with Nestor Canaith. Let's get moving." The two men quickly broke camp and rode off.

Within the hour, they found themselves in the black marsh of the Karghome Fen. The Fen was a place where countless legends of fierce monsters and fallen adventurers had been born. A road ran through the bog, but it was thick with viscous claylike mud that dragged against a traveler's boots and slowed travel to a painstaking crawl. Tall reeds slapped at their legs while the foul-smelling mud constantly threatened to drag them to a suffocating grave. They were plagued by swarms of buzzing insects. The air was filled with the growls and shrieks of creatures that called the swamp their home.

They soon found a relatively dry place in the road and rested. "How about right here?" asked Tyrell. "This is the most solid ground we've seen all morning. We've got plenty of trees to provide cover, or set snares in." Galen appraised the glade with his keen eyes. As a thief, he was naturally more inclined than the mage to laying out an ambush site, and he surveyed the surroundings for potential. Finally, he grinned.

"Yes. This will be perfect. We can set up some deadfalls to herd them into the deeper mud to slow them down, and then we should be able to take them out quickly. Let's get to work." The companions set to their task with the thief directing Tyrell on how to set different types of traps. Soon the area was filled with concealed trip lines, log traps, and other nasty surprises. Galen's coup de grace was made up of two huge logs positioned on either side of the road that would swing together, and pulverize anyone caught between them. The battlefield was set. The rest would be up to the thief and mage.

As they waited, Tyrell's mind turned to their missing warrior. Ambrose had said that success depended on a concerted effort between all three of them. Already, their alliance had broken apart. He and Galen would probably get killed in this dismal swamp by vampire worshipping cultists, while Nestor rode off to gods knew where.

The sound of approaching hooves brought the wizard from his reveries. He signaled to Galen, but the thief had already vanished into the shadows of the nearby foliage. Tyrell watched as four men in black cloaks cautiously rode towards the fallen limbs that he and Galen had planted in the mud. The glint of armor flashed from beneath their robes that were held closed by bright red sashes that wrapped around their waists. They spoke in low voices and kept their hands on their weapons.

Tyrell knew the time to strike had arrived, and he found himself smiling. He opened himself up to the flow of magic and drew upon the very image that was always a crowd-pleasing success when he conjured it forth at dinner parties.

From behind a grove of trees echoed a thunderous bellow followed by a monstrous yellow skinned karg. The beast stood half again as tall as a man and drooled over its wicked tusks. It smashed a nearby tree to kindling with a casual backhand blow then charged at the riders. Two of the horses panicked and ran into the tree limbs. Their riders were thrown into the mud as the unfortunate horses impaled themselves on stakes he and Galen had camouflaged within. The other two riders controlled their mounts, however. They drew their weapons and grimly moved forward into battle.

Galen hid in some bushes off the road and released one of his log traps. A heavy tree trunk smashed into the head of one of the men. The cultist died instantly as the log crushed his skull in a spray of blood and bone. The remaining rider charged the brutish monster and plunged through it before Tyrell could make the image react.

"It's just a damned illusion," called the man to his companions. The other two cultists had regained their feet, and, at their comrade's words, their courage.

"But I'm not," said a voice from the shadows. A thin-bladed sword snaked out of the bushes and stabbed into the rider's neck. Galen rolled out of the falling man's way, coming to his feet beside Tyrell. They grimly faced the two remaining cultists.

"Fair odds," called one of the fanatics.

"We can't have that now, can we," cried a red-haired, buckskin-clad blur. Nestor dove from a concealed place in the sheltering trees and tackled one of the cultists. He snapped the man's neck with a twist of his mighty arms.

The final foe had seen enough and knew he couldn't defeat the trio. He turned and bolted for the marsh road he had come by. Suddenly, another growling karg lurched out of the trees right in front of him.

"You won't fool me with another phantom, wizard!"

Nestor and Galen were puzzled as Tyrell gasped in shock. "That one's not mine," he shouted. The cultist fully expected to run through the mirage as his companion had done. His surprise was complete when he bounced off the creature's fleshy thigh and collapsed in the mud. He shrieked only once as the karg pounded the man's head into the mud with a single strike.

"Maybe we should be going now," said Galen. He looked expectantly at his two companions only to see Nestor draw his sword, and

Tyrell fall into a magical trance.

"Karg would just run you down," said the barbarian. "Wear you out, and then tear you limb from limb."

"I don't have to outrun the karg. I'd only have to outrun you." Nestor ignored the thief's joke and assumed a battle stance.

The beast slowly advanced on the three men. Then, with a surprising burst of speed, it cleared the remaining 10 yards between them with one powerful leap. It took a broad swing at Nestor and struck a glancing blow to the dodging warrior's chest. The barbarian sailed across the clearing, smashing into a tree. Galen dashed frantically into the bushes while Tyrell backed away. He tried to think of how any of his feeble powers might affect the beast.

The wizard remembered the single time that he had seen a karg before. He had been a mere apprentice, and the monster he had seen was in a cage and magically sedated. Even if that one had managed to break free, Tyrell's mentor would have been able to stop the monster with a wave of his hand. The mage wished he had that kind of power at his command.

Tyrell moved behind a tree to keep something, anything, between him and the enraged monster. The trunk above his head exploded into kindling as the karg bashed through the tree, and hurled it into the swamp. The beast roared and raised its arms high above its head, ready to deliver a killing blow to the wizard. Before the fists could fall, however, the karg shrieked and stumbled as Nestor twisted his sword into the beast's leg. The warrior was still dazed, but his face was a mask of fierce determination.

Furious and in pain, the karg grabbed the barbarian's shirt, easily lifting the warrior into the air. With a snarl on its lips, the beast hurled Nestor through the air like a rag doll. Although the barbarian landed with a squish in the mud, he remained very still. Tyrell raced through the trees to the warrior's side. Nestor was still alive, but the karg's ensuing bellow made the mage wonder how much longer that would be the case.

The beast limped forward. The foul stench of sweat and blood filled the wizard's nose. As if clearing an annoyance, the creature kicked over the deadfall and stakes that Tyrell and Galen had placed It roared in triumph before the mage.

Tyrell saw a flicker of movement on a tree limb, just as Galen inched out onto a limb, and cut the rope to another of the log traps. The wizard realized that this was the coup de grace of which Galen had been so proud. The karg, standing in the middle of the road with its arms upraised, was completely oblivious to the trap that it stood squarely in the middle of.

Two giant tree trunks swung down from their lashings from either side of the path, slamming into the beast's body. With a sickening crunch, the mage watched as the monster's ribcage suddenly narrowed on impact under the crushing force. A gout of blood erupted from the karg's toothy maw, and with a wet gurgling noise its knees buckled. As it fell, its arms draped over the logs. The dead monster was left dangling like some grisly marionette.

"Do I have to do all the work," Galen casually called down from his tree branch. "Two riders and the karg to my credit. I want you to know that I do expect a bit more help when we actually face the vampire." The thief nimbly scaled the tree and began searching the bodies of the fallen riders.

Nestor groaned, and Tyrell helped him sit up. The big barbarian rubbed his head, grimacing when he touched an open cut.

"Though we'd lost you," said Tyrell. "Guess we weren't that lucky." He offered his hand to the warrior.

"Karg didn't know any better than to hit me in the head. Otherwise, you might be burying me. Of course, I'd be a lot happier if I'd quit seeing three of you. One is bad enough." He accepted Tyrell's hand

and pulled himself off the ground.

"See three of this then," said Galen with a flourish. He handed an official looking envelope to Tyrell. The mage also noticed how the thief's coin purse seemed to jingle more than it had before. "What do you make of it?" he asked.

Tyrell ripped open the letter and quickly read through it. A broad smile found his face. "It lists four locations in the city. Two of these are street addresses, and the other two are just landmarks. A sewer entrance and a cemetery."

"How convenient," replied Nestor drily. "Since we now have what Ambrose sent us for, can we get moving before any other nasty things show up with the intention of tossing me around?"

"Of course. We've got a long way back to Tarnath. Let's get moving." The men gathered their mounts and started back towards the city.

*　　*　　*

"We should make the city by late tomorrow evening," said Nestor as he poked through the bones on his plate. Night had fallen, and the three men enjoyed the peaceful camaraderie around their campfire. Three days had passed since the attack in the swamp, and the way back to Tarnath had seemed much easier. Tempers didn't flare so quickly now, and they had even taken solo watches on their return journey. Tyrell was thankful that now all he heard from his companions was the young thief's playful boasting and Nestor's groans about his bumps and bruises. It was far better than the taunts and threats that had filled their previous conversations.

"So, why did you disappear on us, Redbeard?" asked Tyrell. "More importantly, what made you come back? I had imagined that you would have been halfway to Del Torac or somewhere farther afield."

"Well, to be honest, at first I had every intention of deserting you and leaving you to your fate. Go off somewhere beyond the reach of Tarnath's authorities, and forget this whole mess. For some reason though, I stayed close to the camp that first day after to see what you two would decide upon once I had left. I thought you might decide to abandon the quest and run too, but you didn't. When I realized that you intended to proceed with the plan, I was impressed. We may not have liked each other much, but I respected your tenacity and courage, and that in turn made me feel ashamed of my own conduct. My people are a proud clan, born and bred as fierce warriors who never back down. What I was about to do was a disgrace to the memory of my ancestors. I followed behind and watched as you set up the ambush. I figured one more surprise held until later couldn't hurt."

"I won't lie, Canaith. I wouldn't have minded another set of hands to help us haul some of those big logs into the trees," added Tyrell. The two men laughed.

"So what happens from here?" asked Galen as he pitched the remains of his meal into the fire. "You have to admit that we work very well together. Maybe this partnership of ours isn't such a bad idea."

"Our assault wasn't exactly graceful," said the wizard. "Nestor and I served as distractions while you crept around, and waited for the right moment to strike. I'm not slighting what you did," he added hastily at Galen's burgeoning scowl. "The entire ambush site was your doing, and I commend you on that. I just don't think I like the idea of being the bait in the trap."

"And nothing personal - anymore, at least" added the warrior, "but I want to finish this vampire business, and be my own man again. I want only to settle my debt with Ambrose so that I can walk the city streets without worrying about a noose around my neck."

"That's just it, though. We aren't finished with Kellen yet," protested the thief. "Not until Darian is gone. So, since we still have more work to do together, why shouldn't we pool our talents, and make a little extra money while we're at it?"

"Spoken like a true cutpurse. You are a credit to your craft, Galen." Nestor yawned and stretched out on the ground. "Take the first watch, will you lad? Seems as though your head is already full enough of dreams tonight." Snores soon broke the stillness of the night.

Tyrell smiled, as he looked at the wisp of the moon. Darkness had come swiftly this evening. He pondered Galen's proposal as he listened to the sounds of the night. He would certainly need to find a new source of earning his keep once this business was behind them. The accusation of thievery would undoubtedly destroy his reputation and credibility among Tarnath's elite. He chuckled. He could never go along with Galen's idea though. The last thing he needed was to become the thief he had been branded as.

The rhythmic chirping of the insects ended abruptly, and Tyrell saw that Galen had noticed it too. The thief looked into the dark forest. "I think we've got some company," he whispered. A shuffling noise and a snapping twig sounded from the shadows. "Whatever it is, it isn't trying to be very quiet."

"Could it be an animal? Some predator inspecting our campfire?"

Galen shook his head. "The movements are too deliberate. Too clumsy." He nodded at Nestor and drew his own blade. "Better wake up our sword arm. I expect we'll need him." Tyrell touched the warrior's shoulder only to find that the barbarian was already awake. Nestor was on his feet with his sword at the ready in a heartbeat.

"It's nice to see that Ambrose picked such capable men," said a whispery voice from the shadowy woods. "I am anxious to see what that fool's concept of a hero is." Six humanoid shapes shuffled out of the trees with slow, lumbering steps. From behind them materialized a powerful figure on a mighty horse. A heavy black cloak obscured the rider's features, but the red eyes that gleamed from within the shadows of the being's hood left the trio no doubts that they stood before Darian. As the creatures shambled forward the smell of death filled the glade around them. The sense of evil that surrounded him caused each man to shiver. "Kill them, my pets," the vampire hissed, "and bring me my list of lairs." There was a sudden flash of light and a puff of smoke that blinded the three companions. When they could see again, the horse and rider were gone.

"So, that was Darian," said Galen. "Did he give anyone else the creeps?" The thief stared into the darkness in a vain attempt to see where the vampire had gone.

"Watch yourselves," yelled Nestor. "Beware the zombies!" The barbarian charged past Tyrell and Galen and brought his sword down on one of the shambling corpses. Galen tried to dodge around the fray to search for traces of the vampire lord's horse, but he was unable to get past the reaching arms of two of the undead brutes. Frustrated that Darian was getting away, the thief gripped his blade and faced off against his foes.

Nestor found himself in immediate trouble. The zombie he had chopped into tore the sword from his grasp, flinging it across the campsite. Undaunted, Nestor threw a punch that would have dropped a horse, but the zombie barely staggered. It and its fellow waded in against the warrior, pummeling him with their dead limbs.

Tyrell put the fire between himself and the two monsters that advanced on him. The mage concentrated on the dancing flames, taking command of the inherent magic of the blaze. He bent that energy to his will and dampened the fire. He remained cautious that he merely suppressed the heat rather than extinguish it. He smiled as the two zombies marched straight through the glowing coals towards him. Tyrell threw the magic back into the tongues of fire. The sudden rush of power made the flames leap up with a white-hot intensity that reduced the walking corpses to ashes.

Galen relied on his speed to keep himself out of harm's way. He poked at the undead with his sword as he dodged and twisted out of their reach. Although he did no significant damage, his minor hits aggravated the monsters enough to follow the young thief as he led them deeper into the woods. The cutpurse had scouted the area when he and his friends had set up camp and knew exactly where he was leading the monsters to. A monstrous fallen tree lay stretched like a slumbering giant deeper into the undergrowth. Galen lured the zombies to the obstacle while he then nimbly scampered up to the top. As the dead men began a slow ascent, the thief looped a coil of rope around his waist and threw the other end over a branch above. He tested his weight on the rope and looked behind him. Beyond the tree, a deep gorge fell hundreds of feet to a rocky slope below. The trick was to get the zombies to fall in.

As the creatures gained the top of the tree, Galen ran parallel to them along the fallen trunk, and then jumped wildly into the air. His momentum carried him around in a wide circle around the trunk of the tree whose branch he had looped his line, and he ended up swinging in behind the two walking corpses. He lashed out with a double kick that caught them solidly in their backs and launched them with flailing arms into the depths of the ravine below. The young thief landed nimbly on the fallen log, grinning to himself as he watched his opponents splatter on the rocks below. Satisfied, Galen turned around and set about freeing his rope.

A thunderous punch in the ribs dropped Nestor to his knees. He grabbed one of his foes around the legs and lifted with a surge of rage. He tossed the miserable wretch far away from him where it landed with a wet thud in the grass. The other zombie hit the barbarian again before he could recover, though, and Nestor fell over on his back as the world spun around him. Never in his life had the mighty warrior suffered through such intense beatings as he had since this whole mess had begun.

The zombie bent over, taking hold of Nestor's throat in a crushing, viselike grip. The barbarian pulled at the thing's wrists but only succeeded in tearing away dead flesh. He tried to call out, but no sound emerged from his constricted throat.

A flaming log suddenly smashed the zombie in the side of the head hard enough to make it lose its grip on the warrior. The rush of air in his lungs restored Nestor enough to shove the foul creature away from him. A hand gripped his arm and hauled him back to his feet. The warrior turned to see Tyrell at his side. The wizard watched as the two zombies slowly regained their feet, and oriented once again on him and his ally.

"Are you okay?" the mage asked.

"I'll survive," croaked Nestor. "Where's Galen?"

"He led a couple of these monstrosities off into the dark. We need to finish these two off and see if he needs help. How do you want to take them down?"

Nestor saw his sword in the grass nearby and scooped it up. "One piece at a time," he growled. "Leave them to me." He started to step forward to attack when Tyrell grabbed his arm.

"We're in this together, remember?" Nestor looked at the advancing monsters, and then back to the mage. A deep sense of respect filled the warrior, and he proudly shook Tyrell's hand.

"Together then," he said. As one, the two men turned to face the dead men.

Tyrell summoned the magic within a nearby willow tree which shook with fury at the abomination that shuffled beneath its boughs.

Slender branches entangled the zombie as it reached for the wizard, and hauled the beast off the ground. Mighty tree limbs thrashed back and forth with the force of a titan's club, reducing the monster to a gray paste.

Nestor was less graceful with his attack. He bellowed and charged at his zombie. The warrior lowered his shoulder into the beast's chest as he raced by, and blasted the creature to the ground. He pivoted so that he stood over the fallen monster and brought his blade down in one wickedly powerful chop. The zombie split down the middle from the force of the attack, shuddered once, and died. Nestor wiped his brow, said a brief prayer to his gods, and joined Tyrell over by the place where Darian's horse had stood.

"Not a single sign that he was even here," the wizard said. "Is his magic so strong that he can spirit himself away without a trace?"

"Forget about that, Tyrell. We'll beat the bastard."

"You don't understand, Nestor."

"What's to understand? Of course, his magic is strong. He's had centuries to perfect it. However, no one said you were to go toe to toe with him throwing spells at each other. We'll find our victory working as a team. You just proved that to me a moment ago."

Tyrell smiled sadly. "I'm not the wizard everyone thinks I am."

"What are you talking about? I've seen you work your craft, and do things that most people would never believe possible."

"I can manage a few simple manipulations and illusions, but I never could master truly powerful spellcraft. Certainly nothing like what he will be able to throw at us. I have some kind of a mental block. Something I've lived with for a very long time now. Ever since…." His voice trailed off as he looked at the gloves on his hands. He sighed. "I've been told before that I have the ability, but that I kept myself from reaching my true power."

"Dammit, man. I just watched you make a tree beat a zombie into sludge. You surely have the aptitude, so just let yourself reach it."

"I want to. I want my skills to grow and develop. I just can't keep from restraining myself though. The only time I ever tried to reach those more powerful levels of magic, I . . . lost control of the power." Nestor could see the anguish on the wizard's face and knew that these words came with difficulty. "The spell had disastrous results that still haunt me. It left scars on me that I will carry forever."

"Well, I'll tell you this. You saved my life tonight, and that's not something I would easily forget. We may have had some fierce moments against each other, but know this. Mine are a proud people. If one man saves another there is a bond of honor formed between them. Whether we are thieves or not, I am a man of honor and will see the end of this with you. I'll do anything I can to help you overcome these fears you may have." A wide grin split the barbarian's face. "Hell, I might even end up liking you by the time this is all over." Tyrell laughed, and the two men shook hands.

"Well, this is a touching scene," called Galen from a tree branch up above. "Now that we've all kissed and made up, can we maybe work on getting ourselves out of here without dying horrible, gruesome deaths?"

Nestor glanced at Tyrell and gave him a sly wink. "I've accepted the mage as my ally. You, little monkey, I intend to knock off your branch." Galen jumped to the ground and sprinted away from the barbarian. Nestor, swift as running deer, took the young rogue down with a flying tackle, then gave him a good-natured thrashing. Finally, as they were all too full of adrenaline from the battle, they decided to break camp and rode with haste towards the city.

CHAPTER FIVE

The trio reached the city gates just after dark the next day, riding casually through the winding streets to Kellen's home. Galen leaped from his horse, taking the short stairs in a single bound ahead of his friends. "I hope that Lorelei is here to greet us again," the young man called to the others as he pounded loudly on the front door.

"Lad's had those copper tresses on his mind since the Fen," quipped Nestor.

Tyrell chuckled. "Marble skin and twinkling firebrands for eyes, if we trust the visions of our lovesick pup. Hope that he isn't disappointed when that door opens up."

The door was opened by a squat, grimy, old woman who squinted to see who disturbed her. "Whaddya want," she growled in the young thief's face. Galen stumbled back in surprise and would have tumbled down the stairs had Nestor and Tyrell not been there to catch him. The woman held her broom in front of her as though she would attack any who came to close.

"Good evening, madam," said Tyrell. "We are employed by Lord Ambrose, and have some business with him."

"His lordship's not here at present, and you'll have to excuse me as we've our own pickle to deal with right now," she replied. She tried to slam the door shut but Nestor held it open.

"What sort of 'pickle', madam? We seem to have had several of our own since making Ambrose's acquaintance. There's the chance that our predicaments are one and the same. Perhaps we could be of some assistance."

The servant looked at the three road-weathered men over and grunted. "This way then," she beckoned as she retreated into the hall, "but mind you don't get mud on the floors."

"I swear she's half goblin," whispered Galen.

"Careful, lad," said Nestor. "I think she may be sweet on you." The barbarian chuckled, though the scowl on Galen's face clearly showed he was not amused.

The three men were led into the study, which was still in shambles from the zombie attack. Lorelei sat in a chair, and forced a smile when she saw the trio. A cup of tea quaked in her hands, threatening to spill its contents onto the floor. The old woman went to her side, whispered something into the girl's ear, then scowled at the companions.

"It's all right, Gildra. I can vouch for them. Please, gentlemen, sit down." She took a deep breath, sipping her tea in a futile effort to calm her nerves. As tears welled up in her eyes, the young woman swallowed hard but refused to let them come. "Things have continued to be exciting while you were away." Galen knelt beside her, and gently took her hand. Nestor kicked through some of the rubble in the room. As Tyrell stepped closer to her, he spied white marks on her neck that conjured the thought of icy fingers that had grabbed her from behind.

"What happened here?" asked the mage.

"I was bringing Lord Ambrose his tray as I do every night when I heard raised voices. My master was yelling at someone, but I didn't think there was anyone else here. I certainly hadn't allowed any other visitors in. Then I heard a second voice." She shivered. "Gods, I'll never forget the sound of it. It was a deep hiss, full of malice and anger. I rushed to the study to see if I Lord Ambrose required the watch. The moment I stepped in, the room plunged into complete darkness, and I felt an icy hand grab my neck." She pointed to the marks on her skin. "Kellen cried out, and then I heard the thud of someone falling to the floor. I was so scared that I could barely breathe. Then I felt his breath, such terribly foul, icy breath, on my cheek. He said 'tell Kellen's trio that should they interfere any further with my plans, that the hangman's noose shall seem a comfort compared to what I shall visit upon them.' I was roughly shaken, and thrown to the floor where I must have fainted. Gildra woke me up only a few moments before you arrived." Galen gave her hand a reassuring pat as Tyrell and Nestor exchanged worried glances. "Could someone please tell me what is going on," she pleaded.

Tyrell went to the broken window and stared down onto the street. "How much do you know about Kellen and his business in Tarnath?" he asked.

"He told me that he came from the eastern baronies, and was here on some personal family business that he had been attempting to resolve for several years. He never told me anything more about it, and I certainly never felt it was my place to ask. I'm just a servant girl that he took in from the streets. Without him, I might have become one of those poor souls getting snatched away by night down at the Docks District." She paused a moment. "Oh, that reminds me. He did mention that should you three arrive while he was away that you had something important to deliver to him. I was to take it and put it with his business papers. Do you know what he was talking about?" Tyrell nodded to Galen who produced the letter he had taken off the cultists.

"Listen to me carefully, Lorelei," said the mage. "Kellen could be in serious trouble, and you may have been endangered as well for that matter. For years he has been chasing the vampire that killed his parents. That is the reason why he needed our help. Of course, we didn't believe him at first, but we met up with it on our way back to Tarnath."

"And it was this vampire's minions who wrecked the study the night before we left," added Nestor. He waved his hand at the debris in the room.

"A vampire?" asked Lorelei incredulously.

"Avenging his family has become Kellen's only goal. He has been chasing this fiend for years, and will not stop until it is dead," said Galen.

The girl rubbed the white mark on her neck. "A vampire," she said again, only this time fear found a way to her words. "It could have killed me without a second thought." She broke into sobs and buried her face in her hands. Galen put his arms around her, helplessly looking up to Tyrell.

"A vampire," called a voice from the doorway. Everyone turned to see Captain Knarya and a host of armed soldiers enter the room. "Making a move from illusion to delusion, are you, wizard? Or are you just trying to get money out of people by making them believe that you have faced the undead as well as bloodthirsty kargs? Well, your lies and deceits won't keep you out of the noose this time. Grab them, men."

"Wait a minute," yelled Nestor. The two soldiers who approached him hesitated at the barbarian's dark scowl. "What the hell have we done now?"

"We just received word that Kellen Ambrose was abducted by three men who matched your description perfectly. It's bad enough that you three condemned souls came here and wrecked his home, but to then go and do gods only know what to the very man who spared your miserable hides, to begin with! What are you waiting for," he growled at his men. "I said round them up." The soldiers advanced again. Nestor pushed and shoved, while Galen dashed behind Lorelei's chair.

"Dammit, Knarya," yelled Tyrell. "Kellen was kidnapped by

Darian, the vampire. The bastard is setting us up, so we can't rescue Ambrose. If you hadn't been unconscious when we were here before then you would have heard the entire story. How long ago did you receive your information?" The mage struggled uselessly in the brawny soldiers' grasp.

"It was delivered by messenger just a short while ago. During daylight, I might add, so your vampire couldn't possibly be the courier."

"He has agents who can work for him during the day. That's why we went to the Karghome Fen. We fought with cultists who worship him. I'm telling you that the vampire is tricking you into helping him. He's trying to frame us. He already has Kellen, and that makes us the only opposition that he has left. If you take us in there will be no one to stop him. The Dockside Slayings will continue for as long as he wants them to."

Knarya thought on the wizard's words. "You told the girl that you saw this creature in the swamp before you got to the city. Why didn't it kill you then?"

Galen rolled his eyes. "Who knows why it didn't kill us? Remind me to ask next time Darian's breathing down our necks."

"Listen to me, Captain," said Tyrell. "Darian has an agenda, some plot that we have yet to see the details of. That's the only explanation as to why it hasn't killed us yet, or why it left Lorelei helpless on the study floor. We have to stop this creature before whatever it is setting into motion is ready to unleash."

Knarya turned to Tyrell. "I don't know why I'm giving this any consideration at all. You three are all condemned thieves." The fat officer sighed and ran a hand through his greasy hair. "All right. I will postpone your hangings. Again. But until I have some other proof that there is a vampire loose in Tarnath, the three of you are still my chief suspects in the disappearance of Kellen Ambrose. For that, you will receive the finest hospitality the city dungeon has to offer. Plus, you'll be safer from the vampire there. He'd be crazy to take on the entire city garrison. Bring them along, men."

The three men shouted and struggled, but the guards overwhelmed them. The soldiers dragged the three men into the streets and threw them into a wagon that carted them off once again towards the city dungeons.

Within a nearby alley, feral eyes gleamed beneath the moonlight.

*   *   *

The cell door slammed shut with a loud bang, and the companions found themselves once again in the cramped, smelly confines of the city prison.

"So now what are we supposed to do," said Nestor. The warrior paced back and forth like a caged animal. "Darian is out there roaming the streets, while we're stuck in this iron box."

"Relax," said Tyrell. The mage stood by the door, studying it for any possible weakness. Finding none, he sighed and leaned against the cell wall. "We need a plan. We have to get out of here so that we can find Kellen. He can straighten out all of this with the guards." He looked at Galen who was settled comfortably against the cold stone wall at the back of the cell with hands behind his head, and his boots crossed at the ankles. "Any suggestions would be helpful. You are the one used to getting past locks."

"What if we overpowered the guard when they bring us our next meal," offered Nestor.

"That would probably only get us in deeper trouble with the authorities. We need to find a way to get out unnoticed." The mage studied the door again. "I couldn't find a weakness that I could exploit with my magic without raising some type of alarm."

Nestor stopped in front of the door, then threw his shoulder against it. He bounced back and rubbed his arm. "My shoulder will give out well before that damn door will."

"You could try using your head," offered the rogue.

"Would you please be serious, Galen," said the wizard.

"I was serious."

"Either pick the damn lock or help us think of some other way out of here. Don't just sit there with that stupid smirk on your face," growled Nestor.

"I can do that," said Galen. He pulled a key ring from out of the back of his trousers, tossing it over to Tyrell. "The jailer's assistant should have paid more attention to what he was doing when they brought us down. The spare set was just hanging on a peg completely unattended."

The warrior stared at the young man for a moment, then broke out laughing. "Galen, I swear I'd shake your hand if I didn't believe that I'd have to count my fingers afterward."

Tyrell winked at the barbarian. "Besides, since no barbarian can count beyond two on his own anyway, we haven't got time for that." The mage knelt by the door handle and tried the key. With a very faint click, the door slowly swung open into the empty hallway. "After you, cutpurse."

The young thief got to his feet and went to peer around the door frame. "Sure, let me open the door for you, and then throw me into the hall first."

"At least we're grateful to you for it," whispered Nestor as he gave the younger man a gentle shove. The trio crept down the hallway with Galen in the lead. The thief kept close to the wall, quickly leading them down the way they had been brought in. The hallway soon came to a junction that offered a left or right turn.

"We came in this way," said Nestor as he started left, but the thief grabbed his forearm.

"Are you planning on going after Darian without any gear?"

"You know where our weapons are?" asked the wizard.

Galen nodded and slipped down the right-hand passage. He beckoned for his friends to follow. The passage traveled on for a few dozen yards, then turned left. Galen stopped, peering around the corner. Tyrell and Nestor watched behind them to make sure that no wandering guards came up from the rear.

"OK," whispered Galen. "There's only one guard. The room he is watching is a storage room. They keep evidence and confiscated equipment in there, but first, we'll need to distract the hired help."

"Leave the distraction to me," growled Nestor. The barbarian ran past the thief and dashed around the corner. A loud smack sounded from around the bend followed by the thump of a body hitting the floor. Galen and Tyrell looked around the corner and saw Nestor poised above an unconscious man who wore a grubby city guard uniform.

"You call that a distraction?" asked Tyrell.

"I'd say that his attention is somewhere other than on us, wouldn't you?"

Galen ignored his two friends as he bent down to the lock on the storage room door. The young thief pulled a thin wire from the heel of his boot and went to work.

"By the way," said Nestor, "how in Alhambra's Hells did you know where this storage room was?"

The thief listened as the tumblers fell into place, then pulled the heavy wooden door open. He motioned his friends inside. "I found it as part of my training for guild membership. We had to devise a daring crime, and pull it off without getting pinched. It was a practice that very few novices ever succeeded at. They get too busy trying to impress guild officers when they should be focusing on the details of the crime. Arrogance gets in the way too often."

"We don't know anybody guilty of that now, do we?" asked Nestor. The man found his sword belt at the top of a pile of gear, cinching it around his waist.

Galen ignored the barbarian's jibe. "Most of them end up getting caught. Those who don't, though, turn out to be some of the best thieves in the land. Anyway, I figured what could be more daring than breaking into a jail, and stealing something from the evidence room? As it happened, the papers I stole could have implicated one of the highest ranking guild officers in some very unsavory crimes. I was handsomely rewarded for my deeds."

The young thief shrugged and took his equipment from the place on the floor where it had been unceremoniously dumped. He threw on his pouches and weapons belt, then hurried back out the door.

"Remind me not to let him near anything I consider valuable," whispered Tyrell. The mage was in awe of the newly revealed daring that his younger companion possessed. Nestor, likewise stunned, could only nod in agreement.

* * *

They slipped past the remaining guards easily enough. Nestor had to provide one more 'distraction', but he was only too happy to do so. They shortly found themselves back on the city streets. The night was still young, and the three friends soon roamed the dock ward.

"So where should we start looking for old sharp and pointy," growled Nestor. The few people that the men had questioned told them that the docks had been mercifully quiet tonight.

"Well," offered Tyrell, "we could always stick to the dark alleys and streets. I imagine Darian would show up sooner or later. I'm just afraid we'll have to wait for him to attack someone before we are aware of his presence."

"Anybody want to be the bait," called Galen into the night. He cupped his hand to his ear. "No? I didn't think so."

"Darian's vanity will make him show himself. He's too proud not to let us find him," said the wizard. "I think he wants to see us struggle along after him. We amuse him. Also, though, if the legends I've always heard about vampires are true, then he has to feed. He'll eventually show up."

"Indeed he will," said Galen. The thief pointed to the shadowed recesses of an alley across the street. A tall, cloaked figure seemed to float in the darkness there. As the figure raised its head, the companions saw the telltale red glow of the vampire's eyes. A hissing laugh echoed in the streets as the creature turned, and disappeared into the alley.

"Let's get him," roared Nestor. The barbarian drew his sword and started to charge past his friends.

Tyrell grabbed the warrior's arm before he could rush by. "Hold on. Rushing in blindly will just get us all killed. He will have some sort of trap waiting for us to blunder into." The mage raised his hands over his head and closed his eyes. The light of the moon seemed to gather around his hands as if he collected the illumination into his palms. He then released a globe of light that floated into the alley, lighting up the tight passage. Nestor let out a low whistle when he saw the dozens of rat-sized spiders that crawled around an open sewer grate. The arachnids were grey with green triangles on their backs.

"Turquet spiders," said Nestor. "Nasty little beasts. I've seen them attack horses, and their venom is deadly enough to take one down." He stomped on one that had crawled too near the party. The warrior took a street lantern from a post and hurled it into the tangle of spiders. The lantern broke, splashing flaming oil all around the grate. The fire shriveled most of the dangerous arachnids, while the three men were able to crush the few that remained.

"So, do we go after Darian now?" asked Galen.

"Do we have a choice," replied Tyrell. The mage examined the opening to the sewer to be sure that no other dangers lurked nearby poised to attack. Confident that it was safe, he lowered himself into the hole. Nestor squeezed his broad shoulders through next, and Galen lightly dropped through into the muck beneath the city streets.

The sewer tunnel stretched off into the darkness both before and behind them. The stench was nauseating. Disgusting things that they didn't even want to think about floated past their legs as they stood in the knee-deep filth.

"So which way do we go?" asked Nestor as he looked down each passage.

"I don't know. Let's start walking," said Tyrell. "Keep your eyes open though. I'm hoping that we can find Kellen quickly, and get the hell out of here. If anyone has another idea, now is the time." He looked at Galen who simply shrugged. "Well, then, the longer we stand around here, the farther away from us Darian gets."

The three men sloshed down the tunnel. They stumbled occasionally, as their footsteps often found less solid purchase than they expected. Moonlight filtered in through grates in the street above every so often, although the sights they saw made them thankful for the darkness again.

Nestor suddenly stopped, clutching Tyrell's arm. He strained to listen and look ahead into the gloom. Galen, who was perfectly at home in the shadows, had vanished, but the mage knew that the young cutpurse was somewhere close by.

"Hold a moment. I thought I heard something splashing around up there." The barbarian walked a little further down the tunnel, beckoning for the mage to follow.

"Do you think it might be more zombies," whispered Tyrell.

"No, something smaller, but it sounds like there are a lot of them." They took a few steps more when Tyrell stopped them again.

"I hear it now also," he said.

"Something just brushed by my leg," said Galen from somewhere off to the side.

"Considering where we are," said Nestor, "you probably don't want to know what it was."

"Gods above, look," called Tyrell. He pointed down the tunnel to the next patch of light. A roiling mass of rats, insects, and sewer snakes raced towards them like a tidal wave. The chirps and hisses rose steadily into a crescendo that drowned out the slurps and squishes of the sewer. Thousands of needle-sharp teeth, claws, and pincers flashed in the brief hint of moonlight.

"Run," yelled Nestor as he shoved the mage back the way they had come from. Galen exploded out of the darkness, running as fast as he could through the clinging slime. The barbarian glanced over his shoulder at the advancing horde, pushing himself faster through the sewer filth as the vermin neared.

Galen reached the ladder first and pulled himself rapidly up the rungs. "Someone closed the grate again!" He hammered his fist into the metal, but a newly forged lock held the portal shut. "Dammit, I can't reach the lock to pick it." He dropped back into the sludge below with Tyrell. Nestor ran up beside them.

"There's no time to stop," said the mage. "Keep moving! Down the other tunnel!" Tyrell sprinted off with his two friends close behind him. The passage turned abruptly after a few dozen yards, and the men found themselves in a dead end. A flow pipe emerged from the wall just above their heads. It looked big enough for them to squeeze into, but another iron grate covered the opening.

"Now what," yelled Nestor. He slammed his sword hilt into the metal. "Those things will be on us any second now." Galen crouched down to catch his breath, looking back down the passage behind them. Tyrell's mind raced for a solution, but only one possibility came to him. The thought of it was just as frightening to him as the horde behind them.

"Back down the tunnel. Stand just around the corner and be ready to run for this pipe when I tell you." The wizard rushed back towards the turn.

"Are you crazy?" asked Galen. "That's where the bugs are!" Nestor grabbed the thief by his collar and dragged him back down the tunnel. The barbarian let the thief loose when they rounded the bend. The slithering, writhing mass was rapidly closing the distance between it and the three men.

Tyrell's eyes were closed in deep meditation. Nestor saw sweat roll down the wizard's brow while the mage's entire frame shook. The warrior realized that his friend was attempting some magic more powerful than he was normally used to.

"Whatever you're doing, do it faster, Tyrell," shouted Galen.

The wizard felt white hot energies burn through him as he fought to shape and control the surge of magical force. He sensed the tempting allure of the power that was offered to him, but he could also envision the devastation he could create. He gritted his teeth and focused his will.

A crablike pincer grabbed at Nestor's boot, and he launched the offending bug against the wall where it splattered in a slimy, green spray. Galen tried to climb the wall to get out of the way, but the slick, wet walls made handholds impossible to find.

Tyrell ignored the snarling fury of the forces that seethed inside of him and shaped the unruly magic in his mind. As his eyes snapped open, he threw his hands out towards the grate in the flow pipe. His friends' cries just barely rang in his ears as he released the built up power within him.

A pinpoint of light zipped from his palm, hovering for a moment before the grate. "That's it," screamed Galen. The thief frantically swatted a snake that tried to entangle his legs. Suddenly, the light erupted into a blossom of flame that hurled them all back against the wall. The wave of heat and concussive force stalled the slithering advance. Nestor recovered the quickest, shoving his friends towards the pipe as they all slowly got back on their feet.

"That bought us a moment," he yelled. "Now get running."

Tyrell stumbled, dizzy from the wave of power that had flowed through him. The wizard felt as if his head would explode, and only the urgency of escape kept him conscious. Nestor wrapped an arm around the weakened mage and heaved him up into the pipe. From the corner of his eye, the warrior noticed the fire-blackened stone and drips of molten metal that had once been the iron cover of the pipe. He gave a low whistle in awe at what his friend had created.

Galen didn't have a chance to be impressed. The thief bolted down the tunnel but tripped as another snake coiled around his ankle. He fell face down in the sludge, choking as slime filled his mouth and nose. He tried to yell for help but the swarm descended upon him.

"Galen," roared Nestor. The barbarian jumped into the middle of the living mass. He ignored the bites and stings as he reached into the center of the horde, and caught the thief's shirt. He hauled the younger man out of the muck, struggling to make his way back to the pipe. As a giant leech crawled up the warrior's arm, Nestor paused just long enough to squeeze the life from the disgusting thing. All around his feet, the sewer waters churned and frothed as all manner of creatures tried to bring him down. Every step he took was a battle, and every time he lifted his foot he sensed how easily he could be knocked into the tangle surrounding him. Nestor knew that if he fell now, he and Galen would never get back up.

Tyrell had caught his breath and saw the danger his friends were in. He knew he had to help. As his eyes fell on the glowing lumps of metal at the edge of the pipe, an idea occurred to him. He pulled the magic to him once again, and slowly, the orange glow of the cooling metal began to increase in intensity. A chill filled the air as the surrounding heat was sucked from the sewer tunnel into the iron. In seconds, the molten lumps had grown to a blinding radiance.

The sudden drop in temperature helped revive the faltering warrior. He also realized that as the air grew colder, the creatures that slithered around he and Galen grew more still. Worms, slugs, insects, and so many other nasty creatures were all caught unawares with the plunging temperature, and they either grew lethargic or fled in search of warmer air. Nestor pulled himself free from the slithering muck and closed the rest of the distance to the tunnel. The barbarian lifted the thief into Tyrell's hands, finally pulling himself up into the tunnel. Galen retched foul water from his bluish lips as Tyrell pulled him to safety.

"Gods above, that was close," swore Nestor. He looked at his two ragged friends. Tyrell rested with his eyes closed. The use of so much magic had drained him. Galen shivered and wiped slime from his face. He occasionally hung his head out of the end of the pipe to throw up on what few creatures remained below.

"Serves the little bastards right," he muttered.

"Are you two going to be okay?" asked Nestor. Both men just nodded.

"And you?" asked Tyrell. He eyed the numerous welts and dots of blood that covered the warrior.

"I've been better, but we're alive, so no point getting grim. Besides, how many men can claim to have broken out of jail, busted up some city guards, and run through the sewers to escape a bunch of slimy vermin set after you by a vindictive vampire all in one day? Hell, I've not had this much excitement in ages!" Nestor began to sing a barbarian victory song.

Tyrell laughed softly. "We have had a pretty full night so far."

"And it's still early," said Nestor as he clapped the retching thief on the back. Galen scowled at the barbarian, then puked again. Tyrell's smile slowly faded.

"You do realize that we are being herded somewhere."

"What do you mean?" asked the thief.

"I mean that Darian sent that swarm after us to drive us in this direction. We're playing his game by his rules."

"You're imagining things," snorted Nestor. "He wants us dead. We barely made it through that iron grate in one piece. If he wanted us to go this way, wouldn't he have left the door open?"

"He's not going to make it easy for us, but I think he did expect us to make it through somehow. Consider his swarm. They're gone for now, but they are still close by. I'll wager that if you set foot down there again, they'll be right back on you. They are standing guard to make sure that we don't go back that way."

"Guard bugs," muttered Galen. "Now I've heard everything."

"Let's get moving then," said Nestor. "If Darian is at the end of this pipe, then let's not keep him waiting any longer. I'm anxious to meet the bastard face to face." The three men finished catching their breath and then started their long, dark crawl.

Chapter Six

"I see a light ahead," said Tyrell as he crawled along the narrow pipe. For an hour now, the trio had been following the twisted maze of cramped passages running beneath the city. Dead ends and looping passages had cost them precious time. The mage led the way with Galen behind him. The thief was less nauseous now but had to pause to scratch the dozens of itching bites and stings he was covered with. Nestor brought up the rear with a steady stream of swearing as he continually banged his head or scraped his shoulders in the tight tunnel.

The crawlspace ended abruptly in a solid iron grate that overlooked a dry stone corridor. Soft, magical lighting illuminated the hallway every few hundred feet.

"Have you got anything less dangerous to open this one with," muttered Galen as Tyrell studied the grating.

"As a matter of fact, I do," Tyrell replied. He gave the iron screen a gentle push, and it fell to the floor with a resonating clang. "Seems someone was kind enough to take the bolts out of this one for us."

"Well at least they know we're here now," said Galen as dug his fingers in his ears to ease the ringing. "Does the word 'stealth' mean anything to either one of you? Let's just make it that much easier for Darian to get his hands on us, shall we?"

"Would you prefer his teeth on you," growled Nestor from behind him. He shoved at the thief's backside. "And if you don't get your ass out of my face, I might just serve you up to him personally."

Tyrell helped his two friends climb out of the constricting passage. He studied the tunnel as they all stretched their cramped limbs. These walls had been made of carefully worked blocks rather than the raw stone that made up the sewer tunnels. Gone too was the reeking smell and moisture of the sewers. The pipe had emptied them into another dead end passageway, so they had only one direction that they could go.

Tyrell beckoned for the others to follow, and they proceeded silently down the hall for about two hundred yards. The hall then turned left, ending at two immense brass doors.

Galen approached the portal, studying them with his trained eyes. "Neither trapped nor locked," he declared. "Pretty ancient metalwork, though. The style of the designs on the brass is about twelve centuries old."

"Should we knock first?" asked Nestor as he put his shoulder against the heavy door. Surprisingly, it opened easily on well-oiled hinges. A tunnel broken by short flights of stairs descended into a cavernous chamber. Jewel encrusted pillars soared into the darkness above. A raised dais with a waist-high stone block stood at the far end of the chamber. Tyrell and Nestor cautiously approached it as Galen attacked the mountings of an emerald attached to one of the pillars with his dagger.

Dark stains covered the stone. "Sacrificial altar," commented the barbarian. "Complete with blood canals to catch every last drop. Do you think Kellen was brought here?" Tyrell shrugged and looked around the gloomy room.

"I smell death here. I don't know if Kellen has seen this room, but the place has definitely been used recently."

"Hey, you two," called Galen. "Come have a look at this." The other two men rushed to the side wall where Galen studied a huge mural.

Various scenes of sacrifice and torture were depicted in graphic detail. "Whoever built this place were not very nice people," he whispered.

The gruesome scenes showed priests dressed in black and crimson robes that stood over people in intense agony. Silent screams were preserved on the wall for centuries. The priests raised bloody hands to a looming darkness at the top of the painting where two demonic red eyes looked over the ghastly proceedings with predatory glee.

"Something is familiar about this," muttered the young thief. Galen studied the eyes of the unseen dark god. "I've seen this before but I can't put my finger on where."

"You probably burgled a demon's art gallery once upon a time," said Tyrell.

"Let's get out of here," said Nestor. "We've still got a lot of sewer to cover, and I'd like to be well away from here before the next worship service begins."

The magical lighting in the chamber suddenly went out, plunging the trio into complete darkness. "You don't want to leave so soon, do you?" The voice was the hissing snarl of the vampire lord from somewhere above them. "The game is just beginning, little friends. Return to me my list of lairs, and perhaps I'll let you survive long enough to see the next round."

"Which copy would you like," called Tyrell. "I took the liberty of making several extras in the event that we misplaced the original." The wizard felt for the magic of the chamber's lamps. If he could relight them quickly enough, they might just be able to blind Darian long enough to get an attack on him. Galen pressed himself against the wall, preparing to strike at anything that seemed to stealthy to be human. Nestor drew a long dagger from his belt, waiting for the vampire to speak again.

"How very resourceful of you, mage. Perhaps I underestimated the three of you, but that is a mistake I will not soon repeat. I have lived for cent-...." The vampire's voice cut off in a sharp gasp of breath after Nestor's throwing arm pumped his dagger through the air.

"We weren't born yesterday either," he growled. The attack distracted Darian's magical focus long enough for Tyrell to punch through the vampire's control. Fueled by the wizard's art, the magical lights flickered on again. A flurry of movement from above caught the friends' attention. A thick, white fog flowed into a small pipe near the ceiling. Nestor's dagger quivered in the mist for a moment, then tumbled towards the floor. The barbarian snatched the blade from the air as it fell, leaping upon the altar stone poised to attack again.

"We've got him on the run," he roared. "Let's finish him!"

"We'll have to find another way," said Tyrell. "We can't follow him through that pipe, even if we could get up to it."

"Over here," called Galen from the corner of the room. "Here's a passageway that seems to go off in the same direction. Maybe they join up somewhere." Nestor raced past the younger man with his sword and dagger in hand. Tyrell grabbed Galen and pulled him along. Nestor set a furious pace, the wizard cursing under his breath as the barbarian raced around the corner ahead without them. There was the sudden noise of a collision, followed by two surprised cries.

"Darian may have set a trap," puffed the wizard. He spurred himself and the thief onward, and they swung around the corner.

Nestor lay flat on his back with his weapons out to his sides. Lying a dozen feet away from him was a pale, dark-haired, young woman. She rubbed her shoulder where the warrior had slammed into her. Her clothes were tattered rags, and tears streaked the dirt that covered her face. As Galen and Tyrell slowed down, she pressed herself back against the wall in wide-eyed terror.

"No, please don't take me back to him," she screamed hysterically. She broke down in frantic sobs. "I want to live. Please, just let me go." Tyrell rushed to her side, kneeling down beside her.

"You're in no danger from us, lady. We are no friends of the vampire lord. He is close by though, so we must be quiet. Tell me what happened to you. How were you brought here?"

The girl wiped her face as her eyes darted to each man with suspicion. Finally, she sighed and grabbed the wizard's arm in relief. "I was dragged down here by these horrible men who tied me up with the red sashes they wore around their waists." Nestor and Galen exchanged knowing glances. "They took me to a dark room and left me. I screamed and pounded on the door, but it was useless. Then I thought I was being watched. There was a . . . presence in the room with me. I screamed and pounded louder, but then something grabbed me. I felt pointed teeth on my throat. I tried to fight, but whatever had me was just too strong. Then just as suddenly it stopped and dropped me to the floor. It was like something had interrupted it. It told me in this horrible voice that it would be back for me. Then he would finish what he had started.

"I felt around in the dark and found a sewer drain pipe that I was able to squeeze into. I scraped and crawled my way through it for hours. When I finally got out I just started wandering these halls looking for an exit." She clutched and clawed at Tyrell's shirt as she sobbed. "You have to help me get out of here, please!"

"Of course. We would never leave an innocent girl down here," assured Tyrell.

"Innocent as a rabid karg," whispered Galen. "That's Alleyway Elenia. Or Any Way Elenia, as some folks call her. She's worked the dock quarter for a few years now. She's every sailor's favorite port."

"Done a bit of seafaring yourself?" asked Nestor. "You sound like you know her well."

Galen shook his head. "She also happens to be a very accomplished pickpocket. I learned of her reputations through the guild, not on the streets. I wouldn't trust her with a lump of sh-."

"She'll have to come with us," said Tyrell. The wizard hadn't heard the discussion, but he scowled when he saw Nestor's smirk. "Anyway, we know we can't go back the way we came, so she'll just have to come forward with us." He took the girl's hand and held it gently. "We'll get you to safety. Don't worry about a thing." Elenia smiled as tears of gratitude welled up in her eyes.

"Well," said Nestor, "if we're finished here, there is still a vampire for us to catch. If we run, we might still close in on him." The barbarian resumed his dash down the tunnel. Galen shrugged and chased after him. Tyrell took the girl's hand, pulling her along behind him as quickly as they could.

Nestor raced ahead like a charging bull. His mind thought of nothing but attacking Darian. Even when the tunnel forked ahead, he didn't even stop to consider which direction to go in.

"Where are you going," yelled Galen from far behind him.

"After my instincts," he called over his shoulder.

The thief hurried after him, rounding the corner just in time to see the floor open up beneath the warrior's feet. The trapdoor closed again on its hinge after Nestor had fallen through. Tyrell and Elenia ran up as Galen knelt to inspect the floor. He pushed the door open with his foot and then jammed a dagger into the hinge to hold it open.

"Nestor, can you hear me?"

"All too well, lad. I'm fine. Nothing injured but my dignity. The cell's table helped break my fall." Tyrell peered over the edge, barely able to see the dim outline of the barbarian below. "By the way, Kellen is here in the cell beside mine. He's been roughed up a bit, but he's alive."

"Greetings, friends," called the nobleman. "You truly have no idea how glad I am to see you. Galen, I don't suppose you would be gracious enough to come down here, and open these cages for us, would you?"

The thief grinned. "I'll be right down." He fashioned his long sword belt into a makeshift rope and climbed down into the pit.

Tyrell smiled at Elenia. "We'll all be out of here shortly. Then you'll be safe."

"I don't trust your friends," she whispered harshly. Her eyes locked onto Tyrell's own. "I think they want you to leave me down here for the monster. If you had to, would you fight them for me?"

Too late, Tyrell felt the touch of magic. He found himself unable to tear his gaze away from the soft red glow that now came from the girl's eyes. His mind screamed for him to resist for the sake of his friends, but his body wouldn't respond. He tried to call out, but his mouth hung open uselessly. As Elenia's hypnotic spell grew in power over him, Tyrell could think only of driving his dagger into Nestor's body before he could hurt the girl. With every moment that his eyes lingered on hers, Tyrell became more her prisoner.

"Okay, everybody out," called Galen as he opened the lock on Kellen's cell. The haggard nobleman clapped the young thief on the shoulder in weary gratitude. "I'll go up first, so Nestor can give you a boost, Lord Ambrose."

Galen pulled himself up the length of his dangling belt, barely noticing the strange look on Tyrell's face. Without warning, the mage lashed out with his foot, catching the thief solidly under the chin. The rogue managed to launch himself to the far side using the hinged floor section to kick off so that he wouldn't crash back down to the stone floor below. He raced to drag himself over the edge but no sooner had he began to regain his feet when Tyrell tackled him with a flying leap.

"Kill him, my pet," snarled the vampiress. She smiled wickedly as Tyrell's dagger flashed across the young thief's leg. She threw her head back, and let out a chilling howl of delight as the smell of fresh blood filled her finely tuned senses.

The evil noise was silenced as Nestor punched her hard in her exposed throat. The warrior drew his sword and took a ferocious swing at Elenia. She ducked just in time as his blade showered her with sparks and stone chips from the stone wall. Nestor knew he needed to end this fight quickly so that he could help Galen subdue the mage.

Tyrell struggled to regain control of his actions, feeling a fleeting moment of hope as Nestor attacked the undead woman. Her magic was strong though, and he could not break his compulsion to attack his friend. He swiped at Galen with his long knife, and then backhanded the thief with his open hand. Words of magic came to his lips, and a blast of sparks burst into the thief's face. Galen cried in pain, blindly lashing out. Only by sheer luck was he able to catch the wizard's wrist before Tyrell could slam his dagger home into the thief's chest.

Nestor made a strong lunge at Elenia, but she easily sidestepped and hurled the warrior against the wall. He rebounded from the impact, countering with a wild swing with his weapon. The vampire narrowly avoided decapitation as she twisted herself out of the way. They squared off again, each waiting for the other to attack first.

Galen grappled with the mage but knew he was in trouble. Not only was Tyrell stronger than he was, but the thief had to hold back for fear of hurting his friend. The mage had no such hesitations. Tyrell fought like a berserker, using every trick he had ever learned. Galen felt his breath explode from his body as the wizard's knee came down hard on his stomach. He lost his grip on Tyrell's wrist, and the mage raised the dagger high above him to strike.

Nestor feinted high with his blade and kicked at the vampire's feet. He might as well have kicked a tree trunk. Elenia laughed and punched the barbarian hard enough to knock him to the floor. She grabbed the fallen warrior's throat and squeezed with superhuman strength when suddenly a piece of splintered wood burst through her chest in a spray of blood. Elenia fell to the ground, writhing and howling in agony. Nestor clutched his throat, gasping for air as he watched the vampire's skin dry up like parchment, and crumble from her bones.

Kellen stood close by with the bloody spike of the cell's table leg in his hand. "Thought you could use some help," he said. He offered his hand to Nestor, pulling the barbarian to his feet. They turned to see Tyrell on the floor beside Galen. The thief had a hand on the wizard's shoulder. Nestor and Kellen carefully made their way around the pit, offering their hands to the other two men. Tyrell looked weakly at his friends and hung his head as he turned away.

"What have I done," he muttered.

Kellen grabbed the wizard's arms and looked him in the eye. "You have now seen another of the devil's tricks. Don't ever fall for it again."

"I could have killed Galen."

"But you didn't," said the thief. Tyrell looked at his friends, surprised to see no ill will in their expressions. "I won't lie about how relieved I am that Kellen hadn't been a second slower, but since he wasn't..." The thief shrugged his shoulders then clapped the mage on the shoulder.

The wizard nodded. "Let's finish him," said Tyrell. His words were softly spoken, but there was a razor's edge in his tone.

"We've all taken a beating tonight, and we found Kellen," said Nestor. "I think we might be better off to find our way out of here and try again when we are fresh."

"I couldn't agree more," said Ambrose. "However, there is one little thing that we can accomplish on our way out. Tyrell, do you have with you the list of lairs that I sent you after?"

"Yes, here is a copy." He handed the piece of paper to Kellen who studied it briefly and then tucked it away.

"I know where one of these is located. It is close by. Follow me." They proceeded down the hallway, making a few twists and turns as they followed Ambrose. Soon, they emerged onto a balcony that overlooked a grand chamber. Tyrell gasped as he saw the dozens of coffins that lined the floor below them.

"How many does the bastard need?" whispered Nestor.

"They aren't his. They belong to the victims he has been harvesting for centuries. Most of them are from Tarnath, but some are unfortunate souls that he cursed with undeath over the span of years." Kellen walked behind the rusty spiral stair that led upwards and rolled out three small kegs towards the men. "Darian brought me here when he first captured me. I think he wanted to gloat before he knocked me around and threw me into that cell. However, I spied these kegs and noticed the familiar pungent smell about them. It made sense to me that he probably kept this stuff close by in the event that he had to quickly destroy evidence of his existence. Tonight, let's destroy it for him, shall we?"

Kellen pulled the cork from the top of one keg and started to douse the coffins below. Nestor and Galen joined in, and soon the entire chamber reeked of the oil. Kellen put flint and steel to a torch, offering it to Tyrell once it was lit. The mage shook his head, and instead held his hands out over the balcony rail. With a word of magic, fire rained down from his hands onto the coffins. The oil ignited, and the flames spread over the entire room. They all couldn't help but smile as the flames crawled and danced over the wooden boxes.

Kellen turned away first and started up the spiral stairs. He beckoned for the men to follow him. The heat and thickening smoke gave them little choice. As he climbed into the passage that the stairs led to, Galen shuddered. He wasn't sure if it was because of the change in temperature from the inferno below, or the thought of how close he had come to being killed by his friend's hand. It might have been the idea of being burned to death in a little wooden box, or perhaps it was just the gruesome scenes depicted in the mural he noticed on his way out. The way that elven warrior was being tortured while the pair of glowing eyes looked on would send shivers down anyone's spine, he thought.

CHAPTER SEVEN

Lorelei sat in her apartment that was located on the outskirts of the Nobles' district. Although it was not as richly decorated as his own home, Lord Ambrose had more than provided for the girl. She lounged back in the soft cushions of a great armchair and felt a sense of peace that she had never known before. She yawned and rubbed her eyes, for the hour grew late, but she knew that soon her inevitable visitor would arrive.

For two weeks, ever since the dreadful night that smoke had mysteriously poured from the sewers, he had come to see her. Despite her senses warning her away, Lorelei had been unable to resist his charm. Every time she looked into his eyes, she felt as though she gave a little more of herself to him. She simply couldn't fight his allure any longer.

She rose and began to pace the floor. She glanced every so often out of the window onto her porch, but there was never anything there but darkness. Then she heard the faint scratch on the pane of glass that always signaled his arrival. She threw open the front door as quickly as she could, just so she could claim to have caught him before he faded back into the night.

He was too skilled for that, however, and the night breeze chilled her skin as she stood alone on the porch. He would not be seen unless he wished to be. She listened intently hoping to catch the clack of his boot heels as he walked, but she had learned that his steps were as soft as the shadows he called home.

A splash of color caught her eye. When she looked down she saw a bouquet of flowers carefully placed on the top stair. Lorelei smiled as she picked up the bundle, and breathed in their fragrance. She strained to see into the darkness one last time, but the porch and stairs were empty.

"They come freshly picked from the gardens of Eferil Durath," he said from inside her apartment. Lorelei didn't want to seem too eager, so she nonchalantly spun, her nightdress flaring out around her shapely legs as she re-entered her home. She set the flowers on a table and shut the door. She looked at him with a raised eyebrow as a grin found its way to her face.

Galen sat in the chair she had vacated with one leg thrown lazily over the armrest. He flashed the smirk of his that always made her melt. She shivered with anticipation but forced herself to maintain her composure.

"Stealing from the garden of the Lord High Governor himself now, are you? Well, milord," she said sarcastically, "I do hope that I am worth such a risk." Galen stood and approached her. He took her hand in his, bringing her fingers to his lips.

"All that, and more," he said with a wink. "And of course there is indeed more." With a flourish, he produced a gem-studded platinum bracelet that sparkled in the light of the hearth fire. The surface was carved with images of entwined lovers in eternal embraces. Galen slid the bauble onto the girl's wrist.

"It's beautiful," she breathed.

"It pales in comparison."

Lorelei put her arms around the thief's neck, kissing him tenderly. "You've been playing these little games ever since the three of you rescued Kellen. Don't you see by now that they are no longer necessary?"

Galen's face grew sad and thoughtful. He stepped away from her, again taking her hands. "I've come closer to dying more times in the past few weeks than I care to think about. I've faced dangers that I never believed could exist. I've always led a reckless life, but have been thinking a lot lately that maybe it's time for me to start living a less adventurous lifestyle." He somberly looked into her eyes. "And I like to think that perhaps I have finally found a reason worth living for."

Her laughter was not among the responses he expected. "Listen to you. Are you now a bard instead of a thief?"

"Well, both can be scandalous professions."

"And more accustomed to taking gifts than giving them." She looked deeply into his blue eyes and smiled. "Galen, you will not be happy unless you are looking over your shoulder for the owner of the coinpurse you've just snatched. You would be poorly suited to the lifestyle of an honest man."

He sighed. "You're right. I can't give up my craft. I have to make a living somehow, so I might as well stick to what I am good at. Besides, how else will I keep my lady showered with tokens of my affection?" He laughed. "And, yes, I do just enjoy the thrill of it."

"Then do what you enjoy doing, and be content with it." She noticed the smirk on his face, and she raised an eyebrow questioningly.

"There's something else I hope to enjoy."

"Well," she said, "we don't always get what we want." She gave him a quick kiss.

"I do," he said, but he noticed that she was pushing him back towards the armchair.

"What exactly do you hope to gain from me tonight, rogue? I don't have enough money to even be worth your notice, and you've already stolen my heart." She pushed him gently into the soft cushions. Galen grinned and snuffed out the nearby candle with a quick pinch of his fingers. The room plunged into darkness.

"Then what else do I need?"

*   *   *

A coin spun high and fast into the air, then exploded into a rainbow cascade of sparks that fell over the astonished tavern crowd. The audience broke into thunderous applause as Tyrell took a bow. The wizard collected the coins that were thrown onto his table, accepted an offered drink, and finally sat down to rejoin Nestor.

The hardships of the past few weeks combined with each man's personal sense of honor had forged a strong friendship between the two men. Tyrell felt now as though the times when they had been at each other's throats were nothing more than a bad dream. He smiled. He could certainly do far worse than to call the massive barbarian his friend.

"Tokens from your adoring public," said Nestor. He pointed to the pile of coins that the wizard stuffed into his pouch. "You haven't already gone through Kellen's reward, have you?" The barbarian belched and wiped beer from his red mustache with the back of his hand.

When they had returned the nobleman to his home, Kellen had given each man a small pouch of coin and gems in gratitude for rescuing him from the sewer dungeon. Although it was hardly a fortune, it was enough money to keep them comfortable for a little while.

"No, I've still got some of that money left. It's just that I've made my living as a performer for so long, it just seems to come naturally whenever I'm around a crowd. Plus it lets me keep in practice." Tyrell rolled a copper coin across his knuckles then made it vanish only to reappear in his other hand. A sad smile found its way to his face. "Not that I'll ever get a job performing again, after this whole thief business."

"Kellen got the charges dropped against all three of us. Less damages, of course."

"Yes, but people remember accusations. I would be regarded as a thief despite my innocence. Every employer would make sure he had the silver counted at the end of the dinner. Crowds don't applaud when they have one hand on their money pouches."

"So give up the theatrics, and practice real magic. And, don't tell me you can't do it. I know what I saw in that stinking hole, Tyrell. I may not know much about your art, but you damn well have the ability. I still haven't grown back all of the hair from that bloody fireball you tossed down there."

"That's precisely why I can't risk it. You don't realize the danger involved, my friend. I could never forgive myself if I lost control of the power, and ended up blasting some innocent bystander to ashes. I know my place, Nestor. I'm an amateur, and I will remain so."

Nestor snorted. He could clearly picture the blossom of flame that had saved his life in the sewer. The wizard had sworn that such a feat was a fluke occurrence caused by the panic and stress of the situation. The warrior also remembered Tyrell's face at that moment, though. All he had seen was a mask of cool control. The mage insisted that he couldn't harness such powerful magic, but Nestor didn't believe that any 'amateur' could unleash such an inferno. If his friend could only overcome his doubts, he thought to himself, would there be any limits to the power that Tyrell could wield?

"Am I interrupting anything?" Galen's voice startled Nestor so much that the barbarian choked on his drink. "What's the matter with him?" he asked Tyrell. "The beer here isn't that strong."

"Pull up a seat, lad," Nestor sputtered. "You're just in time for your own funeral."

"I couldn't help but notice the number of patrons you accidentally bumped into on your way over to the table," commented Tyrell. He pointed to Galen's thickened, and slightly jingling, middle. "Either that or you've been eating too well. I'd say the next round is yours."

"Actually, I need to hang on to a little bit extra right now. I'm on my way to Lord Merkalan's, which should atone for my terrible deeds," the thief said sarcastically. "I plan to repay him for the damages my little misadventure caused in his home."

"What a generous gesture, cutpurse," said Nestor. A barmaid brought over a fresh pitcher then placed an empty mug before the thief. Nestor filled the glass, then pushed it towards his young accomplice. "Magister must have finally caught up with you, and delivered the order, didn't he?"

Galen scowled then nodded. "Yeah, he got me this morning. I tried to duck down an alley, but one of his guards spotted me too quickly."

"You're slipping, lad," said the barbarian. "One too many late nights with your lady fair if I'm guessing right." The big man laughed and drained his cup in one gulp.

"Do you have enough to cover all of the damage?" asked Tyrell.

"I was just barely able to cover the church's broken crystal," said Nestor as he refilled his mug. "Plus I didn't destroy an entire wing of a mansion."

"Honestly, I don't know if I can cover it all or not," he said as he rose from his seat. He patted his jingling waist. "Maybe I'll just have to add a few extra pounds along the way, just to be safe." He took another drink and winced. "Gods above, how do you drink this? Does the barkeep have to hold the pitcher under the horses, or do they fill them up on their own?"

"It's good for you, boy," said Nestor. He grinned. "Puts hair on your teeth."

"Oh, that explains your mustache then," Galen joked. "Anyway, I'll find you two later. If I haven't settled this up before midday, then I might just end up back where we all started again." The thief waved as he disappeared into the crowd.

"Why do I have the feeling that somehow that boy is about to get us in even deeper trouble than we've already been in?" asked Nestor.

"What could possibly happen?" asked the wizard. He tried to ignore his friend's amazed glare, as well as the disconcerting answers to his own question that began to fill his mind.

* * *

Galen was led by armed guards into the vault that had nearly killed him. A large man bellowed at a cringing worker, and Galen knew at a glance that this was Merkalan. The aristocrat's fine clothes dripped with jewels. Years ago, he had been an officer in Tarnath's military. When he came into his inheritance though, he threw down his sword and armor in exchange for a life of luxury and excess. There was still strength evident in the nobleman's frame, though, even if he hadn't touched a weapon in over two decades.

"Why don't you clumsy buffoons go ahead, and finish the job of destroying my home," he shouted at his cowering employee. "It isn't enough that there is broken glass and burned walls, but you idiots have now chipped the statue of my great grandfather! Get out of my sight before I have you drawn and quartered on a bed of hot coals!" He whirled around to see his guard with Galen. "What," he snapped.

"Galen Thale to see you, sir." The guard looked visibly relieved when Merkalan dismissed him with a wave.

The aristocrat looked Galen up and down. "So you are the scruffy street urchin who sought to part me from my treasures." The nobleman scoffed. "Better than you have tried, and failed, boy. I'm sure it was only pure fortune that you made it as far inside as you did."

"I'm not here to take your insults, Lord Merkalan. I'm here

95

because I have to repay you for the damage caused. Let's settle this matter so I can get upwind of you again. After all, it appears that you do have a lot of renovation work to do here." Galen smiled wickedly as the nobleman's face went red with fury.

"If you think that some petty thief with a few high connections can ruin my holiday, destroy my personal property, and then think to satisfy me by simply throwing money in my direction then you are sadly mistaken."

Galen sighed. He had expected this kind of reception. "Then pray tell me what it is you would like from me, milord?"

Merkalan shoved Galen back a step. "I want your head on a plate, boy," he roared. "However, since someone of your acquaintance has greased the magistrate's palm, I am denied such a luxury. I have no choice but to settle for far less than I demand. However, you will still give me more than you have been ordered." He played absently with a thick gem-studded necklace around his neck. "In addition to the cash settlement for the damages you've caused, I want you to tell me in detail about how you bypassed the traps so easily. I will need to design better defenses now so that such an unfortunate incident never occurs again."

Galen bowed, hoping that the gesture hid the rolling of his eyes. "As you wish, Lord Merkalan. First, I simply waited for your incompetent perimeter guards to pass by on their rounds. I knew they were only making their patrols every half an hour or so." The thief grinned as some nearby guards squirmed. "After I climbed the wall, I easily picked that flimsy excuse for a lock you had on the balcony door. Once inside, I made my way down the hall to the gallery. Your pressure plate trap is an effective choice, but only if you are trying to catch a stampeding bull. It was obvious to an experienced thief that it was hidden under the rug." Merkalan scowled, but Galen talked on. He was happy to see that his explanations irritated the aristocrat.

"The dart trap in the archway was, again, only able to catch the unwary. I spotted the trip wire at the entrance well before I was upon it. The false gems were likewise easy to locate since each had a large hole through the middle. Having passed unmarked through all of that, I easily found myself in the main gallery. I quickly located the seam of the false door to the jewel vault, as well as the opening mechanism right along with it. Then I was inside. I must admit that I was surprised by the strength of the crystal case, and even more so by that fire trap. That was a good stroke on your part."

"Yes, I was rather proud of that one myself. Or at least I was until it went off, and burned up the room." Merkalan beckoned a skinny man who carried a ledger with him. "See to it that all of the guards who were on duty that evening are given their severance, and relieved from service. Instruct the house mage to devise something more subtle, and less destructive when it erupts." He turned back to Galen. "Now then, I suppose you've kept your end of the bargain. Pay me for the damages you've caused, and then get the hell out of my home." He held out his hand to the thief.

Galen grudgingly reached inside of his shirt to remove the gems, jewelry, and coins that he had accumulated on his way to the nobleman's house. "I hope this will suffice," he said coldly. Merkalan carefully inspected each bauble with careful scrutiny, nodding his approval over each piece. Finally, he put the payment in a small sack that he tossed to the skinny assistant.

"This concludes our business, thief. Spread the word to the other filth you associate with that the Merkalan family is too clever for common thieves. That's why my family is as wealthy as it is today. Tell them not to mess with us again."

Galen quickly grasped the nobleman's hand and fell to one knee.

"You may rest assured milord, that I will spread the warning among all of those who hunt the night. All shall know of your great wisdom." Merkalan pulled his hand free from the thief's grasp, wiping it on his assistant's shirt as he walked away. He went back to roaring at the help when a fire-blackened statue crashed to the floor.

"Too clever, indeed," whispered Galen as he tossed a gold ring adorned with a great emerald into the air, and deftly caught it. He tucked it into his pouch and wondered how long it would be before the idiot even realized that it was missing. He spun on his heel, then headed for the door.

As he exited the vault into the main gallery, the mural of the elven warrior with the glowing sword caught his eye. The thief stopped and stared. The red-eyed beast that was driven into the dark cave burned away the cobwebs of the young man's memory. It was just like the paintings he had seen in the sewer. He couldn't explain it, but somehow the thief knew that the monster depicted in Merkalan's home was the same creature that adorned the artwork from the sewer. Galen grabbed the sleeve of the worker who scrubbed at the soot and ash adorning the picture.

"Sir," he said as his voice squeaked with excitement, "can you tell me anything about this painting? I am curious as to the history of the image."

The man regarded the thief with annoyance. "If the master of the house catches me talking instead of working, he'll go through the roof." He pondered his words a moment then smiled. "What the hell. It's a copy of some old, elvish painting. The elf depicted there is some ancient elven hero or general. Gilgorad was his name, I think. Was supposed to be a mighty warrior back when Khasharsta was in its glory days. Centuries ago. The stories say that with that glowing sword you see there, he single-handedly fought off some nasty creature that had been hunting down the elves. Pretty gory legend, actually. Everyone is always getting their throats ripped out. Probably wasn't a monster at all. Likely it was just a bear or something with a taste for elf meat."

"What about the sword?" Galen asked. "Is it a legend or did it really exist?"

"Who knows? The legends say that it was created by the most skilled elven smith with the help of the mightiest wizard the elves had ever produced. This hero, Gilgorad, was supposed to have fought some mighty battles with it. Now, I really should get back to work, if you don't mind."

The man turned back to the wall and focused again on his task. A moment later, he felt a tug on his coin purse. Reflexively, he clutched at his belt and looked around, but he saw nothing. It wasn't until several hours later that he opened the pouch and saw a large emerald ring within.

*   *   *

Kellen stared out the window as Galen retold the tale of his encounter at Lord Merkalan's home. The trio had found Lord Ambrose surprisingly receptive to the excited young thief's account of his information on Gilgorad and the elf's enchanted blade.

"The blade was known as Shadow Reaver," said the nobleman.

"Then you have heard of it?" asked Galen when he had finished his story.

"Of course. My father always told me stories of Gilgorad and so many other tales of legendary exploits as he tucked me into bed as a child. However, my research over the years has shown me that the general is not simply a child's fantasy. Much of what your contact told you is accurate, Galen. Gilgorad lived many centuries ago, and Shadow Reaver was given to him for his great service to the elven nation. Khasharsta was a thriving trade and cultural center for the western lands of Belynna. Today it is a ruin buried deep in the Thelvenin Wood. Over the years, I have also found references stating that a 'creature that hunted the night' ravaged the elven lands long ago. I have no idea if it might have been Darian, but Gilgorad fought the beast with his enchanted blade, and saved the lives of many elves."

"Is there anything else you could add to Galen's story?" asked Tyrell.

"Regrettably, no. All I know of the weapon and the general are small bits and pieces. Fragments of information gathered over a lifetime of study. Shadow Reaver was allegedly a weapon that was the bane of great evil. Of course, who can say if it's legendary might came from powerful enchantment or simply because of the wielder's own morality and ability." Kellen looked at the mage and shrugged. "We know it existed once. Whether it does today is hard to say, and doubtlessly harder still to find."

"Yet, I suppose you'll be sending us after it just in case," said Nestor.

"If Shadow Reaver could be found, and the legends about it are true, then it would certainly be a great asset in our fight against Darian." He waved his hand. "However, this is likely a fool's errand, and I certainly wouldn't order you to go on the search. You three saved my life, and our accounts are settled so far as I am concerned. If you were to undertake this quest, it would have to be of your own free will. Be advised, though, that our vampire knows who you are, and now that you have thwarted him, he may still have designs of revenge against you for that."

Galen looked at his friends. "I am the one who brought this up. I guess that sort of obligates me. Besides, what kind of thief would I be if I refused to go on a treasure hunt?"

Tyrell smiled. "I'm in. If we have to search the Thelvenin Wood and the ruins of Khasharsta, then you will need someone along who knows about magic. What about you, Redbeard?"

Nestor threw his hands in the air. "Bloody hell. Why not? What else have I got to do? Besides, there's no telling what trouble you two will get into without me."

Kellen smiled warmly. "Thank you, my friends. I'll arrange for everything that you may need for your journey. You may leave for the ruins of Khasharsta at when it suits you."

CHAPTER EIGHT

"I'd give myself over to Darian for just one day of dry weather," yelled Nestor over the pouring rain. Thunder boomed, and lightning flashed across the sky.

"I'd do the same if you'd quit griping," replied Galen. "We're only a few hours away from Del Torac. There we'll find an inn where we can stay for the night."

Tyrell rode in silence. He was lost in thought, and oblivious to the bantering of his companions. The night before their departure, he had spent many hours in Kellen's library. He read what lore he could find about the lost elven kingdom of Khasharsta and the mysterious Thelvenin Woods. He had found a few passages that related to the life and victories of General Gilgorad, but there was not a single mention of the sword, Shadow Reaver. Kellen had insisted that the blade did exist, but his own records lacked references to support his claim. For all they knew, Shadow Reaver could be a tiny needle in a massive haystack.

Tyrell was also deeply concerned about the ruins of the city, assuming that they could even find their way inside. Specifically, he was troubled by the possibility of potential inhabitants. Since the fall of the elven kingdom, stories had abounded of strange and wondrous creatures that were believed to be leftover creations and abominations of errant elven sorcery. The region where the ruins supposedly lie could be crawling with all manner of unnatural and dangerous beasts.

Of even greater concern to the wizard was the remaining force of any surviving ancient elven magic. Tyrell had no doubts that he would be able to sense any magical emanations, but had time weakened them enough so that his feeble skills could prevent a magical trap from blasting apart he and his friends?

Tyrell played over the same debate he had gone through a thousand times before. How could he risk the safety of those people close to him by tampering with such dangerous powers? His hands weren't the only scars he carried with him. He couldn't live with himself if the screams of Nestor and Galen joined those that already filled his nightmares.

". . . and when I woke up, the wench was gone with all of my clothes and money," roared Nestor. Galen was laughing so hard that he nearly fell from his horse. "I had to walk bare-assed to a tailor, and bargain for a pair of trousers." Tyrell smiled at the end of the ribald tale.

"By the way, lads," added the warrior between chuckles. "We're being followed. I noticed some riders trying very hard to keep a discrete distance for the last couple of hours." Tyrell and Galen strained to see through the downpour, but the curtain of rain obscured their sight. "Trust me, lads, they're back there, and I'll buy the first round in Del Torac if their business isn't about us."

The wizard glanced back over his shoulder as a bolt of lightning flashed. "We better get moving then, and try to put some more distance between us." He spurred his horse, and his friends galloped after him.

*   *   *

They were more interested in escaping the storm than they were their pursuit, and the trio rode hard to the gates of Del Torac. After a brief formality with the gatekeepers, they were waved through, and soon found themselves comfortably seated in the Belching Griffin Inn. The sign that hung above the doorway showed a mythical beast holding up a foaming mug, and the locals considered it a fine compliment to the establishment to belch after a satisfying meal. The noise in the tavern was predictably obnoxious.

"So who do you think is following us?" asked Tyrell.

Nestor shrugged, and 'complimented the house'. "Probably more of those damned cultists. They've likely been told to keep their eyes open for us, and report on any new business we may be about." The barbarian surveyed the crowd, searching for anyone who appeared to be paying them too much attention.

"And where the hell is Galen at now," grumbled the mage. "I sent him after a drink ten minutes. I swear that boy can disappear better than any wizard ever could."

"I imagine he's either got his hand on some poor sot's coinpurse or on some barmaid's. . . ."

"Wrong on both counts, Redbeard," said the thief from behind the fighter. Nestor jumped at the sudden arrival of their friend.

"I wish you'd stop doing that," he growled. "I swear one of these days you are going to get run through."

"So where have you been, and where is my drink?" asked Tyrell.

"Still in the bottle, I'm afraid. I didn't get it because I think we may want to shorten our stay." The thief casually nodded to a couple of rough looking men near the door. "Those men aren't the simple timber men that they appear to be. I caught a glimpse of a dagger with the same design and craftsmanship as the weapons carried by the cultists we fought in the Fen."

Tyrell nodded. "Good work. We'll have to get out of here. Nestor, any suggestions on how not to get ourselves into a barroom brawl?"

"Would I have been in so many if I did?"

"I was afraid you were going to say that."

The two lumberjacks must have realized that they were a topic of discussion for they rose from their seats, and slowly pushed through the crowd towards the table. Their hands were hidden beneath the cloaks they wore, and their once-casual glances at the three friends were now replaced by pointed stares.

"Galen," whispered Tyrell, "vanish in the crowd and meet us over by the door. Nestor, stay seated until I tap your leg. Just act casual. When I signal you, drop to the floor and head for the door as well. Go quickly, but quietly." The mage closed his eyes while Nestor finished his drink. He wondered what Tyrell had in mind. Galen blended into the crowd behind them, vanishing as he lost himself among the numerous faces.

The strangers conferred for a moment. They now stood only a few feet away from the table. Without warning, they drew two small crossbows from beneath their cloaks and fired at Tyrell and Nestor. A barmaid screamed as the quarrels hummed through the air on a direct course for the seated men's chests.

The wicked points punched through the wooden backs of the chairs, yet Tyrell and Nestor showed no sign of injury despite the quivering bolts that had nailed them to their seats.

"Illusion," cursed one of the bowmen. He and his fellow looked around frantically, spotting their quarry on their feet as they pushed through the crowd towards the door. One of the attackers reached for his knife only to find that the blade was gone.

"Looking for this?" whispered Galen in the man's ear as he clubbed the would-be assassin with the hilt of his own dagger. The second man swung his empty crossbow at Galen's head, but the thief easily jumped away from the clumsy attack.

Near the door, Nestor snatched a mug away from a surprised patron and hurled it into the second attacker's face. Galen vaulted over a table landing nimbly near the door next to his friends.

"I thought you said you only caught a glimpse of that dagger," said Tyrell to the thief.

"Well, yeah, the first time, but I liked it so well that I went back for it."

Tyrell threw open the door only to bounce off the chest plate of a giant blond haired warrior clad in black armor. A rain-soaked red sash was tied at his waist. The knight snarled when he saw the mage and punched Tyrell in the face with his mailed fist.

Nestor kicked the door shut and threw his shoulder against it to keep the knight and his companions outside. Galen caught Tyrell as he fell over and dragged him to the end of the bar.

"Wha' happened?" mumbled Tyrell.

"You got punched so hard that your eyes match now," replied the thief. Nestor held the door closed, but the pounding from the other side grew louder and louder. The barbarian also saw the two crossbowmen were back on their feet, and reloading their weapons.

"Someone better come up with a plan fast because I can't hold this door forever," he shouted. An ax blade hammered through the door, narrowly missing Nestor's face.

Tyrell closed his eyes, ignoring the pain that shot through his jaw. He focused his mind on the door as he drew his magic to him. Galen snatched a fallen stool from the floor and drew his sword. He winked at a terrified barmaid who huddled beneath a long table with some other patrons, as he squared off against the two assailants. As Galen advanced, they dropped their crossbows and drew their swords instead.

"Hurry up," yelled Nestor as the ax crunched through the wood again. The wood of the door suddenly swelled and popped as Tyrell's magic warped the boards. The spell wedged the portal tightly in the frame.

The barbarian backed away from the door, clapping the somewhat unsteady mage on the shoulder.

Galen poked the stool into one attacker's face, as he parried the sword of the second man. "Did I ever mention the time I saw a beast tamer in the circus? This reminds me so much of that day. Here this man was surrounded by ferocious lions, and all he had to defend himself with was a whip. Of course, my sword blade doesn't give you the same effect, but you get the general idea." The young thief made a quick spin, tripping one of his lunging opponents towards Nestor. The snarling barbarian's fist timed the attacker's stumble perfectly and drove the man into unconsciousness with one pounding blow.

The ax tore through the door again, this time ripping away a chunk of wood. Nestor and Tyrell exchanged worried glances. "Galen," called the wizard, "quit fooling around, we've got to go."

Nestor dashed to the bar and grabbed the bartender through the crowd of cowering people. "Where's the back door to this place?" The ax hammered again, and Tyrell saw the enraged visage of the blond knight through the breach in the doorway. Galen tripped his other opponent and broke the stool over the man's head.

"It's in the kitchen and unbarred only for deliveries," replied the bartender calmly, "but don't you think your friends outside have it covered too?" Tyrell looked at the door and wiped blood from his nose. More splinters flew as the ax ate away the main tavern door.

From the kitchen, a booming thud resounded as someone bashed away at that unseen entrance. Galen knelt by the fallen soldier, patting down the man's pockets. The thief lobbed a jingling bag on the bar which disappeared under a casual pass of the bartender's rag.

"Go to the wine cellar," the man said with a curt nod to the thief. "Third cask on the right. Twist the tap to the left." The three men ran immediately to the cellar door which was right beside the kitchen door. Nestor's keen ears heard the clank of armor plating, and as he saw the door start to swing open he threw his weight against it. The clatter of the armored foes as they fell in a heap was like a thousand frying pans dropping to the stone floor.

Nestor ran down the stairs of the wine cellar to see Galen duck into the low tunnel behind the cask. Tyrell and the barbarian followed immediately after him. Nestor pulled the secret door closed again, just as the first armored footsteps rang against the cellar stairs.

They followed the tunnel for about fifty yards, where it suddenly ended in an old wooden ladder that led up to a trapdoor. Galen pressed his ear to the wooden planks above, and then carefully pushed it open. As they scrambled out of the tunnel, the smell of horses assaulted them. Quickly, they ran to the stalls where their mounts were quartered.

"No rest for the weary," mumbled Galen.

"You still owe me a drink, by the way," countered Tyrell.

"First round is on me once we get back home."

"We'll hold you to that, cutpurse," growled Nestor. "Right now, let's get out of here." The warrior threw open the stable door and jumped into his saddle as Tyrell led the beast by. They charged out into the courtyard, startling the few knights still outside. They jumped their mounts over a low stone wall and rode into the dark shadows of the Thelvenin Wood.

*   *   *

Thick fog enshrouded the centuries-old trees around them. After their dash from Del Torac, the trio made a madcap path into the forest. They doubled back on their trail, rode in wide circles, and crossed over their own path in an effort to shake off any pursuit from the village.

"Well," muttered Tyrell. "I think those soldiers are the least of our worries now."

"What do you mean?" asked Galen.

"I haven't the faintest idea where we are now."

Nestor gaped at Tyrell. "You got us lost in a haunted forest?" The barbarian glanced around the dark glade and shuddered.

"Cheer up, Redbeard," said Galen. "Only the ruins of Khasharsta are supposed to be haunted. Thanks to Tyrell, we're probably nowhere near there." The young thief swung out of his saddle. "I'll go have a look around, and see what I can see." He disappeared into the mist.

"All of this damn fog has my sense of direction fouled up," growled the barbarian. He dismounted and stretched his tired muscles. "Any landmarks that we might want to look for?"

"I doubt we'll find any signposts saying 'This way to Khasharsta' if that's what you mean. Maybe if we climbed one of these trees we could get our bearings from the stars."

"Might still be too many clouds from the storm, but perhaps we'll get lucky." The big warrior pulled himself up into the branches of an ancient oak, vanishing into the thick foliage.

Tyrell cursed under his breath. How could he have led his friends into danger so blindly? *If I were a real mage, I could have just opened a portal that would have dropped us right in the middle of Khasharsta.* He sighed.

"Tyrell," called Nestor a moment later. "I think I found our signpost." The warrior dropped from the tree branches and landed on the forest floor with the grace of a hunting cat. "Del Torac is over that way," he said as he pointed. "I could see the town lights. Also, I saw some mountains in the opposite direction." He gestured behind him. "Does that help us any?"

"Yes. I remember there being some mountains on one of Kellen's old maps. If Del Torac is back that way, then Khasharsta is vaguely to our right. Good work. Let's try not to lose it this time." Nestor nodded and made a mental note as if he locked the proper direction in his mind.

Galen strolled back into the clearing. He was singing a bawdy tune about a knight who got his group lost in the forest. Tyrell scowled, but the young thief ignored the glare. "I hope we have found ourselves by now. Our friends have set up camp about three hills over there." He pointed in the direction of the town. "By the way, their leader is the big fellow who tried to squish your face, and then hacked the front door to pieces with his ax. I saw him taking out his fury on a fallen oak. That poor thing will be sawdust by morning at the rate he's working on it."

"Duly noted," said Tyrell. He felt a pain in his jaw just at the mention of the knight. "Let's mount up. We can ride through the rest of the night, now that we know which direction to go in. Maybe we'll have lost them by morning."

Tyrell summoned his magic to muffle the sounds of the horses, just in case the knights had scouts nearby. Silently, the three men rode off in the direction where, hopefully, the lost elven nation waited.

Chapter Nine

"The briar bushes are more likely to fall to your blade than your swearing, Redbeard," called Galen from a tree branch. The thief had crawled to this vantage point to look for any indications of the elven city.

Nestor cursed loudly and often as he spitefully hacked away at the wall of brambles and thorns that had ravaged his arms. "Just tell me if I'm chopping in the right direction. I've lost so much blood to these thorns that there won't be any left for the damned vampire to take." He wiped his brow and took another ferocious swipe.

Galen jumped out of the tree, landing beside him without making so much as a whisper. "It's going to take us weeks to get through this mess," he said. Nestor twirled his hatchet, wordlessly offering the handle to the young thief.

"You can put it away now, Nestor. I've found a better way in." Tyrell pushed through the underbrush with a strange smile on his face.

"You couldn't have found it before I had done all of this?" asked the barbarian. He waved his arms around at all the fallen vegetation.

Tyrell turned to the bushes, beckoning to something hidden there. A wizened old man cautiously entered the clearing. His eyes narrowed as he studied Nestor and Galen with suspicion. The two men both noticed something bizarre about the old man. His skin was a honey gold color, and his sharp blue eyes twinkled agelessly. He moved with sure youthful energy despite the mane of wild white hair that hung down to his shoulders. Even though he was clad in rags, there was a certain grace and dignity that he carried about him that belied his tattered appearance. He turned to the wizard, jabbered something in a smooth flowery language, and then cackled madly.

"Great," muttered Nestor. He watched as the old man wandered over to his horse, and started to rummage through the saddlebags. He grabbed something from within, popping it quickly into his mouth.

"He's loopy," said Galen. The thief chuckled as the newcomer pulled a rock out of a pouch on his belt, listened to it intently, and then gently set it down on the forest floor. Afterward, he resumed his inspection of Nestor's belongings.

"He's also possibly the last living elf of Khasharsta. More importantly than that, he knows the way into the city," said the mage.

"You want us to follow a crazy elf into haunted ruins to look for a magic sword that may not even exist, and if it does, will likely be guarded by things just as dangerous as the monster we want to use it against in the first place?" Galen asked. The thief shook his head as the old elf chewed on the stirrup of Nestor's saddle, and then apparently scolded it for being too tough to eat.

Nestor dug his hatchet into a fallen log. "So where did you find him?"

"I literally stumbled over him while I was looking for a path into the ruins. He started babbling, but when I realized that I could understand some of what he was saying, I decided to bring him along."

Galen dazzled the ancient elf by making a coin dance across his own knuckles. The elf let the coin roll from Galen's hand to his own as it reached the end of its trail, and continued it along his own slender fingers. Nestor rubbed his forehead. "I don't suppose he can tell you anything about Gilgorad's sword, can he? Might save us a lot of trouble if he can tell us that Shadow Reaver is just a legend."

At the mention of the elven general's name, the elf pushed past Galen and dashed over to Nestor. He chattered excitedly, but the gibbering ended in a sudden squeal of fear as the old elf fell to the ground curling into a quivering ball. He slowly rocked back and forth on the ground, whimpering and shaking. Nestor and Galen looked to Tyrell for an explanation.

"All I caught was something about 'the ancient evil' and 'bloodthirst'." Tyrell shrugged, "Sounds like our man though, doesn't it?" The mage knelt down beside the elf, speaking haltingly in the same flowery language. He received no reply. "He's scared so badly that his mind is locked up. I might be able to try to touch his mind with magic in order to find out what we need to know."

"I think his mind's touched enough already, but you might as well give it a try," said Galen as he watched the wizard go into a deep trance. Slowly, the cowering elf relaxed, his eyelids closing with longer and longer blinks. Loud snores shortly broke the silence in the glade. Tyrell's own eyes popped open suddenly. He gasped as he fell back on the grass. Nestor knelt beside his friend while Galen checked on the sleeping elf.

"I'll be OK," said Tyrell. He waved away his friend and smiled. "I found the way into the city. There's a secret path that our friend here, whose name is Kershaw, knows about."

"Anything about the sword?"

"Not that I could find. I had no idea how big of a place the mind is. Maybe with a little more practice, I could have, but I really don't want to risk doing any damage in someone's head."

"Could you really damage his any worse," Nestor snorted.

Tyrell ignored the comment. "I'm hoping to find some clues about Shadow Reaver once we enter the city." The mage got up and gently shook Kershaw awake. He said something to sooth the old elf. "We need to go back a bit. There is a glade that we passed through with a huge hollow tree. The tree hides the entrance to an old escape tunnel that leads into Khasharsta. Do we have any idea where the cultists are?"

Nestor nodded. "They can't be more than an hour behind us. With all of the time I've spent attacking these bushes, I'm sure they've closed that distance. Hell, all they have to do is follow the path we've cleared. Should lead them right to us."

"All the more reason to hurry. The tree we're looking for is only a couple of minutes away from here." Tyrell led the elf away while Galen and Nestor gathered their horses.

They found the old tree easily. It stood alone in a small glade, towering above the surrounding trees like it was the king of the forest. Even among the monstrous trees of the Thelvenin Wood, it was a giant. They found a small crawlspace that led into the very heart of the trunk that opened into a chamber just large enough for the four of them to stand in. Kershaw looked around and blinked rapidly as old memories began to awaken. The elf jabbered again and fell to the ground as he pawed at the dirt of the floor.

"What's he after?" asked Nestor.

Tyrell shrugged. "Must be the entrance to the tunnel."

"Well, tell him to hurry," whispered Galen. The thief pointed out the tree's opening. "We've got company." Tyrell moved to the thief's vantage point and frowned. Half a dozen horsemen in dark armor were warily riding down the trail towards them.

"Damn, they must know that we're close," muttered the mage. "They just don't know exactly where."

Kershaw let out an exultant whoop and pointed at an iron ring planted in the ground. The elf tugged at the trap door, but it wouldn't budge. "Galen. Nestor. Clear the edges, and help him get that thing open. I'll see if I can slow down our pursuers." Tyrell closed his eyes, reveling in the feel of the ancient magic of the forest flowing into him. It was an immense swell of power that washed over him, but he bent the energy to his will. Nestor and Galen located the sides of the door buried beneath centuries of moss and dirt. With a heave, the barbarian, thief, and wizened elf pulled aside the massive stone block revealing a short flight of stairs that led into a musty, earthen tunnel. Kershaw chattered again and rushed down into the dark passage. Nestor made a grab for the elf, but Kershaw's speed and nimbleness were considerable despite his age.

"Galen, go after him, and see that he doesn't get too far ahead of us," growled the warrior. The thief nodded, then jumped down the stairs. He too vanished into the darkness. Nestor grabbed Tyrell's elbow, steadying the staggering wizard. "Are you alright?" he asked.

"I'm still a little groggy from the mind reading, and the magic here is a far stronger than I'm used to. I've covered the entrance with an illusion of vines and moss. It should keep them off of us for a little while longer, but won't hold up if they really get curious." He waved towards the tunnel entrance. "Come on, we'd better catch up to the others." Quickly, but carefully, they descended into the tunnel, taking a moment to let their eyes adjust to the gloom.

The light that filtered through the entrance was quickly swallowed up by the surrounding darkness. Though they moved slowly, Tyrell and Nestor still stumbled and tripped as they crossed the uneven rocks along the uneven floor. If not for Kershaw's continuous chattering that floated back to them from somewhere up ahead, they would have considered themselves hopelessly lost.

Nestor yelped as a hand from the darkness grabbed his forearm. "Easy, Redbeard, it's me," said Galen.

"Alhambra's Hells," swore the barbarian. "I thought you were some guardian spirit grabbing after me. Can't see a damned thing down here. Where's Kershaw?"

"He's right in front of us playing in the dirt again. The tunnel is a dead end. He was talking the whole way down to this point, and then suddenly stopped. I think he bumped his nose against the wall."

"I thought elves could see in the dark?"

"Not when it's pitch black apparently."

Nestor pounded his fist against the stone wall before him. "So we're stuck, and with those cultist knights close by looking for us." He drew his sword. "Guess we'll just have to go back the way we came and fight our way out."

"Not if we can find a secret door," said Tyrell.

"What makes you think that there is one?"

"First of all, why build a tunnel all this way under the forest only to make it into a dead end?"

"Maybe they didn't get to finish it," growled Nestor.

"Secondly, the rock ahead of us feels like worked stone, not rough like the tunnel walls. We're almost inside." Tyrell knelt down beside the elf and said something that sounded to Nestor like the wizard swallowed a bug. Kershaw's reply, mused the barbarian, sounded like he hacked one back up. "He says the mechanism is heavily trapped, but he can't remember how to disarm it."

"Of course not," sighed Nestor. "That would be too convenient."

"Step aside then, and give me some light," said Galen.

"If those riders have made it into the tunnel then they'll be on us seconds after we throw up a light," said the warrior.

"Would you rather fight vampire worshippers in total darkness? Light a damn torch, and let me see if I can figure out how to get us inside."

Nestor fumbled for a moment, then pulled some oily rags from a pouch that he kept for just such an emergency. He wrapped them around the end of a long dagger and struck a spark to it.

"Hurry, lad. Don't know how long this will burn." Galen examined the gray stone wall before them that blocked their way. Runes etched in mysterious patterns scrawled across the surface. Galen moved methodically from section to section, his trained eyes searching for telltale signs of hazards that might await the unwary. As he concluded his investigation, he dusted off his hands and grinned at the barbarian.

"Hold that dagger straight out in front of you facing the left wall." The thief positioned the barbarian exactly as he wanted. Galen moved back to the worked stone wall, stomping hard on a rock in the floor. "Get ready," he said with a chuckle.

A half-moon shaped blade shot out of the wall towards the barbarian. Nestor held up his dagger in feeble defense, but it protected him nonetheless. The great blade sheared through his knife but was harmlessly deflected away from the big man's body.

"I thought that locking bar looked broken," said Galen with a wink to his friend.

"I could have been diced, you crazy little. . . . Why didn't you just tell me to stand aside?"

"Consider yourself fortunate that the other locking mechanisms all held. From where you were standing, getting diced would have been pleasant by comparison." Kershaw giggled, which did nothing to improve Nestor's mood. Galen grinned at Tyrell, who just shook his head as his shoulders shook with silent laughter. The thief twisted a root near the wall, and the stone face noiselessly opened on well-concealed hinges allowing the group entrance into the cavernous, gloomy chamber beyond.

Even Kershaw remained quiet as they entered the room. The

vaulted ceiling of the place was lost in the shadows above. "This place feels like a church," whispered Galen reverently.

"Kaariken Tel'duina," said Tyrell.

"Gods bless you," quipped the thief.

"This is the Cathedral of Starlight. I read about this place in one of Kellen's books. This was the holiest place in Khasharsta."

"See," said Galen as he punched Nestor lightly in the arm. "Told you it was a church.

Nestor made a sign of warding as he walked through the sanctuary. "Just don't touch anything," he whispered. "Elven gods probably still watch over this place."

"Well, aren't we here for the purpose of stealing a sword?" Nestor said nothing but glared at the young thief. Kershaw destroyed the solemnity of the moment by cackling gleefully, then dashing off into a nearby hallway. Tyrell closed the secret portal behind them, jumping back in alarm as ominous clicks and whirrs sounded when the stone fell flush against stone.

"The trap mechanism just reset itself," said Galen. "That should slow up our pursuit even more."

"So what do we know about this place?" Nestor started to sit down on a stone bench but thought better of it when he saw a spider as big as his hand scuttle away. "How are we going to find Shadow Reaver?"

"There's supposed to be a library near the cathedral. Elven historians kept chronicles of everything. I suggest we go there and do some research about Gilgorad. He died before the city did, so there should be records of him somewhere."

"Then let's get moving," said Galen. "I want to look around, and I don't know how long those traps will occupy the riders behind us." The three men made a quick check of their personal gear, hurriedly moving out into the hall where Kershaw had vanished. The only traces of the elf were his footprints in the ages-old dust upon the floor. Tyrell figured the elf was better off in the city than they were, so the men moved past the side passageway, and proceeded instead through the massive double doors of the cathedral.

A cool breeze blew over them as they stood on the steps that led down to the street. Twilight had just begun to settle over the forest, and the ancient trees cast long shadows along the cobblestones. The companions looked around, taking their first real look at the lost elven city of Khasharsta.

They were a little disappointed.

Centuries of neglect had left many of the once majestic buildings crumbling into disrepair. Once graceful spires now lay in fallen ruins on the ground. The forest had pressed forward to reclaim the city as weeds, thorns, and brush overflowed once elegant gardens. Tall grasses grew up through the cracked and broken paving stones of the streets and walkways.

"Not exactly my idea of paradise," murmured Galen. The trio stood still for a moment, and quietly absorbed the scene. "So," said the thief at last, "where's the library?"

"I'm not sure. We may have to do some searching around."

"That sounds safe." replied the rogue. "Cultists behind us, and gods know what within these buildings." Nestor lightly cuffed the younger man on the back of the head, then moved towards the nearest ruin.

"Damn, Galen," growled the warrior, "why do you think we brought you along? It's not as if Tyrell and I would come into a place like this without someone to send ahead as bait."

"Will you two stop," snapped Tyrell. "I can't concentrate on the buildings with you two bickering." He sighed. "I'm sorry. I didn't mean to be so sharp. Why don't we spread out a bit? We'll cover more ground that way. Just be careful though. We don't have any idea what else besides the forest may have claimed the city for its own."

The three men fanned out, poking through some of the various tumbled down buildings along the wide street. Tyrell made his way through the undergrowth to the crumbling steps of a once magnificent building. "I found it," he cried out a moment later. "This is it."

Nestor and Galen hurried to his side. "How can you tell?" asked Nestor. He whistled at the obvious grandeur the building before them had once possessed. The stone and woodwork were crafted together with such skill and artistry that it seemed as though one sprang forth from the other. Delicate columns spiraled into the air holding aloft intricately carved archways. The entire structure looked so impossibly fragile to support the canopy of the forested roof. "This place looks more like a palace."

"The elves valued knowledge above their kings. Their academies and libraries reflected that in their design. You could say that this was a palace of sorts to them." He pointed to a moss-covered inscription on the archway. "Harleith Malachor."

"I wish you'd stop doing that," said Galen. "Pretend for one moment that some of us here don't speak elvish."

"Seeker's Hall. This was the great library of Khasharsta. Come on." Tyrell moved carefully over the broken steps towards the door that hung askew from its hinges.

"I think the only thing that could kill us in here is boredom," griped the thief.

"Maybe you'll find a rabid bookworm. Let's go, lad," replied Nestor. Galen sighed, and nimbly picked his way over the rubble. He passed Tyrell who struggled to balance on a few precarious pieces of masonry and approached the doorway. As he peered into the darkness, the young cutpurse gasped when he realized that shining eyes peered back at him.

"Be care-," he began to yell, but a rat the size of a mastiff plowed into the young thief, bowling him over. A second rat scurried from out of the dark portal, hissing angrily at Nestor and Tyrell. Pure luck saved Galen from having his throat torn out as he and the giant rodent tumbled down the staircase. The thief clamped his hands tightly around the rat's muzzle as they rolled. There was a satisfying crunch when they hit the bottom as his knee drove hard against the beast's ribcage.

Nestor sized up the second rat. "This mouse is a little too big to stomp. Have to do this the hard way," he said as he drew his sword. He scooped up a handful of small rocks and threw them at the rat to make sure he had its full attention. "Tyrell, see to Galen. I've got this one under control." The barrage of pebbles did no damage, but they infuriated the rat. Recklessly, it charged across the broken steps towards the barbarian.

Tyrell ran to Galen's side just in time to slam his dagger into the back of the struggling rodent. It squealed in pain and snapped at the mage, but Tyrell leaped back out of reach of the foul bite. The rat's attack gave Galen a chance to reach his own dagger. With a snarl, the thief drove his blade up through the rat's jaw, and deep into the creature's brain. The rodent shuddered once, collapsing on the thief.

Nestor's rat perched on some broken stone, swatting its filthy claws at the warrior. The barbarian deftly parried, and his keen-edged blade sheared off the first knuckle of the rat's paw. More furious now than ever, the rat lunged forward to bite at the warrior. Nestor's foot lashed out at the rock the beast sat upon just as it poised to spring. The cracked stone broke free, sprawling the rat on the ground directly in front of the mighty warrior. With a fast downward swing of his blade, the fight was over.

"Too easy," called the barbarian to his friends. He wiped the blade of his sword on the rat's hide. He smiled as he saw Galen crawl out from beneath the body of the second beast. "Still think going to the library is going to be dull, boy?"

Galen looked at his friend and then grinned. "I take it back. Forget I ever said it."

Tyrell laughed, slapping the thief on the shoulder as Nestor sheathed his weapon. "Just wait until you see the bookworms," he said.

<h1 style="text-align: center;">CHAPTER TEN</h1>

Seeker's Hall was in little better condition than the rest of the city. Many of the ancient bookcases had rotted and collapsed. Their brittle contents were strewn all over the dusty floors. Tyrell winced as Galen poked at one open tome only to see the pages crumble, then blow away beneath the thief's light fingers. The thief shrugged apologetically, dusting off his hands.

"Is anything here even usable?" said Nestor as they looked at the ruin before them.

"There has to be something," insisted Tyrell. The mage gingerly lifted a scroll from an ancient table, but the paper broke into fragments that drifted lazily to the floor. He sighed. "I don't understand it, but I can sense that there is something here that will help us. We just have to be careful with what we touch."

"Tyrell, perhaps we should search the rest of the city first," suggested Nestor. "There have to be some crypts or graves somewhere. If Gilgorad died before the city fell, then maybe we can find his tomb on our own."

"Sure," snorted Galen. "Or maybe we can find something even nastier than the bloodsucker we're trying to stop."

"Just don't go crying to your mummy," returned the barbarian. He ducked the book that Galen hurled at him. Tyrell shook his head, and all three men couldn't resist having a laugh.

"Why don't you two go on ahead," said the wizard. "I don't feel like leaving here just yet. Besides, I'm the only one who can read their language anyway. I still feel as though something here is calling to me. I just have to locate whatever it is." He looked back at his two friends and shrugged.

"We'll stick to the closer buildings then," said the barbarian as he clapped Tyrell on the back. "Are you certain you don't want to come along? This place may hold more surprises than wolf-sized rats."

"I'll be fine. Nothing here but me, and the bookworms," he said with a grin. "You two go. Just stay within shouting distance, and be careful." The thief and barbarian both nodded, then left through the rubble-filled archway back into the darkening street. Tyrell waited until they had left, and then pounded his fist on a desk in frustration. The already fragile piece of furniture collapsed in a cloud of dust and splinters.

Something was here. He knew it, but he couldn't tell where it was calling to him from. Where was he supposed to look? He had felt a subtle power from the moment he had crossed the threshold of the library. It had begun as nothing more than a tickle at the back of his mind, but something with powerful, ancient magic had drawn him into this place as if it knew who he was, and why he had come. Tyrell swore that he wasn't going to leave until he found the source of the summons.

A rickety staircase led up to a balcony, where more rows of moldering books and scrolls sat on rotting shelves. Tyrell carefully made his way up the stair, praying silently that it held together. Floorboards groaned in protest with every step he took, but they reluctantly carried his weight. Tyrell stepped into a dark alcove to go around a huge pile of debris when his senses came alert.

It was close. The powerful magic presence that he had sensed was somewhere near this alcove. The power was centuries old but still stronger than any dweomer he had ever encountered before. The longer he stood in Seeker's Hall the stronger he felt the pull of an awe-inspiring, and somewhat frightening, presence beckoning him onward. Tyrell considered only for a moment that the siren call that pulled him towards the darkened alcove before him was not benevolent, but his curiosity was too keyed up to resist an opportunity to discover a source of magic so old and yet still so powerful.

The wizard gritted his teeth and stepped forward, letting the lengthening shadows embrace him.

*   *   *

"So, just out of curiosity, where do you think that the old elf went?" asked Galen. The two men had wandered back towards the cathedral entrance, having found no evidence of Gilgorad's passing in the other nearby ruins.

"I'm a little more concerned on the whereabouts of those cultists who've been dogging our steps. If they've managed to bypass those traps, then we could easily walk into an ambush. I'll tell you straight up that I'm not anxious to face that big, blond brute who leads them."

Galen looked at Nestor in surprise. "You never cease to amaze me, Nestor. I always thought your people lived for their next fight. Honor, glory, and death in battle. You seem reluctant to even draw your sword sometimes."

"My people are ferocious by necessity. Their lives in the hills are rough, and they must likewise be as tough in order to survive. We wandered after the food we hunted. Oftentimes, that would often take us into territory that others had claimed. Kargs, other clans, and dangerous predators. I learned to fight because it was expected of me to help defend ourselves. I do it well, but that doesn't mean I enjoy it.

"The only fights I have ever looked forward to are against those who have wronged me in some way. Even in most of those, the battle was not to the death. I take no pleasure in taking another life without cause." He chuckled. "Besides, since I've gotten thrown in with you and the mage, I've been pounded on by knights, soldiers, zombies, kargs, and even my own companions. Frankly, I'm getting a little tired of it all."

*   *   *

Tyrell studied the arcane symbols that seemed to crawl along the back wall of the alcove. There was a doorway here, made and hidden by ancient magic. The wizard fell into a meditative trance, gently pushing and probing against the runes that protected the hidden portal. He smiled to himself as he discovered the impression of a subtle yet deadly trap. The rune was still active, but he was sure that the power of the thing was not what it once was. It was possible that he could just trigger the spell, and hope that the runes had weakened enough with the ages to not be fatal. He snorted. And if he was wrong, then perhaps his friends would still find enough of him left to bury.

Tyrell examined the doorway for a few moments longer, then sighed. There was no way around the trap without the word of command created by whoever set the ward. He had no choice but to set off the warding spell and take his chances. Tyrell concentrated on the weakest part of the symbol's pattern. Disrupting the sigil would break the magical circuit of energy, releasing whatever stored potential remained. The thing could quite literally blow up in his face, but he saw no other options. Bracing himself for the magical backlash, Tyrell mentally tore apart the rune.

The resulting explosion of energy hurled the wizard across the library. He slammed through three bookshelves, pulverizing both them and their contents to powder. Tyrell thudded against a wall, rebounded away, and fell face down on the dusty floor. The coppery taste of blood filled his mouth, and his head throbbed as if he had been kicked by a dragon. His back ached, and he felt numerous splinters of wood digging into his flesh. *That's going to leave a mark,* he thought as he pushed himself from the floor. *All in all, I'm pretty damn fortunate to be breathing.*

Tyrell slowly regained his feet. As he dusted himself off, a glimmering light caught his attention. A shimmering doorway now dispelled the shadows that had previously filled the alcove. The siren call that the mage had felt since entering now pulled screamed at his magical senses urging him to explore the space that lay behind the door. He limped over to the portal, took a deep breath, and pushed through the wavering magic before him.

After a moment of disorientation, Tyrell found himself in the long unused laboratory of some elven wizard. A thin skeleton with tattered bits of once fine cloth slumped over a book lying on a high table. Tyrell studied the room, recognizing the telltale dusty jars and bottles full of ingredients found useful in arcane research. He also noticed with surprise, however, that the book on which the skeleton rested was the only written work to be found in the entire lab. Tyrell slowly approached the corpse and looked at the pages beneath the dusty skull.

The pages, unlike anything else in the entire city, were perfectly preserved. The entire book looked as fresh as the day it was bound. No dust settled on the open sheets, and the writing looked as crisp as if it were just off the quill. The ink itself shimmered with a rainbow hue, and the script seemed to dance across the open page.

The mage gasped as he suddenly realized that the magical call he had felt all this time derived from this book. Tyrell could feel the magic as it pulsed from the tome without any need to concentrate. With trembling hands, Tyrell gently slid the skull away from the pages and began reading the scribbled runes within.

*   *   *

Nestor and Galen were back inside the sanctuary of the Cathedral of Starlight. Galen had stealthily crept ahead but found that the secret door remained closed. No signs of their pursuers were evident. Nestor had followed in behind him and sighed with relief at their discovery.

"Well, at least we don't appear to be followed anymore," said the warrior. "I needed some good news."

"Do you suppose there is a catacomb here we could search? I just want to find this damn sword, and get out of here," grumbled Galen.

"What's the matter, boy? Holy places got you spooked? Are the gods going to strike at you for your thieving ways?" Nestor laughed.

"No, I'm comfortable enough in church. Never met a poor box I didn't empty." He grinned back at the warrior. "I just don't like this place. Everything feels so dead."

"Fitting, then, that you will be meeting your end here," called a deep voice from a side hallway. Nestor and Galen whirled around to see the blond giant stride forward with a huge sword in his hand. Three other knights followed closely behind him. All were clad in black armor, and each wore those now too familiar red sashes. The other knights all leveled crossbows at the companions. "I lost a couple of good men, good friends, getting through that damned door," said the leader. The huge warrior tapped his sword casually against his shoulder as he slowly approached the two men. Then his eyes blazed with a sudden fury. "For their loss, as well as for my brothers in the Karghome Fen, shall I now take my vengeance." He flipped his blade down to point at Nestor's chest.

A sudden high pitched wail sounded from behind the altar. Kershaw, now clad in a knee-length blue ceremonial robe, waved his arms frantically at the knights as he raced forward. The youngest of them, already on edge from the deaths of his comrades, turned and fired at the approaching elf. His crossbow quarrel punched into Kershaw's shoulder, spraying the altar behind the elf with blood. The elf screamed in agony and crumpled to the floor.

"Bastards," roared Nestor. He plowed his shoulder into the blond knight's chest, driving the man back into his own troops. As they scattered, Galen drew his own weapon, charging ahead at Kershaw's assailant. The man raised his crossbow as an impromptu shield while the furious rogue attacked.

The blond warrior slammed his knee into Nestor's stomach, then punched the barbarian in the jaw with his mailed fist. The remaining two men held their crossbows at the ready, waiting for the opportunity to take a clean shot. Galen hacked away at the last knight's makeshift defense, scoring a painful cut across the man's knuckles. Before the man's crossbow could hit the floor, Galen reversed his stroke and cut a fine gash across the young knight's throat. Trained reflexes saved the young thief in the next instant as he threw himself forward to avoid the twin crossbow bolts that hummed through the air where he had been but a moment before.

Nestor returned the blond warrior's attacks with brutal fury. Fists flailed as the two men pummeled each other without mercy. Nestor answered the blond knight's strike to the jaw with a mighty blow of his own that caused the armored man to spit blood and teeth. Their battle soon became one fueled by raw hatred with reason becoming lost in the swirling depths of blinding rage. For every successful strike, the other retaliated with an equally savage counterstrike. Each man refused to be the first to fall, and it seemed as though the very walls of the cathedral shook with their anger.

Galen wasn't faring so well. He now faced the remaining two knights alone, and both fought with the obvious skill of experienced veterans. They wove their blades in deft crossing strokes that pushed the thief's guard to its limits. Despite his blinding parries, Galen had already suffered several minor cuts and knew from their sting that it was only a matter of time before he would no longer be able to keep up with them.

A sudden flash of light blinded all of the combatants, causing all to fall away from their foes. When their eyes cleared, they saw Tyrell standing in the entrance to the sanctuary rubbing the black residue of flash powder from his fingers. His eyes burned with anger as he regarded the knights, then boldly pushed past them to kneel at Kershaw's side. The blond giant raised his hand in a silent command to his men to hold their ground.

The old elf gasped for breath as Tyrell lifted his head from the bloody stone. Kershaw clutched feebly at the bolt sticking from his shoulder. As his gaze fell upon Tyrell, the mage saw that the elf recognized him, and for the first time since their meeting, seemed completely lucid.

"Ne tamo ki Kaariken," whispered Kershaw as he grasped Tyrell's hand. The wizard simply nodded. Kershaw smiled and whispered, "Feramik ila fev'amish." The elf stiffened, groaned once, and then lay still.

"Walk eternally in sunlight, my friend," said Tyrell, as he let the elf's head down gently. He covered Kershaw's face with the hood of the blue robe that he wore. He then stood and turned to face the warriors. "I have every intention of fulfilling Kershaw's last wishes. He first asked that no blood be shed within these holy walls. If this fight is to continue then it will be taken outside." The blond warrior nodded respectfully. "His second wish was for us to stop the Dark Enemy. I swear by all of the forces of Heaven and Hell that this damnable vampire will pay for this innocent blood."

The blond knight snorted. "Do you expect us to believe that you would change your allegiance for the sake of a single elf?"

"You had better find a new bloodsucker to worship," growled Nestor. "Your current master dies as soon as we return to Tarnath."

"Worship? The Shadow Lords exist only to destroy such evils.

And those foolish enough to follow such villains," the knight added with a pointed glare.

Tyrell looked puzzled. "You are vampire hunters? But . . . we were told that those who wore the red sash served the fiend. Kellen Ambrose hired us to stop vampire cultists, and deliver the sword Shadow Reaver to him so that he could use it to destroy Darian."

"Who in Alhambra's Hells is Darian?"

Tyrell's jaw dropped open. "Darian is the damned vampire we've been opposing. Who did you think it was?"

It was now the blond knight's turn to look confused. "I have never heard the name Darian before. However, the name Kellen Ambrose is well documented in the records of our order."

"Hold on," said Galen. "What in the hell is going on here?"

"I'd say you've been duped, and set upon those you should name as allies," said one of the other knights.

Tyrell walked up to the blond knight. "Are you telling me that Kellen Ambrose has been misdirecting us this whole time?"

"What I am telling you is that Kellen Ambrose is a vampire lord who has wreaked havoc in these lands for close to a millennium. Ambrose's terrors have been recorded by my brother knights for centuries. His name first appeared at roughly the time of the fall of this city. There is ample proof in our libraries to mark him as the beast that we hunt. We received information that this fiend had recruited the three of you to work for him during the daylight hours that he himself cannot suffer. At first, we only meant to watch you, and determine your intentions. However, after the deaths of our brother knights in the Karghome Fen, we were convinced that our intelligence had been correct."

"Your fellow knights were the men we fought in the Fen?" Tyrell sat down heavily on a stone bench. "I think I'm going to be sick."

"They were en route to Tarnath to deliver a message to some of our other soldiers about. . . ."

"About the locations of Kellen's lairs," finished Tyrell. "Gods above, this all makes sense now."

"Ah," said Galen, "suppose that for some of us, there are still some gray areas. I mean what about the zombie attack, Kellen's kidnapping, and the chase in the sewers? What about the room of coffins that he himself set on fire? Why bring the Shadow Lords into this to stop us from doing what he wanted us to do?"

"Kellen did the whole thing to further his own deceptions," said Tyrell. "We needed an enemy to occupy our attention, so he must have anonymously tipped off the Shadow Lords to who we were. He probably figured that we'd be so busy battling each other that we would never question one another. Also, anyone who was killed in battle was one less enemy seeking to destroy him. The list of lairs was kept out of the hands of the people who could have done the greatest harm to him. He simply had to abandon the places that they knew about, and establish new hideouts before anyone was the wiser.

"In the sewer, he staged his own kidnapping simply to convince us that his feud with Darian was real. We never looked inside the coffins he burned to see if any of his minions were even inside. Damn, I'll bet my life now that they were all empty."

"What about the sword? Why not just leave it unfound, and go on about his business?"

"He probably would have if you hadn't heard the story of Gilgorad, and mentioned it to us all. Since we knew of the weapon, he must have decided that he would be better off having it in his own possession so that no one else could use it against him. We all supposed the sword was a legend, but he swore it was real. The reason he knew was because Gilgorad had used it against him centuries before."

"But why did he choose us though? Why not get someone who really was interested in helping him?" asked Galen.

"He told us that himself. Our skills complement each other well enough to let us succeed at tasks he couldn't undertake himself. We can function by daylight, unlike him. Also, we were conveniently thrown together on the same night, and left without a choice of refusing his offer."

"We need to be absolutely certain of this, Tyrell," said Nestor. "I mean we can't just kick down Kellen's door, and attack him. If we're wrong, we'll end up on the gallows for certain. Of course, if you're right, then I personally want to ram 3 feet of steel through his bowels."

"We need more to go on, Tyrell," added Galen. "In my line of work, I know the value of evidence."

"We've never personally met with Kellen during the day, we've never seen him eat a morsel of food, and I can't recall ever seeing a single reflective surface anywhere in his home. All of these are traditional signs of vampire lore. But if you want proof, I think that this confusion with the Shadow Lords as well as their own histories should give anyone a pretty clear idea that Ambrose has been lying to us from the beginning."

The blond knight coughed lightly. "Now that we've cleared all of this up, and we all realize that we both want to destroy the same creature, perhaps we should consider uniting our forces. My name is Drayton. My two surviving companions here are Krieger and Berthis. If you truly seek the destruction of Kellen Ambrose, then our swords are at your disposal." The knight extended his hand out to the mage. Tyrell clasped it and shook.

As the introductions concluded, Tyrell lifted Kershaw's frail form from the stone floor and placed the elf on the great altar of the cathedral. He bowed his head reverently, then returned to the group. The knights did likewise with their fallen man, with Drayton offering a brief prayer of blessing over his dead soldier. When all were finished they joined together at the entrance of the sanctuary.

"Now, then," said Nestor, "all we have to do is figure out where that damn sword is. We still haven't found a single clue."

"Yes we have," said Tyrell. The wizard reached into his pack and drew forth the beautiful leather-bound book he had discovered in the city's library. "What you are looking at is the Book of Torax'alamien. He was the most powerful wizard that the elves, and arguably the entire world, has ever known. Everything he ever learned about the arcane arts was written into this mystical book, which apparently never runs out of pages. I can turn right to any topic I concentrate on, provided that he wrote something about it in here."

"Is there anything in it about Shadow Reaver?" asked Drayton.

Tyrell nodded. "Torax'alamien was the mage who enchanted the sword. This book says that Gilgorad's body was carried to a particular crypt in the heart of the city soon after his death in the Battle of Southmead. His sword rests at his side."

"Then you know where the crypt is," said Galen. "Is it close by?"

The wizard grinned. "My friends, we're practically standing on it."

Chapter Eleven

The tunnels to the crypts beneath the Cathedral of Starlight were choked with cobwebs and dust. The group proceeded slowly and cautiously. As the knights cut through wall after wall of ancient webbing, Galen would scout ahead for traps. Nestor watched the passage behind them, although nothing appeared n the centuries abandoned halls. Tyrell walked in the middle of the group, thumbing through the Book of Torax'alamien for guidance.

At last, the twists and turns came to an end at a short stairway that emptied out into a wide chamber filled with row after row of stone sarcophagi. "We are now in the Chamber of Kings," said Tyrell softly.

"Elven royalty only received simple brass plaques and plain stone to mark their passing?" asked Drayton indicating the simply adorned monuments. "Doesn't seem very fitting." The knight absently ran his hand over the dusty stone that housed a long forgotten elven monarch.

"The elves put less importance on their aristocracy. They understood that a bloodline didn't make someone either good or wise. So, King Curealane the Humble set forth the practice of requiring the elven people to be buried according to their accomplishments and merit, rather than by their station. The more decorative burial chambers will be deeper in. Come on." The mage led the others through aisles of the dead to a low opening at the far end of the chamber.

Fewer sarcophagi were in the second room, but the carvings upon the stone were more detailed, displaying inlays of gems and precious metals. The nameplates attached to these were made of pure gold. Galen's eyes gleamed as he took in the small fortunes used to mark the last resting places of those entombed. The thief rubbed his hands together, stepping towards a slab when Nestor grabbed him roughly by the collar.

"We're only here to loot one grave. Don't touch anything else," the barbarian growled. Drayton nodded his agreement and clutched his sword hilt a little tighter. Galen grinned sheepishly, holding his hands out wide in silent apology. He knew that he was in the wrong company to commit any acts that might be seen as irreverent or a desecration.

Tyrell looked up from the book again. "This still isn't the right place. This is the Vault of the Sage. All of the great elven scholars and artisans are buried here. The next chamber must be the Hall of Heroes. That is where Gilgorad was laid to rest." The wizard hurried forward and descended another short flight of stairs that led into the final burial chamber.

Only three sarcophagi were in the last room. Each was studded with jewels, and made from the finest quality of marble. The light from the group's torches made dazzling reflections as the flames danced over the surface of each tomb.

"Hero must not have been an easy title to achieve in elven society," mused Drayton.

"Only the greatest contributors to their culture earned a place in this room," replied Tyrell. "This was King Khasharas," said the mage as he touched the first stone. "He united the warring tribes of elves and brought peace to their race after six centuries of violent war. The city Khasharsta was named in his honor, and built by the unified elven nation. His laws formed the basis of not only the elven courts but were adopted by many other cities that Khasharsta dealt with." The wizard moved to the second stone slab.

"This is the tomb of Lady Hylissa. She was a priestess who offered herself as a hostage in lieu of an elven prince. For forty-three days she was tortured and beaten by the general of a bandit army that threatened the city. She not only endured the agony, but prayed to the elven gods throughout her ordeal to forgive the aggressors, and let them see how the elven people could live in harmony with their kind. The enemy general was so moved and ashamed by her display of compassion that he recalled his army from their siege, which had very nearly defeated the elves. Not only did he attempt everything in his power to make amends for his actions, but he also threw down his sword forever, and became the first Archbishop of Tarnath." Tyrell walked to the final sarcophagus that sat upon a raised dais.

"And this is the tomb of General Gilgorad. He wrote the book on elven warfare and tactics. His strategies are still required reading in most military academies around the world today. He led the elven armies to more victories than any other general in history. He fell during the Battle of Southmead while single-handedly holding back a troop of kargs. The ground had become so slick with blood that he eventually slipped, and that was when one of his opponents got in a glancing blow. It was heavy enough, though, that he fell to the ground. It was only then that they could set upon him. His second in command brought in a cavalry charge right at that moment that decimated the remaining creatures, but the damage was already done. Another of his important feats was when he drove off a despicable evil that threatened the elven nation by night." Tyrell's eyes met Drayton's. "I think we all know who that was."

"Something with big, sharp, pointed teeth, I suppose," said Nestor. He squinted at the end of the sarcophagus. "What the hell is this nameplate made of?" Tyrell and Galen knelt down to see better. The metal plate glittered like a rainbow even in the dim light of the flickering torches. The etchings, written in the elven tongue, were infused with diamond dust.

"I've never seen anything like it before," whispered Tyrell. "It's beautiful though."

"It's called elvensteel," said Galen. All eyes turned with surprise to the thief. He shrugged. "Read about it at the guild. Supposed to be the most precious metal in the whole world, and damnably hard to work with. Only the elves knew how to make things out of the purest form of the metal. It's thought to exist only in legends."

"And in the tombs of their greatest heroes," said Drayton reverently. He gave a slight bow to the sarcophagus.

Tyrell frowned. "Well, let's get this grim business over with. There's something about this place that I don't like."

"Well, the guests of honor aren't exactly great on conversation," quipped Galen. The thief knelt to examine a stacked pile of armor at the foot of the stone slab. He noticed a second identical suit at the far end as well. Their style was ancient and bore such elaborate trim and markings that the suits gave the clear impression that they belonged to no common soldier but were more likely those of an elite honor guard.

Nestor and the knights lifted the heavy stone lid from its place, revealing an ancient coffin within. Krieger reached in and knocked on the wood, drawing scowls from Drayton and the barbarian warrior. "Anybody home?" he asked with a chuckle. Nestor started to open his mouth to rebuke the Shadow Lord when a Galen interrupted.

"Wait. Do you hear that?" A faint scratching noise came from beneath the exposed lid of the coffin. "Something is alive in there."

"It couldn't be. No one's been here for centuries," said Tyrell. "It has to be insects or something."

"Krieger, get that lid open, but be cautious," ordered Drayton. "Something seems amiss here."

Krieger took a pry bar and leaned over the coffin. Splintered wood blew outward as a rotting hand punched through the top, and clamped down on his wrist. The sound of crunching bone was only drowned by the knight's howl of agony. A rattle of armor drew everyone's attention to the suits at each end as they suddenly rose from the floor. The spectral eyes of long-dead elven warriors could be seen through the visors, as they drew wicked looking swords.

Drayton and Nestor immediately squared off against the armored ghosts as Berthis tried to break the iron grip of the monster that held Krieger. The captured knight screamed in agony as the bones of his wrist snapped with an audible crunch. The lid suddenly blew upwards with a powerful blow, stunning both of the knights but knocking Berthis away from the horrifying monstrosity that rose from the tomb.

"It's a ghoul," shouted Tyrell.

"Great," yelled Galen. "How do we kill it?" He saw that Tyrell's eyes had already closed as the mage went into the realm of magic to seek that very answer. The ghoul snarled at the thief then turned back to Krieger. The knight smacked the undead monster on the side of the head with the pry bar he still held, but if the ghoul even felt the blow, it didn't show it. With blood encrusted black talons, the fiend ripped through the knight's breastplate, spilling Krieger's innards onto the floor. Berthis had regained his feet but stood in mute terror as his friend fell lifeless to the floor.

Tyrell's eyes snapped open, and he grabbed Galen by the arm. "That thing is not Gilgorad. It just took up residence in his crypt. I sense some very powerful magic within that tomb. It has to be the sword. We have to get Shadow Reaver."

The ghoul stepped past the body of the fallen knight and stalked Berthis. It hissed and spat, waiting for the knight to make some foolish move. Meanwhile, the ghosts of Gilgorad's elite company showed their formidable swordsmanship against Drayton and Nestor. The two men fought frantically but were soon frustrated as their attacks were repeatedly turned aside by the skilled undead.

Galen raced around the room careful not to draw attention to himself as he leaped into the sarcophagus. As he pulled away a piece of the shattered coffin, he felt a strange chill run up his spine as he crouched within the tomb. He quickly discounted his uneasiness as adrenaline, as he began digging through the debris. His keen eyes found a hidden catch that he triggered with a flip of his thumb. When a panel slid open in the bottom of the casket, the thief was amazed to see the perfectly preserved body of a middle-aged elf. The body was clad in the most elegant armor that Galen had ever seen, but the battle scars and gouges that ran along it told that it was far more than ornamental. Across the corpse's chest, his hands resting upon the hilt, lay a sword of glittering elvensteel that the thief knew in an instant could only be Shadow Reaver.

The thief snatched the sword from the dead elf's hand and jumped out of the sarcophagus to land behind the ghoul. The beast didn't notice Galen's approach as it batted Berthis' sword aside, and ripped open the poor man's throat with a backhand swipe of its filthy claws. As Galen raised the sword to slash across the monster's exposed neck, the shimmering sword flared with a sudden brilliant light. The ghoul shrieked and shielded its eyes as Galen's stroke sheared through the creature's forearm like paper. The ghosts that pressed against Nestor and Drayton staggered as the sword flared like a noonday sun in the young thief's hand.

Drayton attacked with renewed vigor as his foe faltered. His sword rang as it struck the ghost's armor, but the blow only drove the specter back a single step. The ghost recovered too quickly and batted aside the knight's defenses. It howled in victory as it slammed the point of its blade deep into the Shadow Lord's shoulder, and then backhanded the wounded knight. Drayton fell to the ground as his weapon skittered across the stone floor. He clutched at the bleeding wound in his shoulder, glaring defiantly into the ghost warrior's gleaming eyes behind the ancient visor. As it towered over him, it slowly raised its sword in a two-handed grip high above its head.

Nestor had been forced back into a corner of the room by his opponent but fought with the fury of a caged animal. Tiny cuts covered his body from the relentless assault of the undead guardian. As Shadow Reaver flared, Nestor took advantage of the momentary weakness of his attacker. He knocked the ghost's sword high, spun about, and slashed hard and fast across the neck of his foe. He snarled in frustration as his blade met little resistance. He lashed out with a ferocious kick to the creature's breastplate, though, opening a path to the middle of the room. The barbarian saw the second ghost raising his sword against the downed knight, and threw his shoulder into the back of the unsuspecting creature. With a crash of metal, the ghost slammed against the sarcophagus of Gilgorad.

Galen feinted at the ghoul, which caused the beast to lunge forward in a futile grasp. The thief brought the elvensteel blade back in a flashing arc that sliced a deep wound across the beast's chest. The ghoul shrieked in agony as the weapon burned it with a pain unlike any it had ever known. It turned to run from the dangerous weapon, but Galen moved faster. He reversed the sword and drove Shadow Reaver into the fleeing ghoul's back.

The sword shrieked in triumph as it sent purging flames through the ghoul's innards. The monster thrashed back and forth as greasy smoke rolled from its mouth. Its screams were hideous as its pallid skin burned to ashes. In seconds, the ghoul crumbled, and Galen snatched Shadow Reaver before the enchanted blade could hit the floor. It was surprisingly cool to the touch and pulsed within his grasp.

Nestor fell into a defensive stance beside Drayton as the two tomb guardians turned to face him. "Do something," growled Nestor over his shoulder to Tyrell. The barbarian raised his guard although he knew it would do him little good against his insubstantial opponents. Galen closed in with Shadow Reaver at the ready drawing the attention of one of the guardians.

Tyrell raised his hands, and cried out, "Su ne niala arken'duisa. Su vorcara fev'amish." The wizard prayed that he had spoken the phrase correctly. Their only chance to survive this encounter was if the guardians realized that their group was not an enemy to the elves. He sighed with relief as the two warriors turned to face him.

"Et morak'tha viellin dorush?" The voice of the guardian spirit sounded like wind howling through a deserted catacomb. Galen swallowed hard, clutching Shadow Reaver's hilt a little more tightly. Nestor remained unmoving but alert, and ready to spring. His eyes flicked only once to Drayton who had fallen unconscious. Blood flowed freely from the knight's wound, and the warrior knew that he had to help the man soon or he would die.

Tyrell bowed deeply to the spirits. "Su ne tianalin Gilgorad qui'ellis." The mage spoke haltingly. The twisted inflections of the ancient tongue made it difficult for him to get his point across. One misspoken syllable, and he could go from explaining that he was an ally to Gilgorad's cause to calling the general a thick brained pig. Happily, he noticed that the ghosts took no offense at whatever he had managed to say.

One of the specters lowered its sword, reaching out a hand towards the wizard. A low buzzing sound began to drone in Tyrell's mind. He could feel the presence of an otherworldly consciousness contacting his own. The mage forced himself to quell the natural reflex to defend against such an invasion, though, and opened his mind to allow the ghost to see the truth of the group's intentions. He let his mind fill with the thoughts of Kellen's lies and deceit. He thought of the suffering that so many had faced at the vampire lord's hands.

The buzzing presence abruptly disappeared, and the ghosts backed away to their positions on either end of the sarcophagus. With a clatter and crash, they collapsed back into neatly piled suits of armor. All three men let out a sigh of relief. Nestor dropped his blade beside him and immediately knelt to check on Drayton.

"Will he live?" asked Galen.

"He's injured badly," replied Nestor. He took some rolled cloth bandages from a pouch and began to clean and dress the Shadow Lord's wound. "He's going to need rest and far better attention than we can give him here though."

"We have what we came for," said Tyrell nodding to the glittering sword in Galen's hand. "Will he be well enough to ride back to Del Torac?"

The barbarian shrugged. "He'd better be. That's the closest place where we can find any help." He continued his work on the knight's wound.

"What the hell happened with those ghosts?" asked Galen.

"I told them that we were not evil men or common looters. I tried to show them that the ancient evil had returned and that we needed Shadow Reaver to defeat Kellen. I think they drew a large piece of our tale directly from my mind. Once I convinced them of the sincerity of our intentions, they backed away."

"So they'll let us take the sword out of here?"

"As far as I can tell. Honestly, I believe the power of that blade would have destroyed them even though their intentions weren't evil. It's as if they knew it was time for the sword to drawn for noble purposes once again."

Nestor stood up and brushed off his hands. "Fine by me. If they want us gone, then I for one say we should take their advice. I've had enough of tombs, ghosts, and things going bump in the night. Let's get back to Tarnath with this weapon, and stick it all the way to the hilt in Ambrose's gizzard. We can put this whole nightmare behind us."

"Nobody would like to finish this more than I, my friend," said Tyrell. "First, however, I think we could all use some rest, even if only a short one. We've been run ragged lately, and we lose any advantage we might have should we go against Kellen weakened and exhausted. Secondly, as you pointed out, we need to see to Drayton's care. I believe his part in all of this is at an end now. Finally, I would like some time to examine this book that I found. There are secrets of magic locked away in here that haven't been seen for centuries. I might even find the key to unlocking my own mental block. Maybe figure out how I can draw upon some magic that will really shake Kellen up."

"Then let's get our gear together, and set out for Del Torac as soon as possible," said Galen. "The sooner we leave here the sooner we can all get back to living a normal life. I miss lifting coin purses, and breaking into aristocrat's homes."

"That's your personal definition of a normal life, then?" asked Nestor wearily.

"Galen's right," said the mage. He took Shadow Reaver from the thief, and carefully examined the blade. "We'll get going, rest up briefly, and then show up on Kellen's doorstep with a surprise in hand for him. He'll never know that we've succeeded in finding the sword. By the time he knows it, we should be driving it through his black heart." He handed the sword back to Galen who had found a cloth to wrap it in. "Nestor, I'll help you carry Drayton. We leave immediately for Del Torac, and from there to Tarnath.

"We have some unfinished business to settle."

CHAPTER TWELVE

Their departure from Khasharsta was without further incident. Galen easily bypassed the reset trap mechanism in the Cathedral of Starlight, and the four men made their way into the cool evening breeze of the Thelvenin Woods. They rode as hard as they were able, considering Drayton's condition, setting camp a couple of hours later. The Shadow Lord regained consciousness while Nestor sat beside the injured man to check the bandaged wound. The barbarian proceeded to tell of the remaining events of the battle, including the tragic deaths of Drayton's brother knights.

"They fought as well as they were able," he said. "They fell in battle, and no doubt sit in a far fairer place than we have ever seen."

"They are two more tally marks against that devil, Ambrose. Two more lives that bastard will answer for." The knight struggled to sit up, but Nestor gently pushed him back to the ground.

"And if you start trying to jump up and down too soon, you'll be the next. Your wound won't take that kind of excitement right now. Hell, we're all lucky to be out of there without some sort of grievous injuries."

"How did you escape?"

"Tyrell, talked the spirits out of hacking us to bits," said Galen, "and we found this." The thief unwrapped the scintillating elvensteel blade allowing the knight to see the reflected campfire dancing like a rainbow across the weapon. After it was passed around among them, Galen carefully and reverently covered it again, cradling the magnificent sword in his arms, as if afraid to put it down.

"He couldn't have tried doing that before I got stabbed then," quipped Drayton. Tyrell hadn't heard the jibe though, as he was lost in study over his prize tome liberated from the Seeker's Hall.

"All I know is that I don't want the responsibility of using Shadow Reaver on Kellen. I mean, whoever is going to use this needs to get a lot closer to Kellen than I find comfortable." The young thief looked back and forth at the two swordsmen with a raised eyebrow.

"Then give it to me," said Nestor. "I'll be more than happy to give Ambrose the business end of it after all of the tricks he has played on us."

"We must still be careful," said Drayton. "Having a magic sword won't counter the centuries of experience and cunning tricks that Kellen has mastered. I warn you that when the time comes to face Kellen Ambrose, you will find yourselves hard pressed." The wounded knight was seized by a fit of coughing that wracked his entire body. When it passed, Nestor saw flecks of blood on the Shadow Lord's lips. Nestor dipped a cup into a foul-smelling brew that he had placed on the fire and lifted it to the knight's mouth.

"Here. Drink this. It smells terrible but it cures quite well," he assured Drayton.

"It certainly won't cure bad breath," said Galen who backed away from the mixing pot. Nestor flipped a cupful into the face of the young thief. Galen's look of surprise and revulsion even brought laughter from Drayton. The thief stripped off his shirt and threw it away from him.

"Now I'll have to go wash that," he complained. He glared at Nestor, who only grinned. The thief picked his shirt back up and walked towards the nearby creek while a steady stream of muttered curses rolled back to the barbarian.

"That lad will scare away skunks for the next day or so," he mused.

Tyrell sat away from the others, silently watching his bantering friends. As his mind swirled around with thoughts of their upcoming battle, he wondered to himself if his companions were taking the approaching dangers seriously enough. Or perhaps, he was simply taking everything too seriously. He smiled a wistful smile. He longed to share their enthusiasm and enjoy their raucous behavior, but he hadn't been able to escape the terrible sense of foreboding that had been with him since leaving Khasharsta. Some great tragedy still loomed before them. You're being foolish, he chided himself. The last thing we need now is a doomsayer among us. He closed the book on his lap, and finally joined in Nestor's raucous laughter when Galen fell over into the stream.

The next day's journey was slower than they had hoped for. Drayton's wound had turned an ugly shade of grey, and the blood that seeped from the cut was cold and thick. A fever had taken hold of the knight, and he thrashed about so fiercely that they had needed to tie him to his horse.

"He won't survive another day like this, Tyrell," said Nestor during a rest break. "You and I have both done all we can for him, and he's getting worse."

"There is something unnatural about his wound that is draining his life force. This is something beyond a simple infection."

"Some side effect from the guardian's weapon perhaps? But why then wouldn't I have suffered the same from all of the minor wounds that I received."

"I can't say. Perhaps there was something that the spirit consciously did or channeled into Drayton that the other apparition didn't get a chance to do to you. Maybe you're more resistant. All I know for sure is that we are going to have to stop long enough to cure this sickness, or else we'll bury him before we reach the town."

"Can't you use some kind of magical healing on him to keep him from getting worse?" asked Galen. "You patched me up pretty well the night that we were in jail together."

"This is something much more complicated though. You suffered from natural injuries. His wounds are caused by a mystical energy not from this world. That makes them more difficult to drive from the body. It's harder to direct his natural defenses to fight against whatever's making him worse." He sighed. "A powerful wizard could easily heal him, but . . . ." The mage looked at his friends helplessly and shrugged. The three men sat in silence around their campfire until the knight thrashed and groaned.

Nestor said softly, "Tyrell, he's a dead man if you don't at least try. If the worst thing that you could do is kill him accidentally, then he has nothing to lose." The warrior looked at Tyrell, surprised to see tears streaming down the mage's cheeks.

"My master once told me that I had the potential to be one of the most powerful wizards the world had ever seen. Despite his teaching, despite his belief in me, I could never control the kind of power that was at those higher levels. The first time I tried was such a disaster that I…." The mage looked down at his gloved hands and clenched his fists tightly. "I still wake up screaming from nightmares to this day. I convinced myself that I couldn't reach that power without someone else getting hurt, so I abandoned such efforts altogether."

"You handled that power pretty well in the sewer," replied the barbarian. "Drayton doesn't have any other chance for survival, Tyrell."

"But if the magic runs loose, this entire glade could become a smoking crater with no trace at all that we ever even existed."

Galen grinned. "Then we'll just stand back a bit once you start casting." He clapped his friend on the shoulder, and Tyrell smiled sadly.

Finally, he nodded, bolstered by his friends' encouragement.

"Alright, then. Let's see what I can do."

*   *   *

Tyrell finished drawing the last rune on Drayton's forehead. The unconscious man shivered beneath a blanket, totally oblivious to the risk Tyrell was about to undertake on his behalf. The wizard again read over the focusing exercises that he had discovered in the Book of Torax'alamien. With one final deep breath, he closed the tome. His every nerve was on edge, and he already felt the grip of fear closing on him. He pulled off his leather gloves, studying the webs of scars that crisscrossed his hands. He shook his fingers vigorously, trying to drive away the memories of the damage that he had inadvertently caused so many years ago.

Galen leaned against a stump nearby, absently poking at their campfire, when Nestor marched out of the forest. The barbarian was covered from head to toe in paint and feathers. The thief stifled a laugh though as the solemn warrior's gaze fell over him. The cutpurse knew that if he dared to make a joke at Nestor's expense now, he would likely end up in far worse shape than Drayton was in.

Nestor sat down with his legs crossed in front of the fire. He pulled out stones, strange pungent herbs, and a jagged knife. With an air of ceremony, he arranged the items out before him. "I don't suppose you'd mind telling me what you're doing?" asked the thief.

"Hosai del Tre'al," replied Nestor.

"Thanks, that cleared it all up."

"The Ritual of Strength. I will call to my gods, and beg them to aid Tyrell and Drayton." The warrior shrugged. "I'm not a shaman, but I figured that they can use all the help that they can get."

Tyrell focused himself and began a slow rhythmic chant. Magic of this kind required a gradual stair stepping climb through the tiers of magic into the highest realms of power. He would have to make absolutely certain he was in control of each plane before he could ascend to the next. The mage immediately felt the alluring tingle from the power around him that beckoned him to rush into its turbulent embrace. His words nearly faltered, but Tyrell forced his mind to ignore the call, focusing on bending the magic to his will.

Nestor began a chant of his own, as his hands unconsciously swirled the stones before him into patterns of summoning that would draw the attention of the gods. Galen watched as each man performed their individual rituals, and noticed that their chants did not sound entirely different.

Tyrell opened himself to the next realm of power. In combat, a wizard had to hurl himself to those higher planes so quickly that it seemed instantaneous, but Tyrell had to be absolutely certain that he made no missteps. He could now feel the sickness in Drayton's body, and could actually see the dark infection draining away the knight's life force to some other shadowy dimension. If he had any doubts before that Drayton would die without his help, the spectacle before him dispelled them. With an even greater sense of urgency, Tyrell drew still more of the power surrounding his consciousness into himself and pressed on.

Nestor started to feed herbs into the fire that caused a sweet smelling bluish smoke to rise into the sky. The barbarian raised his hands to the heavens, his chant increasing with vigor. Each growling word was a primal snarl building to a crescendo of awe-inspiring power. The warrior swayed to the rhythm of a music that only he could hear, and the thief wondered briefly if his friend had actually entered the mead hall of some patron deity.

Tyrell reached now for the greatest pinnacle of magic and could feel raw untapped energy flood his being. The very workings of the universe were bare before him, and he sensed himself surrounded by a force that could create or level entire continents. The energy had a peaceful and soothing feeling, yet it remained ferocious and deadly in its might. The mage drew the magic to him, reveling in it as it flowed through him. It was as if he had been promised unimaginable bliss in exchange for excruciating agony. He burned without pain and seethed without anguish.

Nestor picked up the knife by his side. Galen watched carefully, wondering what his friend meant to do with the cruel instrument. The barbarian's chant had slowed in tempo. His face was sweating, and his skin was flushed. As the thief glanced back at the mage, he saw that Tyrell had the exact same look. Galen's eyes opened wide and his jaw slackened as the mage's hands began to glow with an intense white light. Slowly, Tyrell placed his hands on Drayton's chest.

The mage could see the knight's fever as if it were a living entity pulsing and throbbing as it drew away the man's strength. As the blinding power of magic coursed through him, Tyrell directed the energies gathered within him into a bolt of white-hot cleansing flame. The magic poured into Drayton's body, ripping into the supernatural infection that consumed him. The rush of such incredible power through his hands made it harder and harder for Tyrell to concentrate on his chant. He wanted to give himself to the flow and become one with the magic he now wielded. To do so now would be catastrophic, but the lure was so terribly powerful. His bolt of energy flickered momentarily as the forces that tore through him tried to convert his body into an open conduit for its own raw destructive force.

"Come on, Tyrell," whispered Galen. The thief saw the internal struggle that the mage was fighting with. He swallowed hard as the glow around the mage's hands faltered, then came back. "You can control this. Show yourself who is really the master." Galen didn't know if Tyrell could even hear his encouragement, but the blazing light of the wizard's curative magic seemed to intensify, and Tyrell's chant resumed although the syllables sounded more like the same growls that Nestor spoke nearby.

Nestor held his hand over the flames of the fire, and, with an easy flick of his blade, he cut a deep slash into the palm of his hand. Blood dripped into the coals and hissed with an angry sizzle. Galen jumped at his friend's sudden self-mutilation. He started to reach out to grab Nestor's arm but hesitated for fear of interrupting. Although Galen had no practice in either magic or religion, he could feel a very tangible force pervading the campsite, and surrounding them all. The air around them seemed alive and charged enough that the hairs on the back of his neck stood up. He decided that no matter whether the energy present was magical, divine, or both, he wasn't about to interfere with either.

Tyrell felt the last of Drayton's infection burn away under the healing blast from his hands. The wound in the knight's shoulder began to knit together, and his revitalized natural defenses began to go back to work on their own as strength flowed back into the Shadow Lord. The mage faced a new problem though. The danger wizards faced when using such magic wasn't finding one's way into it, but rather in finding one's way back down from the incredible power. Few of those trained in the arts had the necessary force of will to break away from the seductive pull that Tyrell now found himself battling. The wizard could see his way down, but did he have the strength of will to walk that arcane path?

Tyrell focused all of his might on closing the magical conduit. He thought of Kellen Ambrose and his upcoming role in destroying the vampire lord. His friends needed him. Without him, they would have no chance of surviving the vampire's own deadly magic. In the depths of his mind, the mage screamed in defiance as he fought to break free of the energy surrounding him.

Nestor had grown silent although his lips still moved in a now silent chant. His eyes remained tightly closed, and blood dripped freely down his forearm. The barbarian sensed Tyrell's inner struggle, and he knew that their strength was somehow tied together now on some higher plane. The wizard had the ability to save himself, but he needed to be shown where such indomitable might dwelt within his own mind. With the echoes of Kellen's own words of praise regarding his might in his head, Nestor thrust his blood-soaked hand into the fire, grabbing a handful of red-hot coals. With a snarl, he raised his hand high in the air for his gods to see the real measure of his strength. No cries of pain passed his lips, but only the low feral growling like a hunting cat stalking its prey as he continued his chant.

Galen whistled softly in appreciation for the barbarian's display. The smell of burning flesh filled the air, but if Nestor was in pain, he made no sign of it. The thief saw the lines of strain on Tyrell's face gradually begin to soften, and the light around the mage's body dimmed.

Tyrell felt a surge of warmth flow into him, a reassurance that came from his nearby friend that such strength was his to command as well. With new resolve, he slammed shut the gateway that the magic poured through. In moments, he was back to the levels of power that he was familiar with, and in seconds after that, his eyes snapped open as he ended his magical trance. The mage fell backward on the ground. He was drained, and completely exhausted. As he struggled to look around the camp, Galen knelt beside him. Just before the blackness took him, Tyrell saw Nestor open his hand, and blow ashes from his palm into the fire pit.

*　　　*　　　*

Tyrell awoke to the sounds of low voices around the camp. Drayton was awake, and, although still weak, was obviously well on his way to recovery. His face was no longer pallid, and he was eating some broth with Galen's help while the thief retold the events that had led to the knight's healing. Nestor sat nearby with a grim smile on his face as he checked the dressing on his hand. The barbarian rose when he saw that the mage was awake, and came over to his side.

"How are you feeling?"

"Like a flight of dragons just stampeded through my skull. I've heard though that it's normal whenever a wizard tries to use that much power for the first time. It will pass."

"Well, as you can see, you didn't manage to blow us all away. That was quite an impressive bit of spell weaving for a self-proclaimed amateur."

"I had help," he said after a moment. He recalled the sight of the barbarian in his ceremonial outfit. "I know enough about the barbarian cultures to recognize that was a ceremonial outfit you were wearing."

Nestor snorted. "It was improvised from what I could remember our tribal shaman wearing on such important occasions." He paused thoughtfully. "I won't deny, though, that you and I somehow worked together throughout the ordeal."

"It's called cooperative magic. One participant is the focus, and any others involved offer supportive boosts. It's usually only mentioned in legends about the creation of great magical artifacts."

"All I know is that you removed all of my doubts that you are capable of that caliber of magic. Powerful magic, I mean." Nestor noticed the scowl that came quickly to Tyrell's face. "You have faced some terrible trials in your past, my friend, and one day I hope that you may share your burden with me. Today, however, you threw aside your fears and performed like a master spell thrower. You know your craft, Tyrell."

"I wouldn't have been able to resist though if you hadn't been able to assist me. It is incredibly dangerous. You can't be there to help pull me back every time I try to use magic."

"You fought, and resisted the pull of that power on your own.

Yes, you came out of there with my help, but I only showed you the strength that was already within you. Now that you've fought your way back once, the next time will be easier. As will every time after that. Eventually, you'll be able to walk those planes as you please, but only if you keep going to them. If you turn away from your talent now, then the next time that you again have no other choice but to go there, you will face the same struggle all over again."

Tyrell looked away from his friend. "You don't understand what it was like. I could see visions of myself using that magic to destroy continents. I don't want to be drawn into something as dangerous as that. You didn't get to feel the seduction of all of that power."

"I know exactly what you felt, Tyrell," said Nestor. Fury flashed in his eyes. "I too have felt the pull of something so strong that all you could do is revel in the feeling. My people have a rite of manhood that they call 'Lar ka ofin'. Young warriors drink a liquor that instills a battle lust so intense that all they can think about is slaughtering the tribe's enemies. It's a bloody ritual performed as young men come of age, and participate in their first raid." As the barbarian lowered his eyes, the edge in his voice softened. "It is a terrifying experience. You are only aware enough to separate enemies from allies, but all else feels as though you are a puppet on a string. When you come out of the haze, all around you is death. Death that you had helped bring about.

"It was the reason I left my people," he said as he wiped tears from his eyes. "I came back from my own raid covered in so much blood. When no one was watching I stole away from the crowd and vomited. Worst of all was that my chieftain planned to bestow honors upon me for my glorious actions in battle. Too well do I remember the rush of adrenaline, and the grisly hiss of my sword slicing throw sinew and bone. I was powerless to resist the allure of that damnable brew, and I went from one victim after another." He paused again, looking his friend in the eyes. "And even now, years later, I still can hear the screams of every man, woman, and child that I slaughtered that day.

"So, yes, Tyrell Amalcheal. I do indeed know the danger of such destructive power. You and I were each given gifts that impose difficult choices upon us. I am a born warrior, and you, my friend, whether you choose to believe it or not, are a talented spellcaster. I made the decision to walk away from my home and family, and become an outcast rather than be revered as a slayer of innocents. You have strength in your magic, but only you can decide how and when to use that power. The choice you make will determine how you live the rest of your days. Will you use your skills to learn what benefit they can bring to yourself and those who would look to you in time of need, or will you wonder forever if there might have been something you could have done to make a difference if you had only made a stand?"

Tyrell thought on the barbarian's words but made no reply. Finally, the warrior clapped his friend on the shoulder, offering his silent support to the troubled man. Galen came over to the wizard and held forth a bowl.

"You should eat something. I have no idea what Redbeard here put in it, but he claims its safe enough to eat, and it doesn't smell too strange." The wizard smiled weakly and accepted the bowl from the young thief. He spooned some of the stew into his mouth, and then sucked in air to cool his burnt tongue.

"How's Drayton?" he asked between bites.

"He's a tough one. I expect he should be back in shape in no time at all. In fact, he's already insisting that we get back to Del Torac as quickly as we can. He says that he fears we've already lost precious time against whatever Kellen is planning next. I have to agree with him. The longer we're out here the more time that lying bastard has to work some other scheme against us all."

"No argument here," said Nestor. "Drayton, do you feel well enough to sit a horse?"

The knight waved a hand to the warrior. "I feel well enough to get us moving again, although I fear I would be of little use in a battle. I'm ready to be on the move unless my doctor has other orders." The blond warrior held his fist over his heart and nodded to Tyrell. "Master wizard, I am deeply in your debt, and humbly thank you for my life. From now until the end of my days, my sword is yours."

Tyrell bowed his head graciously to the knight, knowing that to refuse Drayton's pledge would be an insult to the proud man's honor. "I am grateful to have you with us, my friend." He cleared his throat. "Alright then. Everyone rest tonight. Tomorrow morning we'll make up some lost time." He looked back to Nestor and Galen. "The time to settle this account is long overdue."

*   *   *

A day and a half of riding saw the group inside the walls of Del Torac. The ride still proved difficult though, and the riders were weary when they finally dismounted. Tyrell, in particular, was still exhausted from his use of so much magic. Drayton, even though he was now healing, remained pale, and leaned heavily on Nestor's arm. Galen rushed inside the inn to secure a room for the giant warrior and ordered food for all of them to be brought to the chamber in short order. Payment was made for the accommodations by a slovenly drunk whose coin purse strayed too close to Galen's nimble fingers.

Finally, all four men were settled into the room with plates of warm bread, fresh cheese, and roasted meat in hand. Drayton lay back on the bed, his back propped up with two thin pillows. He wiped crumbs from his mouth and looked gravely at his companions.

"Thank you for everything, my friends. We started off as the victims of a cruel and tragic misunderstanding, but that is behind us now. I owe each of you my life, but I am afraid that this is as far as our mutual roads shall travel for now. You have wasted too much time watching over me, and tending to my sickness when you should have by now arrived back in Tarnath facing down our devil." His eyes met the gaze of each man. "I bid you go, and destroy Kellen Ambrose. His evil has carried on for too long. Too many have suffered by his hands, and his terror must come to an end. I only wish I could be at your side when you finally confront him."

"I'll be certain to get in a clean strike for you, and each of your men who have fallen because of him," swore Nestor. He shook the knight's hand firmly.

"Do not underestimate him, though. He is powerful, both physically and magically. Expect no quarter to be given by him."

"He'll certainly get none in return," said Tyrell. Nestor solemnly drew Shadow Reaver from the sheath belted around his waist, and the men all gazed reverently upon the weapon as it glittered like a dancing rainbow in the low light of the room. "Join us in Tarnath as soon as you are well." The barbarian resheathed the elvensteel blade, farewells were made, and arrangements for Drayton's care were provided. As the sun set slowly over the horizon, three very determined riders raced southward towards Tarnath.

*　　*　　*

Tessarin stumbled down the darkened street toward his apartments. The young nobleman didn't think his recent luck could get any worse. First, his father had nearly disowned him for losing his family signet ring, he had lost heavily at the gaming tables tonight, and now worst of all, he was going home alone.

"Things just can't get any worse," he slurred to no one. His unreliable vision could barely make out the stairs to his rooms yet fifty yards away. He staggered, turned his ankle in a hole, and crashed heavily to the ground. Mud spattered his face and clothes. "Damn it," he cried out.

In the distance, something hissed. Tessarin looked around but saw nothing in the dark gloom of the alley.

"Hello?" he called, but only silence answered him. The young man quickly forgot to lament that he was sitting in the mud with a nearly empty coin purse, and stood up. He strained to hear something, anything, but the alley remained as quiet as a tomb. Truly frightened now, Tessarin limped down the road toward his door. He glanced repeatedly over his shoulder for any sign of pursuit, but there was no one behind him.

Something crashed in the shadows ahead. Rats squealed and scurried in search of new holes to hide in. "Please, is someone there?" he called out again. Tessarin guessed that he was still about forty yards from his door, but decided to let dignity fall second to terror as he bolted for the stairs as fast as his injured ankle would allow. Thirty yards, then twenty, now only ten.

His ankle betrayed him, and he fell again. He sprawled face first on the cold ground. His cheek stung from where the cobblestones had rubbed away his skin. He began to rise but froze when he saw a dark silhouette in the shadows only a few strides beside him. The shape crouched down, and he saw cold red eyes gleaming from beneath the cowl of a black hood.

"Took a nasty fall, didn't we, milord?" The voice was a harsh, hissing whisper whose tone assured malevolence to the nobleman's ears. Tessarin jumped to his feet, racing past the thing in the shadows. The throb in his ankle was pushed aside as he dashed up the stairs with terror driven speed. He grabbed the door handle and pushed only to rebound off the heavy locked portal. Tessarin fumbled at his belt for his key pouch when his terror reached new heights. The silken bag where he kept his keys was lying on the street in the muck where he had fallen.

"Such a pity," came the hissing whisper from somewhere nearby. Tessarin spun frantically, searching in vain for either his stalker or an escape route. He saw neither.

And then the darkness descended.

.

Chapter Thirteen

Night had just fallen when the companions reached Tarnath. Two days of hard riding had brought the trio to the city gates, weary and saddle sore. Yet despite their fatigue, fury and determination pushed them forward to the avenue that led to Kellen's home.

"So what do we do when we get there," growled Nestor. "Knock first and then skewer whoever opens the door?"

"I was hoping for something a little more discreet," said Tyrell. He wasn't certain whether the barbarian was joking or not.

"Right," said Galen. "Don't even bother to knock. Just kick in the door and start swinging."

"Sounds good to me," replied the warrior.

The mage shook his head helplessly. "Could you two be serious for a moment? We need to catch him unaware. If we can make him believe that we are none the wiser, then we can get close enough to take him completely off guard."

Nestor scowled at his friend. "I'm not going to waste time coaxing him into revealing his master plan. The bastard gets the sword between the ribs at my earliest convenience."

"Sounds as though thieving wasn't enough. Have you moved on to murder now, gentlemen?" Tyrell turned in his saddle and saw Captain Knarya closely followed by four guardsmen. "There's enough trouble in this city without the likes of you hunting down the natives."

"Believe it or not, fat man," growled Nestor, "you will be thanking us once we finish our business."

"If your business is murder gentlemen, kindly save me the trouble and come along quietly with us now. Men," the officer said as he waved his hand forward, "take them into custody." Knarya's soldiers advanced slowly and with weapons drawn towards the riders. It was obvious to even the least skilled of them that the men they faced were no strangers to combat, and the utmost caution was called for.

"We have no time for this, Captain," called Tyrell. "We intend to stop the Dockside Slayer for you, but we can't do it if you continue to detain us here."

"The Dockside Slayer has already been caught," said Knarya. "I personally apprehended him."

"How the hell did you manage that?" asked Galen. "The only thing you could apprehend on your own is a rogue sandwich."

Knarya ignored the jibe. "Last night, young Lord Tessarin was caught in the act of tearing apart a sailor down at the Dock Quarter. Covered in blood, he was. Chewed the poor bastard's neck to shreds. He must have been mad. His eyes were all glazed over, almost like he wasn't in control of himself, and he didn't even put up a struggle when I arrived on the scene."

"Tessarin?" Tyrell felt a sinking feeling in his stomach. "Oh, gods above, Knarya. You have the wrong man. Tessarin is a simpering little fop." Nestor could see the fear in the wizard's eyes. "He's no murderer. He has been set up by the real killer, who happens to be a vampire. Take me to him, and perhaps I can break whatever enchantment he is under."

"If you wish to see him, then go to City Square. He's still swinging from the gallows since he was executed there this morning." Knarya glared quite pointedly at each man. "That's what we do to murderers in this city.

Now unless you lads intend to join the young nobleman, I suggest you make your way to a tavern somewhere and drown your aggression."

Tyrell sat in mute shock. What had Kellen done to Tessarin? More importantly, why had Kellen given the guards a killer? "Oh my god," whispered the mage after a moment of reflection.

"What is it?" asked Nestor.

"We have to move fast. Ambrose is about to make some sort of play."

Galen cocked his head quizzically. "How do you know that?"

"He has decided he doesn't need to hide behind the identity of the Dockside Slayer any longer. Whatever his scheme is, it's about to erupt. I only pray we aren't too late to stop him." Tyrell wheeled his horse and spurred the animal into a gallop. Galen and Nestor followed right behind him leaving Knarya and his men in a cloud of dust.

"Hold it just one damn minute," yelled Knarya, but his cries were ignored by the riders. "Come along swiftly, men," he ordered. "Something big is about to happen." I just hope we can handle it, he added silently.

The companions' path met no further resistance, and the three men soon found themselves at Kellen's townhouse. Tyrell took the stairs three at a time and pounded loudly on the door. Nestor and Galen flanked him with weapons drawn and ready.

The door opened slowly to reveal a thin, old manservant. "Yes?" he asked in a raspy voice.

"We need to see Kellen. Tell him that Tyrell Amalcheal and company are here. It's extremely urgent."

"My lord has asked that he not be disturbed this evening by anyone as he has rather pressing business that cannot wait. Perhaps you could try him again tomor-."

Nestor grabbed the little man by the front of his shirt. "Disturb him. Now." The servant, cowed by the barbarian's sudden fury backed away from the door. He did not move to fetch his master, but the way inside the house was now clear. Tyrell pushed past him and the three men found themselves once again in the grand foyer.

"Try the study first," said Tyrell, pointing to the closed doors nearby. The companions charged the doorway, and Nestor shouldered the portal with such force that one of the doors was blasted from its hinges. Kellen looked up from behind a new desk where he had propped up his feet as he read over some papers.

"Do you three have some deep seeded hatred for my furnishings or just an embarrassing lack of manners?"

"Please, sir," said Nestor mockingly, "would you be so kind as to hold still while I run you through?" Kellen took his feet from the desktop and looked at the warrior with knit brows.

"Oh, that's subtle, Nestor," muttered Galen.

"I do trust there is an excellent explanation for all of this. Tyrell, you are generally the most reasonable of the group. Explain yourselves."

"Why Tessarin, you bastard? How many innocent people have died because of you? Nobody uses us as pawns, Ambrose. We've done your dirty work, but now we're here to set things right."

Kellen regarded each man with his mouth agape. "I am at a complete loss," he said at last. "Would someone please explain to me why the hell the three of you are behaving like lunatics?"

Nestor ripped Shadow Reaver from its sheath and punched Kellen across the jaw with the hilt. The nobleman spun from the blow and collapsed to the floor. "We know the truth about you now, you bloodthirsty murderer. We've found the blade that chased you from Khasharsta, and tonight we'll finish the job that Gilgorad couldn't." As he spoke, the elvensteel sword began to pulse and hum in the barbarian's hand. The shimmering blade glowed with a pure pale light that steadily grew brighter and brighter.

Kellen drew himself up slowly from the floor with his back still to the companions. As he turned to face them, though, Ambrose's look of confusion had melted away into a snarl of unbridled fury and murderous hatred. Despite the warnings of the true nature of the man before them, the trio gasped at the sight of the glistening fangs that slowly grew in Ambrose's mouth.

"This is unfortunate." Kellen's voice had lost the cultured formality to which they were accustomed, but took instead a more ferocious hissing quality that the friends knew all too well from their previous encounters with 'Darian.' A gleam like red hellfire burned in the depths of the vampire's eyes that was a stark contrast to the light from Shadow Reaver. "I had hoped to retain you as my agents for a bit longer, but it is of little consequence. My forces await my command to strike. For all your bravado, tonight Tarnath will be mine."

Nestor raised the elvensteel sword, but Kellen moved with supernatural speed. The vampire grabbed the corner of the desk and flipped it at the lunging warrior. The barbarian ducked far enough to avoid getting his skull caved in, but still sailed through the air when the huge missile clipped his shoulder. He slammed against the hardwood floor while Shadow Reaver skittered across the study.

"Did you expect to find me unprepared for this?" roared Kellen. "It was inevitable that you would learn the truth. I chose the three of you for one simple reason. Although you are formidable, you would never have the necessary might to defeat me." Ambrose grabbed the edge of a towering bookcase and launched it across the room where Tyrell and Galen stood. The two men narrowly dodged aside as the bookcase splintered on impact. The mage spared a glance at his friend who raised his eyebrows in awe. Nestor pulled himself back up to one knee and cradled his bruised shoulder.

"You have no hope of stopping me," snarled the vampire. "My strength is superhuman, my magic is born from timeless evil, and my cunning has kept me alive for centuries. I am invincible!"

"Shall we add arrogant?" asked Tyrell.

Kellen moved in a blur and grabbed Galen as the thief tucked and rolled towards the sword of Gilgorad. He tossed the thief over his shoulder like a rag doll, and the young man slammed into the far wall with such force that the beams within groaned. Ambrose whirled to face Tyrell, throwing out his outstretched palm to the mage. Tyrell's mind raced to prepare a defense as arcane syllables rolled from Kellen's fanged mouth, but the vampire lord's casting proved faster. A dark fog coalesced around the wizard, and Tyrell collapsed to the floor as the mystical energy sapped the strength from his limbs.

"Thus the Night of Terror begins," said Kellen. The vampire dusted his hands off in arrogant insult to the fallen trio. Tyrell boldly met the vampire's gaze as Kellen knelt beside him. The wicked smile on the vampire's face melted however as he saw hatred rather than fear in the wizard's eyes. "And even now you think you may win," he hissed. He grabbed Tyrell's hair and drew back his fist when a crossbow bolt suddenly zipped past the monster's face.

"Halt in the name of the ...," Captain Knarya started to yell as he and his guardsmen charged into the room. Kellen bared his teeth and tore through the room like a black shadow. He crashed through the window and disappeared. "Search the grounds," commanded Knarya. "I want Ambrose brought back here for questioning."

With Kellen gone, the black fog dissipated around the mage and Tyrell found his strength returning to him. He sat up and shook his head.

Across the room, Nestor helped pull Galen from the wreckage of the furniture.

"Thank you for the timely entrance, Captain," said Tyrell.

"Shut up. I want some damn answers, and I want them now. What the hell is going on here?"

"We already told you that Ambrose is the Dockside Slayer and a vampire. After what you just saw him do, surely you can believe us now," replied the mage.

Knarya rubbed his forehead under his helmet. "I am not going to say I believe in vampires, but I will agree with you that what I saw wasn't natural." His brows knit together as he regarded the three men. "I don't suppose there is any chance that I could persuade you three to help us catch that . . . thing?"

A rasp of metal filled the room as Nestor scooped Shadow Reaver from the floor. "It would be my genuine pleasure, Captain. Galen. Tyrell. Let's go. He couldn't have gotten too far yet, no matter what he is." Galen nodded, falling in behind the big warrior as he moved towards the door. Nestor looked over his shoulder and paused as he saw Tyrell standing in reflection. "Are you coming, Tyrell?"

"There's something he said that is nagging at me. He called tonight the 'Night of Terror'. He also told us that his forces were ready to strike."

"Perhaps it was a bluff," suggested Knarya. "What fool would be willing to serve in a vampire's army? Too great of a chance that you might get called to feed the general." The officer started to chuckle but stopped as he saw Tyrell's face turn pale.

"You have to alert every man you have in the city. Alert every garrison. Kellen plans to take control of Tarnath, and he will do it with his army of fledgling vampires."

"Do you ever have any good revelations?" asked Nestor.

"Fledgling vampires?" asked Knarya.

"You mean like the girl in the sewer," said Galen.

"Exactly, only gods know how many people he's turned. Every murder he committed as the Dockside Slayer was done to add to his ranks. In the sewer, he mentioned something about bringing vampires from other places also. There could be no limit to the number of undead waiting to attack at his command. We have to find him and stop him immediately, or the entire city is doomed."

"Tarnath is a big city, Tyrell," said Nestor. "Just where the hell do you think he's hiding them?"

"He's right," said Galen. "They could be anywhere."

"The list he sent us to recover from the knights in the Fen. There were graveyards, old warehouses, and abandoned buildings. Those were the types of places on the list. Those are the places you should have your men start searching, Captain."

"And what do we do if we find something?"

"Put a stake in anything with pointy teeth," said Galen.

Knarya nodded. "Where will the three of you be?"

Tyrell looked at his two friends. "We're going back into the sewers."

*   *   *

Tyrell held a torch high above his head as he and his two friends moved down the slimy corridor beneath the streets of the city. They easily retraced their previous path, and the three men soon found themselves standing outside of the dark temple. The sewers were eerily quiet, without any trace of the foul denizens that had plagued their prior journey.

Nestor carried Shadow Reaver, and the blade glowed softly as they approached the evil sanctuary. Galen melted into the nearby darkness as Tyrell and the barbarian boldly marched through the great doorway. The room was lit by the flickering glow of thousands of candles that made eerie shadows tremble and shudder across the gruesome murals.

Upon the altar was the still form of a pale young woman. The tattered rags of her simple dress looked as though fierce claws had shredded the material. Tyrell's fists clenched, and a silent snarl found Nestor's lips as they looked on yet another of Kellen's poor victims.

"A pretty thing, isn't she?" Ambrose's chilling voice broke the stillness of the chamber. The vampire lord flowed from the shadows behind the altar. "However, I have always been an admirer of the aesthetic beauty of such baubles." He caressed the woman's cheek, and then regarded the two men. His fury blazed as his eyes met Tyrell's. "You should have left Tarnath when you had the chance. I cannot allow you to live, nor can I even afford now to make you my servants. I could never trust you. Did you not realize that now your only course is to die a cruel death at my hands?"

Galen sprang suddenly from the nearby shadows, while Nestor sprang forward to catch Kellen from the other side. Tyrell reached out with his magic to the cobwebs behind the vampire lord. The silken strands pulsed with arcane power as they thickened and stretched towards Ambrose. However, Kellen had not survived for centuries only to be taken so easily. He grabbed the young thief by the wrist and hurled him over the altar into the charging barbarian. Nestor caught his friend, but they crashed into a tangled heap on the cold stone floor. Ambrose snorted in contempt as he ripped through Tyrell's webs. With a puff of smoke, the magical energy backlashed in a surge of power, staggering the mage.

Kellen brushed the dusty remains of the webs from his shoulders. "I told you before that you have no hope of defeating me. I have killed men far greater than you without even breaking stride. Accept the fact that you are as good as dead, and this all becomes so much simpler."

Nestor disentangled himself from Galen and resumed his attack stance. "I hate to disappoint you, but we're still kicking."

"An unfortunate circumstance that will soon be corrected." Nestor growled and lunged across the stone altar, the glimmering point of Shadow Reaver arcing towards the vampire lord's chest. Suddenly, the woman on the altar moved like lightning and grabbed the warrior's wrist. Shadow Reaver teasingly quivered a hair's breadth away from Kellen's breast. Ambrose's contemptuous laughter echoed throughout the temple.

The girl bared her gleaming fangs in a fierce snarl as she anticipated her first kill. Her eyes blazed with hunger and hatred as she drove her elbow into Nestor's stomach, and shoved the warrior away from her master. With supernatural agility, the vampiress sprang from the stone altar and landed on her feet with feline grace.

"I would truly love to stay and watch as this child of mine tears you to shreds, my friends, but I have an army to lead against the feeble defenses of the city. I would bid you farewell," said Kellen as a cruel smile crossed his face, "but I really don't think that you will." The vampire lord faded back into the shadows of the alcove behind him and vanished.

Nestor regained his fighting composure and spared a glance at Tyrell. "Any suggestions?" he growled as he held the point of the elvensteel sword pointed at the vampire's breast. Tyrell looked around frantically for some weakness he might exploit.

"I suppose sweet talk is out of the question," said Galen. The thief had his sword in hand as he tried to edge around behind the undead woman.

"She's not really my type," quipped the barbarian. "This wench strikes me as a bit too cold for my liking."

A smile flashed across Tyrell's face. "Then let's warm her up." The wizard jumped forward just outside of the vampire's reach. With a feral growl, she swiped her wicked claws at the mage's face, but the wizard easily leaned out of harm's way. Despite her speed and agility, however, the girl lacked Kellen's centuries of battle training and overextended herself. Tyrell countered her swipe with a thrust of the blazing torch in his hand igniting the girl's hair into a crown of fire. The wizard forced the inherent magical energy of the flames to burn downwards, and in seconds, the shrieking vampire was wreathed in a shroud of flames.

As her agony and terror paralyzed her, Nestor leaped forward, bringing Shadow Reaver down in a mighty two-handed chop, that cleaved the vampire from her collarbone to her stomach. The blade hummed as it struck the beast, but as it slashed through bone and sinew, the noise rose to a wail that matched that of the dying monster. The sword's scream died off slowly as the woman's body crumbled to ashes that drifted to the floor.

"Quite a blade we've found," said Nestor in quiet awe. He kicked the pile of ashes, and let out a low whistle. Tyrell and Galen ran behind the altar to the alcove where Kellen had stood moments before. The thief's trained eyes scanned the stonework.

"Found it," he said as manipulated a stone projection that caused the crease of a concealed door to pop open.

"The bastard won't escape us that easily," swore Tyrell as he pushed past his friend, and into the sloping tunnel. Galen and Nestor followed close behind with the same grim determination that possessed the wizard. The tunnel twisted back and forth as it led them deeper into the city's underground, but it ran without any side branches to confuse them. Shortly, the passage opened into a wide chamber where Kellen stood atop of an aged sarcophagus and addressed an assembled host of ragged vampires. Two score men and women knelt before him and swayed in a religious fervor as their master addressed them

"I shall make the first kill, but you shall know the instant that my victim is taken. The moment you sense my victim's death, carry out your instructions. Go forth from these hidden catacombs and attack Tarnath." The vampires snarled and howled. "Go forth and feed that your strength may grow." The ragged group's snarls rose to growling cheers. "These people are cattle and we are gods before them," shouted Kellen. "We shall rule this city or see it destroyed by our might!" A deafening roar arose as Kellen looked over his minions. They writhed before him as if he was a snake charmer before a field of serpents.

"This can't be good," whispered Galen as he looked past Tyrell's shoulder.

"Even I don't like these odds," growled Nestor. "And I have a terrible feeling that this isn't the only assemblage Ambrose has in hiding." The barbarian sheathed Shadow Reaver as it began to hum as if the blade sensed the nature of the force assembled in the room ahead. "He could have a whole damn army down here waiting for a signal to attack. Every location on that list of lairs we found could house groups like this."

Kellen threw his hands to the ceiling and arched his back. "Let the Night of Terror begin," he roared. The vampire lord leaped away from the sarcophagus and raced up a stairway at the back of the room that led back into the main sewer tunnels. His worshippers filed in behind him, pressing against one another to get as close as they could to their master, but those at the top of the stair paused to await the signal to charge forth.

Tyrell's brow knit in concentration. "Kellen said they had to wait for his signal. I have a hunch that if we move fast, we can at least rid the city of this group, and possibly get back to the surface in time to warn Knarya's guards." He glanced at Nestor. "Are you ready for a fight?"

The barbarian only grinned in response as he once again drew forth the humming elvensteel sword. Without a word, he slipped past the mage and charged the rear rank of the undead. One vampire curiously turned around as he thought he heard a buzzing noise, only to have half of his face removed by a glittering razor of metal.

Nestor let loose with a savage fury, as he hacked and sliced at reaching arms. Vampires on the stair saw the charge of approaching death and leaped over the stair rail to avoid being trapped. Galen and Tyrell desperately swung torches at anything that got too near them. The smell of burned flesh and the piercing wails of dying monsters filled the room.

Nestor took a kick to the ribs that drove him back into the mage. Tyrell caught his staggered friend, but a nearby vampire took advantage of the distraction to snatch the torch away from the wizard. Galen fell back against his comrades and poked his own torch hesitantly at a suddenly encircling mob.

"That didn't work as well as expected," the thief said. Nestor regained his stance and looked around at the closing throng. Demonic claws clicked and long bared fangs gnashed, but the remaining undead simply hovered and waited.

"Well we almost got half of them," said Nestor as he held Shadow Reaver defensively before him.

"It's the other half that has me worried, Redbeard," retorted Galen. A daring vampire lashed out and grabbed the torch from Galen. The thief was thrown to the floor by the rough yank, and the monster kicked the fallen man's ribs twice. Galen felt cold claws play teasingly over his face and throat, yet none pierced his skin. Nestor roared and slashed the face of the beast that loomed over his friend. Tyrell pulled Galen to his feet Nestor held the creatures at bay.

"We'd better think of something fast," said the warrior. He lopped off the arm of a foolish vampire who strayed too close to his deadly weapon.

"Kellen hasn't struck yet. We still have some time. He must have chosen his victim carefully."

"Well, the suspense is killing me," growled Galen.

"If he gets where he's going before we can get out of here, the suspense will be the least of the things killing you." Nestor's eyes grew wide and he lunged at Galen. Shadow Reaver passed a hair's breadth away from the thief's face as the barbarian skewered a lurking vampire through the eye.

The circle of vampires tightened around the three men. The fiends were intent on making these three enemies of their master suffice as their first kill of the night. Fangs snapped, icy fists clenched, and feral snarls filled the air. The soldiers of the Kellen Ambrose were ready. All they needed was the signal.

For the master demanded the first kill.

*   *   *

Lorelei sat in the plush chair that had become Galen's favorite in her home. She absently wondered about her lover and mused about what he might be doing. So many lonely nights had passed since she had last seen him, since he had left on an assignment for Lord Ambrose, and he still hadn't returned to her door. She chased away her girlish fears. Galen was not only capable of taking care of himself, but he was in the company of two other skilled adventurers who would see her young thief safely through whatever they faced.

She sighed and stretched lazily, extending her feet toward the warm fire. Well, she thought to herself, at least if he's working for Lord Ambrose, then he is working for a good cause, regardless of whatever else it may be that he is up to. She regarded for a moment the platinum bracelet that the thief had given to her just before he and his companions had left. She smiled at the memory of all of his romantic babble about the purity of the metal being symbolic of the purity of his affection, and the circle being some other symbol of something or another that she couldn't remember. She'd have to ask him to repeat it all over to her again. It made her feel all warm inside, a feeling which she longed for every time now that her mind dwelt on her young cutpurse.

A knock on the door brought her away from her daydreaming, and she jumped from her chair with hopeful expectations. Galen was the only person who she could imagine calling at this late hour. Lorelei scolded herself to be ladylike and not race to the door. Better to make him think that I didn't even miss him, she thought. Too eager, and he'll think he can have whatever he wants from me. She smiled again. Even though he could, of course.

She walked to the door and casually opened it with all of the nonchalance she could muster. The face that stood before her was not at all who she had expected to be there.

Lorelei blushed, and quickly checked her robe to make certain that she wasn't too revealing. "Forgive me," she said quickly, "I wasn't expecting company this evening. Frankly, I'm surprised to see you here. I didn't think you even knew where I lived. Oh, but where are my manners. Please come in. I had thought that you didn't need my services for a while." She paused, nervously regarding her visitor. "Do you have need of me for something tonight?"

Kellen Ambrose smiled as he stepped across the threshold, and entered her room. "Oh, yes, my dear. Tonight I have a very special need of you," he said with a wicked chuckle as he closed her door.

CHAPTER FOURTEEN

Tyrell ducked the wild swipe of a vampire's talons, driving the end of his torch into the beast's stomach. The wizard racked his brain for any solution that might save him and his friends quickly, or else they were surely doomed. He spared a glance around the circle and realized that for one brief moment all of the vampires had paused in their fight. Their gleaming eyes dulled as they looked off into empty space as if they watched the goings on of some faraway place. The moment passed, and the blank stares turned to looks of predatorial glee as undead eyes refocused on the trio. There was no mistaking what had happened.

Kellen had found his victim.

Tyrell snatched a pouch from his waist. "Nestor, push hard for the stairs, now," screamed the wizard. The warrior slashed the face of an attacker with Shadow Reaver as the mage hurled the leather bag to the floor. A blinding flash of light caused the vampires to shriek and stagger back as the pouch full of flash powder exploded. Tyrell shoved Galen ahead of him while Nestor took advantage of the distraction, and charged for the stairs like a maddened bull. Galen stumbled once, but the thief's natural grace and agility kept him moving in the right direction.

"This way, lads," yelled Nestor as his foot touched the bottom stair. The barbarian turned to hold at bay the vampires' pursuit while Tyrell and Galen raced to the top of the stairs. He took a few tentative swings at a couple of overly bold undead, then bolted up the stairway after his friends.

Snarls and howls of rage echoed after him, urging all three men to greater speed. Galen rounded the final landing first and yelped as he saw a wooden panel in front of him. The thief was unable to slow his pace and crashed into the barrier. Rotten wood gave way with a splintering crash as the thief plowed through. He fell into a tumbling roll and came to his feet in time to see Tyrell leap through the opening into the room. Nestor threw himself up the last four steps, guarding the entrance to delay the expected horde.

"They're coming fast," he yelled over his shoulder. "Find something to hold them back!" Tyrell looked quickly at their new surroundings. Old wooden crates of musty cloth surrounded the hidden door.

"Throw these in their path. It might slow them down," cried the wizard as he tumbled a box down the hidden stair. Nestor quickly overturned a couple more into the opening.

"This isn't going to slow them for long. With their strength, all it will do is irritate them that much more."

"But maybe it will buy us enough time to think of something else." A hiss echoed from the dark stairwell and Nestor saw the first telltale glow of a vampire's eyes. He raised Shadow Reaver in a salute and kissed the blade. Tyrell shuddered as he recalled the barbarian people's custom of kissing their weapons before they entered their final battle.

The stairwell was cluttered now with broken crates and piles of cloth. Galen reappeared suddenly, rolling a barrel in front of him. He smiled as he came to a stop before his friends.

"I think this may be just what we were looking for." He kicked the barrel through the opening, and the cask shattered as it struck the stone wall. A sickeningly sweet smell filled the corridor, and a splash of thick, syrupy fluid struck Nestor's boot.

"OK, Redbeard," said the thief. "Hold them on the landing just long enough for me to get this lit. When I tell you, get the hell out of there." The thief pulled a rag and his flint and steel out of a pouch. Nestor jumped back into the hole and kicked an advancing vampire in the face, knocking it and several of its fellows back to the next landing.

Tyrell watched as Galen ignited the rag, and wrapped it around the blade of a throwing dagger. "You'd better stand back," said the younger man to the wizard. "Nestor, get back now!" The thief whipped the flaming blade past Nestor's head as the warrior made a hasty retreat to the doorway. The missile glanced off the wall and landed on the soaked pile of cloth.

Flames roared to life, and the resulting explosion threw the barbarian to the ground. Shrieks filled the tunnel as the undead caught in the blast burned and flailed into other vampires who strayed too close. Tyrell smashed one burning fiend in the teeth with a broken board and knocked it back into the inferno.

Galen pulled the warrior back to his feet, and Nestor noticed that his boot was aflame where the strange liquid had splattered him. He stamped out the fire and glared at the thief. "What in Alhambra's Hells was that stuff?"

"Vanasian siege oil. An old guild master of mine received a barrel of it once. He eventually blew himself up experimenting with it and nearly burned down the guild hall. It's pretty potent stuff, and I'm actually amazed that someone had a barrel of it just lying around."

"I wouldn't be surprised if Kellen had stashed it here in the event that he needed to cover his tracks," said Tyrell.

Galen shrugged and looked back into the raging inferno on the stairwell. "Could be. At any rate, those flames will burn hot enough and long enough that any of those bastards that survived the blast won't be able to come up behind us from that direction for a good long while." The thief clapped the barbarian on his smoldering shoulder. Nestor winced and gave the younger man a shove.

"Excellent," said Tyrell. "Let's get moving and find Kellen. Somehow, I can sense that his vampire army will be fairly helpless if we can stop him." The other two nodded in agreement, and Nestor threw wide the heavy warehouse door. The salty smell of the waterfront drove back the fumes from the oily smoke and cooled their sweaty brows. A sudden scream tore through the night air, spurring the men forward. They had to prevent the citizens of Tarnath from being overwhelmed by the vampire army of Kellen Ambrose. As they dashed into the darkened city streets, a moment of singular purpose crossed the face of each companion.

It was time to bring their business with the vampire lord to its conclusion.

*   *   *

Knarya rallied his men against an almost hopeless assault. Vampires poured forth from the sewers, springing from the shadowy doorways of abandoned buildings. All around him, his soldiers died as they fought the vicious horde capable of rending a man to pieces with bare hands. Maces and swords caused minor damage that healed almost before a backswing could even be brought to bear. Despite their courage, Knarya's troops had done little more than draw the fiends' attacks away from the citizenry, and on to the city guards.

"Damn Kellen Ambrose for this mess," swore the Captain. A young lieutenant who fought beside him nodded quickly. "If I ever get my hands around that noble bastard's neck, I promise that, vampire or not, he will regret ever crossing my path." The younger officer struggled to hold at bay a young sailor whose bared fangs gleamed white in the moonlight. Knarya shoved his junior man aside and brought his own blade in a savage arc that whistled with the promise of cleaving the head of any who were so unfortunate as to be under the stroke.

The vampire moved with supernatural speed though, and he caught the descending blade in his bare hand. Black blood welled up around the blade, but if the strike had done any serious damage, it failed to show on the creature's face. It wrenched the weapon from the captain's grasp and took the officer by the throat in its free hand.

Knarya tore at the clutching hand, but the crushing strength of the icy fingers held him fast. Desperately, he reached for anything nearby that might serve as a weapon. With a choked cry of pain, the captain's hands closed on one of the hot braziers that served to light the city streets by night. Ignoring the searing heat and the smell of his burning flesh, the officer swung the bowl of coals around into his attacker's face.

Like a candle, the vampire's head burst into flames. The burning embers choked off the agonizing screeches of the creature, as it flailed around helplessly. Knarya kicked the beast away from him, gasping for breath. As he watched the monster struggle and writhe in its death throes, a grim smile crossed his face.

Maybe Tarnath had a fighting chance after all.

*   *   *

Galen raced up the stairs to Lorelei's apartment. The young thief had insisted that they needed to check on the young woman before chasing after Ambrose. Tyrell chafed at the detour, but he was even more reluctant to split up their group, so he and Nestor had no choice but to follow the young man.

"Lorelei," screamed Galen as he threw her front door open. Tyrell and Nestor nearly bowled the thief over, as he came to an abrupt halt just inside. As Galen sank slowly to his knees, the other men got their first look into the girl's home. Tyrell covered his mouth in shock, while the barbarian bowed his head in reverence.

Lorelei had been carefully laid out on her table. Her long reddish brown curls were neatly piled around her shoulders, and she held a bouquet of flowers to her breast. Her open eyes stared sightlessly at the ceiling as if in silent supplication for divine aid. A vicious slash creased the creamy white skin of her throat, but not a drop of blood spilled from the wound.

Galen pulled himself back to his feet and staggered over to her. His shoulders shook as uncontrollable sobs wrenched his body. Tyrell motioned for Nestor to keep alert, while the mage approached his grief-stricken friend. Gently, the mage closed Lorelei's eyes and whispered a quick prayer as he laid his hand on Galen's shoulder.

"I will make him pay," whispered the thief.

"We all will, my friend," replied the mage. The somber moment was suddenly shattered by the keening of Shadow Reaver as the elvensteel blade lit up like an exploding star.

"I have been preparing her for this night for a long time now," said a familiar hissing voice from the front doorway. Tyrell and Nestor whirled around to see Kellen leaning casually against the door frame with his arms crossed over his chest. "Please don't think that I chose her simply to spite you. She was a part of my plans long before you three were." The vampire's eyes glowed with a hellish light as he looked back and forth between wizard and warrior, silently daring either to make a move.

Galen turned slowly, and squarely met the vampire's gaze with a distant look in his eyes. "I swear by all the gods of heaven and hell that I will see you die, Kellen Ambrose." The thief's voice was soft and strained but held a previously unheard edge to it that even startled Kellen.

Ambrose quickly regained his composure though. "I grow weary of this. Make whatever oaths you wish, boy. Issuing threats and carrying them out are two entirely different things." His sneer dripped with contempt. "I defy you all. Even now, my army is sweeping through this city, paving the way to make me its master. I am a force of pure evil.

Something timeless, something deathless. I am eternal."

"You are long winded," growled Nestor as he sprang into action. The glittering rainbow of Shadow Reaver flashed in his hand, as Galen drew his own blade and lunged forward. Tyrell summoned his magic, bending the room around Kellen in a way that warped the vampire's perception of the actual location of his surroundings.

The vampire blinked and tried to clear his eyes. He heard the piercing shriek of Nestor's blade as it neared, and knew he was doomed if he couldn't break the spell. Kellen tried to bolt for the door, but disoriented as he was the vampire smashed into the door frame instead. The barbarian's battle cry boomed around him, and then a line of agonizing fire cut across Ambrose's back.

Galen never knew a cry of pain could sound as sweet.

*   *   *

Knarya shouted orders to his archers as they prepared their next volley of flaming arrows against the approaching horde. Word had spread around Tarnath to the city's defenders that the vampires were susceptible to fire, but so vast were the numbers of the powerful undead that they swarmed over the city faster than the news could travel.

Vampires burst into homes and shops. Everywhere they went they destroyed property, and mercilessly attacked the citizens in a bloody frenzy. In one home, a man raised an iron poker against the undead intruder who had smashed through his door. His wife could only stand in stark terror as the vampire blasted through her husband's futile attack and broke his neck with a savage backhand blow.

A serving maid fled the tavern in which she worked, as the patrons tried to fend off the six fiends that dropped in for drinks of a more grisly nature. Blindly, the girl ran from the carnage, unaware of the fact that one of the tavern's attackers had set his eyes on her alone. Her panicked flight was no match for the creature's supernatural speed, and her screams echoed through the night as chill fingers grabbed her by the hair and dragged her to the ground.

A man out for his evening stroll in a serene park stopped to help a child doubled over on the pathway. As he knelt down to check on the young girl, he saw too late the gleaming white of her fangs. An explosion of pain tore through his chest as she punched him, and he coughed up a gout of blood as his shattered ribs tore through his lungs. His last sensation before he lost consciousness was of icy, delicate lips closing over his own bloody mouth.

Knarya turned to lend his support to a hastily made barricade that the vampires were smashing through. Cold fingers raked over his forearms as he waved a torch back and forth. Despite the blood that flowed down his arms, the captain ignored the pain of his wounds and drove the undead back from his besieged men. He simply didn't know how much longer he and his men could keep this up. As he bashed another attacker in the face with his brand, he wondered briefly if those three thieves had fared any better.

*   *   *

Kellen shrieked as he fell against the doorway. The pain from Shadow Reaver's bite had broken Tyrell's disorienting enchantment, but the vampire lord knew he was not out of danger yet. He batted away Galen's blade with a bare hand, thankful that the thief's weapon lacked the magic that the accursed elvensteel sword carried. With a snarl, Kellen backed out of the apartment and hurled himself over the railing into the cobblestone street below.

Nestor charged through the door right behind the vampire, hitting Kellen in a flying tackle as he too soared over the stair rail. Kellen sprang to his feet with catlike grace and recovered a mere moment before the barbarian. With all of the strength his arms could muster, Ambrose punched Nestor with a punishing blow to the barbarian's jaw.

The force of the blow lifted Nestor from his feet and smashed him into the stone wall of Lorelei's apartment. He felt like he had tried to catch a catapult boulder with his teeth. With a groan, the barbarian fell to the ground on his hands and knees and tried to clear his throbbing head while the magical blade fell into the mud beside him.

Kellen lunged forward to finish the warrior quickly but he saw Galen and Tyrell already closing fast upon him. The thief's eyes found the dropped elvensteel sword, and the light of gathering magical energy glowed around the wizard's upraised hand proved menacing enough to make the vampire pause. Swearing under his breath, Kellen turned and bolted down the street away from the approaching men.

Nestor's hand grasped Shadow Reaver from the mud just as Galen arrived. The thief paused only long enough to help the warrior to his feet and then sprinted into the darkness after Kellen. The barbarian staggered, his cheek broken and bleeding, but the low growl that escaped his lips was one of hatred and fury rather than pain. A gloved hand grabbed his shoulder, and a cool healing warmth flowed through his body. The pain in his jaw eased, and the assaulting dizziness cleared his head. When the mage released him, Nestor gave Tyrell a quick nod of thanks, and then the two men dashed down the street after Galen.

The cries of anger and frustration caught their ears and they found Galen throwing his shoulder against the door of a small shop. "He ran inside and threw the bar," said the thief as his friends ran up. Nestor pushed the younger man aside and then, fueled by true berserker fury, he hurled himself against the portal. With a thunderous crash, the door exploded from its hinges and fell to the floor in pieces. Galen and Tyrell rushed into the room pausing only long enough to catch the sound of footsteps fleeing to the second floor. Wordlessly, they gave chase, pounding up the small staircase.

The dark shadows of the second floor gave the illusion that the room was far larger than it actually was. Around the three men, numerous vats and flasks surrounded a strange piece of machinery that faintly reflected the light from below. There was no sign of Ambrose as they peered into the gloom. Tyrell felt a chill race up his spine as he waited for some insidious trap to be unleashed against them. Nestor's nose twitched, and like a bloodhound, he sniffed the pungent spicy aromas that filled the room.

"This thing is some sort of a still," he mumbled. The only partially healed bone of his cheek made his words slur, and his voice a growl of pain.

"Indeed it is, my friend," said Ambrose from the darkness ahead of them. Nestor and Galen spread out slightly to try to corner the vampire lord, but Tyrell stayed right at the top of the stairs. There was no other means of escape from the room that he could see, and he meant to block that path from Kellen against whatever the vampire had up his sleeve.

The rushing sensation of magical energy being drawn forth surged through the mage, and Kellen began a soft chant. "Be ready," yelled Tyrell. "He's up to something."

"Thanks for the tip," quipped Galen. He and Nestor tried to follow the sound of Ambrose's voice but the incantation echoed throughout the room making it impossible. Suddenly, Kellen's voice stopped, and in a blur of movement, the vampire lord leaped between the two men, dashing for the top of the stairs. Tyrell began to summon his own magic, but Kellen brutally knocked him aside and fled back down the stairs before the wizard could bring his powers to bear.

Heartbeats later, before the three men could recover from Kellen's flight, the room exploded in a blossoming ball of heat and flame. Nestor and Galen were thrown in the direction of the stairs, while Tyrell was blasted through the doorway and down to the floor below. The mage dragged himself to his hands and knees, gasping for air and choking on the superheated air in his lungs. On his hands and knees, he dragged himself back over to the stairs.

"Galen! Nestor," he cried out over the roaring sound of the inferno above. He reached the top of the stairs, wincing at the heat. The small attic was engulfed in flame. He saw Nestor lying still on the floor. Galen sat nearby clutching his arm where a shard of broken glass had slashed him like a sword. Tyrell pulled the thief to his feet and shoved him in the direction of the stairs. "Go on! Get out of here." Galen nodded and lumbered off to the top of the stairs before turning to see if Tyrell needed any help with Nestor.

"Nestor! Come on, my friend. Now is not your time," yelled the mage as he shook the barbarian. He sighed in relief as the big man groaned. "Thank the gods," he whispered, but the praise died off quickly as his eyes fell upon the contents of a large barrel that had been splintered by the shockwave of Kellen's fireball.

The grayish-green powder that now lay spilled all over the floors quickly triggered in the wizard's memory a string of long alchemical lectures he had endured on volatile substances. Of these, one of the most dangerous he had learned of was refined auralesea dust. His master had shown him how just a few grains of this potent powder could start a raging bonfire with the touch of a mere spark. It was mostly used by the military for siege practices or signal fire communications. Another common use for auralesea dust, however, was as a hallucinogenic agent used in some illegal liquor brewing recipes, and here in the burning attic of a Tarnathian distillery was an entire barrel full of the stuff.

Tyrell grabbed the barbarian and threw him over his shoulder. In a panic, he turned and ran for the stairs. The cracking of the burning timbers above told the mage that the roof of the building would come down on them any minute.

"Galen, run. Get out of the gods forsaken building now, dammit!" He shoved his friend down the stairs, crashing down behind him with Nestor on his back. Upstairs, a blazing rafter broke away from the ceiling and fell end over end into the pile of dust. With the doorway to the shop just ahead of them, Tyrell heard the roar of hell itself unleashed above him. Then he was hammered by a cascade of fiery debris and knew no more.

*　　　*　　　*

Knarya and the city guard had finally turned the tide of the battle. Something had disrupted the advance of the vampire horde. The watch captain had no idea what that something might have been, but he had pushed his men ferociously to take advantage of the monsters' chaos. The creatures had fallen victim to the pain and doubts that now tormented their dark master, and the victory that had once seemed inevitable now lay perilously close to disaster.

Knarya poured another jar of pitch on the bonfire he oversaw. For all of the damage that his men had caused the ranks of the vampires, the demons had given back as good as they got. The captain's thoughts dwelled a moment on the faces of those men he had trained and served with who he had watched die in agony tonight, torn apart or beaten to death as they valiantly stood to defend friends and families from the undead terror. He wiped his eyes with the back of his hand, focusing his mind on matters at hand. The time for grieving would come later. Right now, he had a city to defend.

"Captain," called out a young archer from his rank. "Sir, we need more fire if we're to hold them off. The arrows are hurting them but just barely."

"You just keep firing, son. We've arrows enough to last the night, and the courage to face these bastards even with our bare hands if need be." He cheered as the young soldier put a flaming shaft through the eye of an approaching monster. Knarya knew, however, that his words were just bravado. The arrows would run out before long, and all watchpoints were reporting that the fires were beginning to burn low. They needed more flame, he thought to himself.

The night was ripped open then as a colossal fireball erupted like a volcano in the middle of the city. Fire rained down all over the city as if a flight of dragons had joined the attack. Buildings ignited and both soldiers and vampires were struck by flaming debris from the blast site.

Even from this distance, Knarya staggered from the force of the blast and felt the wash of heat from the conflagration. He cried out in frustration as he realized that the horde of vampires wasn't the only problem he had to deal with now.

The great port city of Tarnath was burning.

CHAPTER FIFTEEN

The fires raged across the city as the auralesea flames, far hotter than of any normal blaze, were fanned by the winds that blew in from the sea. At the center of the blast, the distillery had been completely leveled, and a few smoldering stones were the only evidence that the building had ever been there. For one hundred yards around, the surrounding buildings were also blasted into rubble. Screams filled the night air as citizens fled from the dangers around them. Many fell to the fires. Many more fell to the lurking remnants of Kellen Ambrose's army.

The vampires who fought nearest to the distillery had recoiled from the light and heat of the blast but had blended in well with the rest of the fleeing citizens. Once their initial disorientation passed, they resumed their conquest on the panicked population who tried to escape the engulfed dock quarter. The citizens found themselves fleeing from one deadly menace into the waiting arms and drooling fangs of another equally deadly one.

Knarya looked in horror as his city burned. A volley of flaming arrows took down the few struggling vampires in his immediate vicinity, and Knarya quickly regarded his exhausted and frightened men. The guard captain wondered, not for the first time, if this night was ever going to end.

"All right," he yelled. "Bailey, get your archers to provide some cover fire. Nail down anything with fangs. Sartor, bring your foot soldiers to the harbor's edge. If we don't start some kind of bucket line immediately, there won't be anything left of the city for these pointy-toothed bastards to claim." The pudgy captain absently swung his torch into the face of a lurking vampire. As the beast's clothing and hair ignited, Knarya's men fell upon it with a savage fury.

"Captain," called one young soldier, "couldn't we make good use of this fire as well?"

"We don't have time for roasting sausages and singing campfire songs, boy," Knarya growled.

"No, sir. What I meant was that perhaps we could drive the vampires back into the fires. We could still take steps to control the spread of the burning, but let's push this scum back in there, and not give them a way out."

Knarya looked at the young soldier with pride. "Excellent idea, son. When this thing is all over, I'm going to recommend you for a commendation." Provided we all live through any of this, he added silently. "Archers," he ordered, "concentrate your fire and push these devils back into the hellfires that spawned them!"

The archers began to release volley after volley, steadily driving the vampires towards the flames. With their numbers being cut down by the encroaching blaze, and the unexpected tenacity of the city guard, the vampires had decided enough was enough. With their link to their dark master inexplicably severed, and the growing likelihood of a looming defeat becoming reality, Kellen's minions broke off their attack and retreated into the shadows.

Knarya's soldiers gave an exultant whoop of victory and charged ahead with renewed vigor. They quickly sorted fleeing citizens from the undead, pulling the frightened townsfolk behind their lines. The captain ordered up a fire brigade and was surprised at the number of able-bodied men and women who volunteered to face the flames while still exposed to the threat of Kellen's minions. It was a true testament to the will and determination of the people of the city.

As the remaining vampires steadily fell back, desperation overcame them. They were monsters, but not unthinking ones. They drew their ragtag numbers together until all of the remaining unholy force was gathered together, numbering some fifty strong. Behind them, the auralesea flames burned hot at their backs. Ahead lay the fiery arrows that hammered their ranks. These creatures were once citizens of the port city, though, and they too were possessed the same tenacity and courage as those men and women who stood arrayed against them.

In a show of defiance, the snarling vampire horde stormed the lines of the city watch with a terrible battle lust. Glittering fangs and rending claws ripped into the city defenders with the ferocity of those who had nothing else to lose. Soldiers and citizens fell before them as they joined together for the brutal common purpose of survival.

The undead army of Kellen Ambrose had already tasted death once. They were reluctant to do so again.

*   *   *

Tyrell's ears were ringing as he slowly regained consciousness. His head throbbed, his body ached, and he could feel burns all along his backside. As he looked around, he sighed in relief as he saw Nestor and Galen lying nearby, the slow rise and fall of their chests allaying his fears, although they were yet a long way from safety. All around them, flames hotter than a blacksmith's furnace decimated buildings, spreading out like a living thing in search of prey.

The wizard choked on the thick black smoke that blanketed the area. He had to get his friends out of here. As quickly as his body would allow, Tyrell crawled over to Galen and shook the young thief. Slowly, he opened one eye, then groaned. "Are we dead yet?" Tyrell could barely hear the thief's words over the roaring fires, but he had to laugh at his friend's ability to find a moment of levity even in the direst of circumstances.

"We aren't that lucky," replied the mage. "But that could very well change if we don't get moving. Can you walk?"

Galen nodded and painfully got to his feet. He swayed a moment, and put a hand to the back of his head, rubbing a knot that he had received from some piece of flying debris. Tyrell knelt beside the warrior. Nestor's pulse was faint, but present. Muttering a quick prayer of thanks, Tyrell dragged the big man away from the fires.

"We may need this," said Galen as he examined a pile of burning rubble. With a heave, the thief rolled aside a blackened timber, lifting forth the glittering rainbow of metal, Shadow Reaver. "It's not even warm," he commented as he slid the blade into an empty sheath. "Let's see if we can get clear of this, and pick up that bastard's trail." Tyrell nodded, and Galen began to pick his way through the wreckage in a direction that he hoped led to the nearest edge of the fire.

They made slow progress since Tyrell had to carry Nestor, let alone the fact that they were simply exhausted. Galen scouted ahead, seeking the easiest and safest routes for his friends to follow behind. Many times, burning buildings and debris forced them to backtrack, and the heat from the auralesea flames was beginning to take its toll on them.

"Look out," cried Tyrell the creaking of a nearby building gave him just enough warning of the structures impending collapse. He shoved Galen back far enough so that the thief only got singed rather than crushed. "We've got to get off these streets," the mage shouted. "We're not going to last much longer like this."

"Even the sewers would be preferable to this," said Galen. Tyrell started to respond when Nestor, slung over his shoulder like a sack of potatoes, coughed and sputtered.

"Why am I face to face with your ass," growled the barbarian. Tyrell lowered his friend to the ground, steadying the warrior as the blood rushed out of his head. Nestor looked at the bruised and bloody faces of his friends. "Hell, this view isn't any better." He looked around and rubbed his temples. "So where are we?"

Tyrell could see the pain on the warrior's face. Through the night, Nestor had taken the worst of everything that Kellen had thrown at them, but the warrior stoically refused to submit to his injuries. "This isn't the best place to talk right now. Let's keep moving, and I'll fill you in as we go."

Nestor nodded, aware of how his unconsciousness had slowed his friends down. "Lead on. I'll be right behind you."

"I hear yelling in that direction," said Galen as he pointed past a tattered jumble of burned out shops. The thief dashed forward to find the easiest way through the mess. Tyrell came next, pausing when needed to lend Nestor his silent support. Just as silently, the warrior accepted his friend's assistance. He was too pragmatic, and too exhausted to let pride come in the way of survival.

"I found the way through," said Galen as he reappeared through the smoke. "It's this way. Follow me quickly." The three men moved through a burning archway, crawling on their bellies through a narrow space that was so hot that they could scarcely draw a breath. Tyrell worried that Nestor might pass out, but the stubborn warrior forced himself to stay alert.

The cries of battle and the clash of steel rang out in the night. "Look," called Tyrell, as he pointed at two members of the city watch fighting a desperate battle against one of Kellen's minions. One of the soldiers made a ferocious swing at the vampire's head with his ax, but the creature caught the haft in his hand and wrenched it from the man's grasp.

With a savage backhand swing, the soldier's head was removed from his body with his own weapon. Snarling with glee, the monster turned on the remaining soldier.

"We've got to help," said the mage, as he quickly opened his mind to the forces of magic. The sudden flow of power staggered him, and he realized that he was hardly ready for another fight, but there was no time to rest. He could only hope that his friends were in better shape than he was.

"The only one of them I give a damn about is Ambrose," growled Galen. The ferocity with which he spoke was so alien to the young thief's demeanor that Tyrell was shaken from his magical trance. The mage knew the words stemmed from the young thief's grief and rage over Lorelei's death, but Galen's tone frightened him nonetheless.

"We will get him," swore Tyrell, "but right now there are others we have to help or else they might share her fate. Let's move."

The thief nodded and drew Shadow Reaver from the scabbard at his side. To everyone's surprise, Nestor snatched it from the younger man's hand and stumbled off to fight. "Strong as a horse," muttered the mage. As Nestor, sank the glittering elvensteel blade into the back of the vampire, Tyrell noticed more fighters, both vampire and human, had come closer.

The main group of vampires stood in front of a burning building that teetered on the verge of collapse. Losing himself again in his magic, the mage felt the fire's intensity as it ate through the supports of the building. The mage drew on his powers to make those flames burn even hotter. Timbers creaked and groaned as Tyrell's magic ravaged the already doomed building.

Galen caught a glimpse of a lone vampire creeping through the shadows towards Tyrell. Quickly, the thief blended into the flickering shadows created by the nearby flames. As the vampire leaped from its hiding spot to attack the concentrating wizard, Galen bashed it in the face with a burning piece of lumber, driving it to the ground.

"Don't try that again," snarled the thief. The monster replied with a savage grin of its own and swept Galen's feet from under him with a sudden kick. Galen fell flat on his back, the wind knocked from his lungs and embers burning his back like tiny needles. He tried to sit up but was slammed back to the ground as the vampire jumped on him. Gasping for air, and aching from so many battles, Galen fought on to keep the beast's fangs away from the flesh of his throat.

Captain Knarya stood over the body of a young soldier. With dismay, he recognized the lad who had suggested that the watch try to push the vampires into the flames. Tears of pain and grief streamed down the captain's face as he fought. With his torch, he bashed the vampire who had killed the brave youth, sending the murderous beast staggering back, trying to pat flames out of its scraggly hair. Knarya pressed his attack, but the night's toils made him too slow for the vampire's uncanny speed. The monster easily ducked, and grabbed Knarya by the throat, lifting the man from the ground in one crushing hand.

"All for nothing," hissed the vampire as his clawed forefinger tapped teasingly at the vein in Knarya's throat. "You will die no better than the rest of these." Knarya's vision started to dim from lack of oxygen, and spots danced before his eyes. A sudden rainbow of light whistled through the air near his head, and in the next moment, he felt himself falling.

He realized that he hadn't died and looked up to see a familiar red-bearded face, though covered in soot and battered like a man who had been through hell and back. Knarya shook his head and cleared his vision, fully recognizing Nestor as the one who now helped him to his feet.

"Thank the gods," Knarya said. "If you had been a moment later, Redbeard, I'd be . . ." The captain's words died off in exhaustion and fear.

Nestor thrust Knarya's torch back into the captain's grasp.

"Your men need their leader. Show them victory." The barbarian clapped Knarya on the back and turned to find another vampire to cut down.

Knarya felt a rush of hope and strength flood back into him at the sight of the warrior. He had no idea what horrors Nestor Canaith had seen this night, but he recognized instantly the man's adamant refusal to surrender. He slapped the torch into the palm of his hand. "Come on, lads," he cried. "We've got them on the run. Let them taste your flames!"

Tyrell felt the last of the support timbers burn through, and not a moment too soon. The vampires had scattered many of the disarmed and battered guardsmen who frantically raced off to find safety. As the remaining group of vampires began to pursue, the building fell with a mighty groan into their midst, sending a great column of fire and embers high into the night sky. Screams of fear and agony of the trapped vampires filled the night air as they were incinerated. To the watchmen that he had saved, such salvation was nothing greater than sheer coincidence, but Tyrell smiled to himself as the brave men quickly regrouped and moved off to find more undead.

Galen wrestled with his vampire, rolling around on the ground as he struggled to keep away from the monster's teeth and claws. The undead's breath was hot and foul against his cheek, and Galen gagged on the stench of old blood, and who knew what else.

"We'll destroy you all," the vampire taunted. "We'll kill every last one of you. All of your men, women, and children. Everything that you ever loved. Do you hear me? Everything that you ever loved!" As the vampire threw its head back and cackled into the night, Galen grabbed the end of the timber he had first struck the vampire with. The vampire's words triggered in the young thief's mind thoughts of Lorelei and his brief time with her. With a surge of strength, the thief hammered the vampire with the splintered timber, rolling the beast into the dirt beside him. In a flash, Galen found himself sitting on the vampire's chest with the stake in his hands.

"Your master already took the only thing I ever loved from me, and I intend to pay him back," growled Galen. With a battle cry inspired by pure hate and rage, Galen slammed the stake home into the vampire's chest. The creature bucked Galen off as it screamed in agony, and writhed around on the ground. The thief walked over to the thrashing vampire and pulled the beast to its feet. With a bitter smile on his face, Galen Thale shoved the monster back into the flaming rubble of the building Tyrell had brought down.

Nestor hacked and slashed in a wide circle as the vampires diminishing numbers tried to close in on him. The undead could feel the power of the weapon in the barbarian's hands, and they knew that the warrior was the greatest threat to them all. Exhausted beyond reason, Nestor fought on instinct, and never once felt a pounding blow or rending claw as he spun Shadow Reaver in a glittering rainbow of death. Undead flesh, although proof against normal iron and steel, was no match for barbarian savagery and the magical elvensteel sword wielded. It was only a matter of time before Nestor found himself looking for new foes to bring the blade against.

Tyrell and Galen moved around the battlefield, giving whatever support they could. They quenched fires, put vampires to the torch, and eased the suffering of the men and women too wounded to survive the night. Every such instance made Tyrell swear a silent oath to make Kellen Ambrose pay for the torment that he had created. Galen's own hatred for the vampire lord was matchless. Even though he pitied the poor citizens of Tarnath, his mind burned with the image of Lorelei's bloodless face as she lie on her sacrificial altar.

The night winds were filled with the howls of furious combatants, cries of the wounded and dying, and the roaring of the auralesea flames. The vampire horde, now only a mere dozen, drew together into a tight circle. Although escape would be difficult at best, the monsters knew that every living person they killed was one less to oppose them. They hissed and growled as the city defenders surrounded their evil throng. Both sides studied each other with contempt and malice evident on every soot-stained face. The ranks of the soldiers broke as Nestor came to the front of the ring. He raised Shadow Reaver to his brow in the traditional salute to those who were about to die.

The vampires were creatures of fury and hate, and so it was with these same emotions that the valiant people of Tarnath fell upon them.

Chapter Sixteen

Knarya went among his surviving soldiers, assessing their losses, and comforting those who needed it. The final charge had still cost many brave men their lives before the last vampire fell. They had won the night, but the cost had been staggering. As he looked around at the still burning city, the captain knew he still had a great deal more to do. He sighed in weary relief as he saw three figures shamble out of the smoke. Tyrell, Galen, and Nestor looked haggard and spent, but each man's face bore its own expression of dogged determination.

"Captain Knarya," said Tyrell, "these flames are caused by auralesea dust, and will be very difficult to put out. We need to get every able-bodied man, woman, and child on a fire brigade line. I will do everything I can to extinguish the flames with my magic, but my powers are not that great, and . . ." Tyrell looked around at the devastation and shrugged. "It has been a long night."

Knarya nodded. "You're telling me. If the cutpurse and Redbeard here will lend their backs to the bucket lines, it would be greatly appreciated. I know already the debt that the city owes you for tonight. For what it's worth, I promise I won't forget it." The captain shook hands with both Galen and Nestor, who then ran off to find a place in the forming water lines. Knarya looked back to Tyrell and grinned. "I never thought we'd see the end of this night. You probably didn't either, from the looks of you."

"Thank you, Captain," replied the mage. "You look like hell also." Tyrell wiped his brow as Knarya gave a short, barking laugh. The mage could see that the dock ward was virtually destroyed, and the flames had spread into the city's marketplaces and residential sections. "Well, shall we finish this?" the mage asked. Knarya clapped the man on the shoulder, hurrying off and shouting orders to anyone within earshot.

Tyrell found a position near the front of the nearest bucket line and lowered himself into a deep meditative trance. On many occasions, the wizard had needed his magic to enhance the power of flame. Now he needed to do the opposite. His body groaned with aching muscles as he drew in the power around him. While far too weary to outright quench the auralesea flames, the mage knew that he had strength enough to bring the heat down to normal levels. Even with that small help though, the fires were now so far spread throughout the city that the fire brigades would be working until dawn.

As Tyrell felt the flow of power through him, he could sense the presence of his friends in the brigade lines. Nestor was nearly unconscious on his feet, but the big warrior wasn't one to complain or fall when he knew so many lives depended on his assistance. It was a trait that Tyrell had come to admire most about this man he had once fought so bitterly. Nestor was someone who could always be counted on, regardless of the situation. Tyrell realized at that moment that Nestor Canaith would always be there to assist him if he was sorely needed.

When Tyrell's mind found Galen though, the wizard nearly recoiled. The young man's thoughts were awash with sorrow and anger. Gone was the boyish prankster. Galen had faced a terrible trial by fire, and now bore the scars of the experience. The mage could only hope that time would heal the thief enough to rekindle Galen's zest for life. He would miss the cutpurse's impish grin and perfectly ill-timed wit whenever situations were at their worst.

The mage briefly touched the minds of other people in the lines as well. Awe and shock prevailed in the citizens' thoughts. Here was a man whose life had been spared by the timely arrow of a city guard. Here was a woman whose only son had given his life so that she and her daughter could escape their besieged home. Here was a shopkeeper whose entire livelihood had been gutted by vampires and flames. Everywhere Tyrell looked, he sensed loss and despair, but with each touch, he still sensed hope in the thoughts of the forlorn townspeople. Homes and shops could be rebuilt. The fallen would be mourned.

And, he thought solely to himself, justice will be served.

*   *   *

Kellen Ambrose watched a group of firefighters from the depths of a distant alleyway. Pure fortune had allowed the vampire lord to remain undetected. For all of his strength and cunning, Kellen had no desire to be drawn into another battle tonight. The explosion at the distillery had blasted him into unconsciousness, and burns now scarred him badly along one side of his body. He would be a long time in healing despite his regenerative powers. How could he have not known that auralesea dust was in that attic? His own bloody trap had nearly killed him.

A snarl crossed his lips as he caught sight of Galen, Nestor, and Tyrell. The slash across his back throbbed as he watched them working to extinguish the city fires. He truly had forgotten how hard that damned sword could bite. Why hadn't he been able to beat the barbarian as easily as he had thrashed that skinny elf all of those centuries before?

The answer, of course, came to him in his own prophetic words. He had told the trio that only together did they have a chance of defeating the vampire lord. They had nearly done that very thing. They had thwarted him successfully at every turn, destroying all of his plans and gains for conquering the city. Even in the sewers, they had managed to escape his vampire vanguard. Their luck was absolutely infuriating.

Now his army was gone. His bid to rule had been shattered by three men who would have hung from the gallows so many weeks before. All of his scheming and careful attacks to build his forces had all come to nothing because of the actions of a trio of petty thieves, and a few sword swinging militiamen.

Kellen found himself surprisingly undaunted, though. The vampire lord watched the teams at work against the fire and smiled to himself. He had hurt them all very badly. With time, he could rebuild his army, his spy network, and correct his strategy for any more unseen contingencies. All he needed was time, and, after all, what was a couple of centuries to a vampire?

Ambrose laughed out loud and drew the attention of a couple of bystanders who quickly gave him a wide berth. It was time for Kellen to go home, and start his plans anew.

*   *   *

The last fires were finally under control. The auralesea dust had burned itself out, and the flames were all but extinguished. The resulting devastation, however, was enormous. The dock quarter was gone. Most of the marketplace was lost, and that which remained was covered in soot and ash. The homes of hundreds of people, rich and poor alike, had been completely consumed.

In the streets, casualties of the night's battle lay all around. People who had been torn to pieces by the vampires, people who had died from their burns, and those who had succumbed to the thick blanket of smoke were fallen throughout the city. Those people who could went among the fallen, looking for survivors, and gave aid where they may.

Knarya lifted a body onto a wagon and wiped his soot-covered brow. The daylight brought a measure of relief, but also had revealed the extent of the damage around him. Tarnath would be rebuilding for years to come. He turned to lift the next body when he noticed Nestor, Galen, and Tyrell leading their horses towards him.

"Hallo," he called to them. "Actually found your horses, I see. Well, you've done better than me. Think mine ran for the hills. Can't say I blame the little fella."

Tyrell smiled sadly. "They weren't where we had left them, but they hadn't gone far. More importantly, none of our gear was disturbed." Tyrell pondered a moment on what the loss of his newly discovered book of magic would have meant to him.

"So, I take it you three are for leaving?"

"We still have some unfinished business with Ambrose," said Galen. "He has a date with Shadow Reaver, and I'm a little anxious to stick my own blade in him as well."

"We could sure use your help cleaning this up, but I suppose your own tasks are just as important. Besides," Knarya said with a grin, "I don't expect we'll have finished up by the time you return."

"We'll return and help as soon as we are able, Captain," said Nestor. The barbarian's broken jaw only made his grim visage look more fierce, and Knarya couldn't suppress a shiver.

"My men said that Kellen's house was taken in the blaze, but I don't suspect he has stayed in the city anyway. How do you propose to find him?"

"When I cast a spell on him last night, I was able to touch his thoughts. Somehow, I created a link between us. I can use that feeling to sense where he is heading. He's moving quickly, Captain, so we really must be off." Tyrell shook Knarya's hand. "We'll fill you in on everything when we return."

Galen absently fingered the petals of a flower from the grave they had made for Lorelei that morning. Knarya also noticed a bracelet on the thief's arm that he couldn't remember ever seeing before. The thief looked at the sun climbing in the sky. "We'd better get moving."

"Farewell, Captain Knarya," said Tyrell as he pulled himself into his saddle. "We're riding north."

CHAPTER SEVENTEEN

The atmosphere that surrounded the trio was much different than on their previous ride to Del Torac. The nervous excitement that abounded during their quest for Shadow Reaver was now replaced by malice and grim determination. The three friends said little as they each remained lost in the depths of their own vengeful thoughts.

Tyrell had used his magic to repair some of the damage to Nestor's jaw, easing the barbarian's pain and allowing him to speak more clearly. Nestor had refused to let the mage try to fully heal his wounds, asserting instead that the lingering pain would sharpen his focus and anger. The wizard sighed as he regarded the young thief, and wished there was some magic he possessed that could heal Galen's wounds.

Galen had changed dramatically since the Night of Terror. The mischievous glint of his eyes had been replaced by a scowl of sorrow coupled with abject rage. What dreams of past joys haunted the young man? What gazes into a now impossible future tore through his heart, thought Tyrell? When Galen looked at either of his companions now, the laughing trickster gave way to someone driven by a far more malevolent purpose.

Tyrell pulled the Book of Torax'alamien from his saddlebag and opened it across his knees. "I'd have thought you'd have that book read by now," said Nestor as he pulled his horse closer to the mage. "You've been thumbing through it every chance you could get."

"I just hope to gain every possible advantage against Ambrose as I can. When I touched Kellen's mind in Tarnath, I saw a glimpse of just how ancient and evil his magic is."

"And you are afraid of failing if you have to go spell against spell with him."

"I know my limitations. At my present level of skill, Kellen could incinerate me in a spell duel."

"And you still aren't giving yourself due credit. No matter how stunted you believed your skill was when we started this thing, Tyrell, your powers have grown considerably. I don't need some magic book to prove that to me."

"It's more than just hoping to stumble across some new spell that I can use against him. I want vengeance on that black-hearted bastard just as badly as you or Galen. When I think of how many people suffered because of him..." The wizard left the thought unfinished. "I can picture Lord Tessarin swinging from the gallows because of Ambrose. I can hear the screams of terror and pain as people were attacked by his horde of minions. I can still feel the heat of the roaring flames as Tarnath burned around us." The wizard met his friend's gaze levelly, with a look of cold steel. "It is for all of those innocents whose lives have been lost or overturned that I will stand against him."

Nestor nodded and looked away. He let his friends words fade as he watched ahead, and listened to the sounds of the road. The barbarian expected an ambush from the vampire lord, despite the fact that Kellen had been sorely wounded and was in a panicked flight. Nestor's thoughts drifted back to the moment where Kellen's fist had broken his jaw. The warrior knew that he had felt the full strength of the vampire with that one blow, and he had sworn upon Shadow Reaver that he would return with a strike of his own. He rested his hand on the hilt of the sword, as he had done so many times since they had left Tarnath, reveling in the jolt of arcane power that flowed into his arm.

The gates of Del Torac appeared as they crested the next ridge, and the men rode through without incident. The taproom of the Belching Griffin warmed the chill from their bones, and after ordering food with instructions to send it up to Drayton's room, the three men found themselves once again in the company of the blond knight.

"You look well, Drayton," said Nestor as he warmly grasped the knight's hand.

"In truth, I still wobble like a newborn when I go to the taproom, but I am alive and recovering, thanks again to your efforts, my friends. Tell me how things went in Tarnath."

"Kellen escaped us," commented Tyrell. "He attacked the city with legions of vampires that he had been creating for months. We fought him several times, but the cagey bastard still managed to slip away. His army was stopped, but a huge part of Tarnath was leveled, and the loss of life was staggering."

Drayton lowered his head in a moment of reverence. "And now you follow Kellen on a road of revenge."

"We go to finish what we started," said Galen. "Kellen set us on this path to kill a vampire lord. Now his death will finish that job." The thief's cold gaze met the worried glances of his friends. Finally, he turned away to look at the flames in the hearth.

Drayton looked at Tyrell and Nestor. "And what of you two? Will Kellen's death satisfy you?"

"Nothing can ever repair the damage done by his evil. What we go after is not satisfaction, but justice. We want a reckoning for what he has done," said Nestor.

"Be careful, my friends, for many times justice is simply revenge in different clothes. I also caution you, do not go blindly into Kellen's den. Wherever Ambrose flees to, you may expect it to be well fortified with the ingenuity of centuries. I fear that should you rush in foolishly, his lair may tear the lives from your bodies as easily as he might himself."

"Your order has hunted him for centuries," said Tyrell. "Have you learned anything about his home that might help us?"

Drayton shook his head. "Precious little, as none of my brothers have ever found his hideout and lived to tell the tale. I could send for some of my men to go with you, but they would not obey you even at my direction. Damn, I wish that I could go along with you myself, but I can barely get out of bed unaided let alone sit a horse or wield my weapons." He balled his fist, and lightly pounded it against his thigh.

"Still, I'll tell you what I may, and counsel you against the vampire lord's cunning. Kellen is a shrewd opponent as you undoubtedly already know. Though I've never seen where he lairs, you can bet that it is a virtual fortress, if not an actual one. As he has known of our order for centuries, I would imagine his home to be capable of repelling an army. This may prove to be his undoing. Where an all-out assault of mounted knights might prove incapable, the three of you might manage to approach by stealth.

"It will be his traps and bodyguards that will give you pause. He could have anything from vicious animals to the most fearsome undead horrors watching the pathways into his home. And I will promise you also that his innermost sanctums will be more insidiously trapped than the fabled Vault of the Nine Kings." Drayton winked at Galen. "However, the treasures within should prove no less precious."

Nestor rose from his seat. "Then I'll chop the heads off of anything that he sends to us with Shadow Reaver, while Galen and Tyrell can see us through his traps, whether mechanical or magical. The only question I have left is would you like his head on a pike or a platter?"

"You sound dangerously close to underestimating him, my friend." The knight laughed sadly. "That is what my men kept doing with you, and look how that ended. Kellen Ambrose has proven himself time and time again that he is a power to be reckoned with. So much so that he was able to nearly level one of the mightiest cities this side of the Fire Plains. If you underestimate him, then you'll die."

Drayton's words left Tyrell and Nestor in somber silence. The men sat in silence until Galen lifted his head from hands. "Someone should send him the same warning," he replied.

*   *   *

Two days of hard riding found the men slightly northwest of the ruins of Khasharsta. Tyrell's magic had fed their horses the strength to run on with little rest. The terrain whipped past them as they covered the ground with a pace that they had never dreamed of.

As they settled into camp that night, Nestor drew out an old map that the knight had given to him. "Drayton said to look for a place that an army would find hard to reach." He scratched his beard as he studied the brittle parchment. "Tyrell, are you still getting some sense of where the devil is headed?"

The wizard nodded. "Kellen is still to our north, but I don't sense that he is moving any longer. I suspect that he has reached whatever lair he sought."

"Then there's only one place he could be given the amount of time he had to travel." The barbarian tapped the map before him. "He's somewhere in the Pillars of Heaven. It lies in the direction we're headed, and it just makes good tactical sense. Those rocky crags are the highest peaks around, and they're right in the middle of the northern Thelvenin Woods. No army would march in there. Takes too many troops to guard the supply lines."

"Why would they need so many guards?" asked Galen as he looked over the warrior's shoulder. He identified the rocky terrain but failed to see what Nestor was implying.

"The northern Thelvenin is rumored to be filled with creatures every bit as fey and foul as the black-hearted fiend that we're chasing." The barbarian gave the thief a wicked grin. "They say that all the misfired experiments of Khasharsta's elven wizards loom in the shadows. Beasts that the gods toyed with and cast aside dwell in the depths." He chuckled as he watched sweat bead up on Galen's brow. "Probably some simply nasty natural critters too. I suppose that simply referring to the place as a haunted forest was too plain for the storytellers."

"Rumors more likely started by Ambrose himself to keep away unwanted visitors," said Tyrell. The mage took the map from the warrior's hands. "The Pillars are situated close enough to the elven kingdom that he could have struck at their villages from his lair, and retreated to safety when he needed to. I would guess that whatever place Kellen is calling home is likely to be near some of these sunken passes. There are bound to be high cliff walls that he would use to keep watch over his domain."

"That's right," said Nestor. "Drayton said the lair would be a fortress that no army could reach, surrounded by strange guardians. I'm willing to bet that Ambrose probably has some kind of keep way up on a cliff wall. Most likely with one tiny, solitary bridge to get to the door, and every beast with claws or teeth in the vicinity standing in front of that watching out for intruders."

"Perfectly logical from a tactical standpoint," muttered Galen. "So how in Alhambra's Hells do we get to him? Call it a professional quirk but I'm not accustomed to walking up to the front door and giving a rap with the door knocker so that some pet of Kellen's can eat, I mean, meet us at the gate.”

“We’ll have to figure that much out once we actually get there. Finding the place in question is still the first task.” Tyrell looked again at the map and frowned. “According to our estimates, we’ll be passing the edge of the northern forest shortly. I probably need to stop enhancing the horses so that I can save my strength against anything that may go bump in the night.”

“We’ll slow our pace down when we head out. Take it slow and easy for a while. Things will be safer that way anyhow.”

“I have a deeper concern though,” added Tyrell. “I’m afraid that Kellen knows we’re coming.”

“I imagine that he sort of expected that part,” said Galen.

“Yes, but I have a bad feeling that if I can sense where he is, then most likely he can sense my presence through the same bond. That most likely means that he is already gathering his forces for his defense.” Tyrell rolled up the map and handed it back to the barbarian.

“So you expect an attack soon,” said Nestor matter-of-factly. He looked around the camp, peering into the shadows.

“Soon, and then with ever-increasing frequency until we arrive at his doorstep.” Tyrell looked into the solemn faces of his friends. “No one ever said this was going to be easy.”

“Wouldn’t be worth doing if it was,” said Nestor. Galen nodded in silent agreement.

Tyrell shook his head as his friends began to lay out their weapons. It was all too plain from their grim faces that, in order to reach Kellen, they would charge into a fight with anything and everything that the vampire lord threw their way.

*   *   *

The foothills sloped upwards before them as the green of the forest fell away to the rear. Despite the fact that they had passed through the darkest part of the Thelvenin Woods, no attack had yet come at them. Rather than relief, the three men felt ever more apprehensive at the fact that they remained unchallenged. A rustle in a nearby bush caused a dagger to fly from Nestor's hand, but rather than some undead horror, a scrawny rabbit bolted from its hiding place to the safety of some nearby rocks.

The trio moved even more cautiously now. They were certain that every rock outcropping and every shadowy crevice hid a servant of Kellen Ambrose who only waited for some cue to unleash an ambush.

The rocky ground now forced the men to walk their mounts. As night fell in the mountains, a chill fog settled over the craggy slopes. Before long, the friends' visibility was reduced to only a few yards, and they were forced to huddle closely together to avoid getting separated in the mist. In the distance, a wolf howled at the pale moon that cast an eerie sheen through the dense clouds.

"Now isn't that hellishly appropriate?" muttered Nestor as the wolf's cry faded into the night. "Keep alert, lads. I've got a feeling that the action we've been waiting for will find us this night."

Galen strained to see the trail ahead. "This is ridiculous. If we keep trying to travel through this, we're either going to find ourselves trapped in a box canyon or tottering off the edge of a cliff. I for one am in favor of neither."

"Galen's right," said Tyrell. "We'd better find a place to settle in for the night, and hope this fog burns off in the morning."

"You were unwise to pursue me to my home." Kellen's voice echoed through the fog with a sinister hiss. Nestor jerked Shadow Reaver from its sheath, and the elvensteel blade began to hum softly. The fog distorted the direction of Kellen's voice, making it impossible for the warrior to determine where the vampire stood.

"Show yourself, coward," cried Galen. "Come out and answer for your crimes!"

"And are you willing to do the same, little thief? How many times over could the magistrate of Tarnath send you to the gallows if he knew the extent of your career history? No, Galen Thale, my account shall not be tallied for many more centuries to come, and certainly not by the likes of you three," Kellen hissed.

"Tyrell," whispered Nestor. "Can you sense his position?"

Tyrell closed his eyes and then shook his head. "No. At this close range, I'm getting impressions of him from all around us. It's as if we're surrounded by his influence."

"Actually, you are surrounded by my minions," purred the vampire. "Call it a parting gift for you. I have grown weary of your persistence. You thwarted my army in Tarnath, and have proven yourselves to be worthy adversaries. Now, face my elite guard." A dozen shadowy forms suddenly materialized in the fog, but even though they moved closer to the trio, they grew no more substantial.

Shadow Reaver began to glow as the creatures neared. Galen lunged with his own weapon, but his blade passed harmlessly through the nearest specter. A smoky, wraithlike arm shot out and slapped the thief across the face leaving a frosty handprint emblazoned on his cheek. Galen fell to the ground, a silent scream on his lips as he trembled from the supernatural cold.

The wispy creatures closed their ranks. Nestor lashed out with Shadow Reaver, tearing through one of the ghostlike minions. The sword whistled through the apparition, yet still, the beast fell back from the blade's touch. "Any idea what these things are?" yelled the barbarian as he leaped to stand guard over the fallen thief. Shadow Reaver danced back and forth, holding the monsters at bay. Tyrell knelt down beside Galen who only shivered as he stared off blankly into the darkness.

"Haven't a clue. Just don't let them touch you."

"I figured that part out already," grumbled Nestor as he drove the elvensteel blade through another wraith that drifted within his reach. Tyrell's mind raced. He had studied a number of spells from his magical book that were said to be of particular use against the undead, but there were none that seemed to fit this predicament. Their attackers were little more than living shadow, and even the mighty Shadow Reaver needed something more tangible to strike.

An idea suddenly struck the mage. If the undead were creatures of darkness and drew their power from the shadows, then why not take it away from them? Tyrell raised his hand to the sky and called forth an explosion of light that blossomed out in all directions from him to pierce the darkest reaches of the surrounding fog. Shadow Reaver swished through the air at that precise instant, biting into a wraith like a woodcutter's ax into an oak. An unearthly wail of agony tore through the night as the specter was blasted away into smoky wisps.

"Hit them fast," groaned Galen from the ground. The young thief struggled to his feet. Nestor, invigorated by the sudden success of Shadow Reaver against the wraiths, went after the creatures in a rage. Galen drew his own blade and lashed out at the nearest beast. Although not nearly as effective as the elvensteel weapon, the thief hacked and slashed his way into the now vulnerable undead.

Still, the specters pushed forward, despite the fact that the three men were thinning their ranks one after another. Banishment from this plane of existence was far less punishment than what their dark master would inflict upon them for failure. One after one, they attacked with claw and fang. One after one, they were blasted away into nothingness.

When the last of the creatures' dying wails echoed from the

surrounding hills, the three men collapsed to the ground, exhausted. No words were spoken as they gasped for breath. After several long minutes, Tyrell broke the silence. "Kellen's gone back to his hiding place. He must have thought his minions would finish us off." The wizard struggled back to his feet. "We've got to move fast. If he gets a chance to throw anything else at us, you can rest assured that he'll do everything he can to make absolutely certain that he finishes us off. Our only hope is to find him tonight before he can conjure up another surprise."

"Then quit talking, and start tracking," muttered Galen. The young thief rubbed at the fading handprint on his face. The painful, beyond-the-grave chill that the monsters had employed seemed burned away by Galen's fiery rage. A dark scowl passed briefly across the young man's face that spoke of hatred and anger beyond what Galen Thale had ever known before.

The men quickly gathered their gear and set out with Tyrell in the lead. The mage ran as fast as the fog would safely allow while he followed the magical pull that he knew led towards Kellen Ambrose. As the trio moved on, Tyrell sensed that Kellen was no longer moving farther away, but was climbing, as if up the side of a cliff.

Suddenly, a howl broke the stillness of the night.

Nestor looked over his shoulder, but the fog distorted sound in such a way that none of the men could truly discern which direction the noise had come from. "Let's keep moving," said the barbarian. "That sounded close." He gave his friend a gentle push in the direction they had been going. They started off again, all of them hoping to put some distance between themselves and the wolf.

Another howl split the eerie night this time undoubtedly from ahead. A third sounded louder than the others directly off to their left. Sweat covered the brows of all three men, as they raced forward. Shadowy forms on four legs loped in and out of the mist-shrouded night. Low growls rumbled close behind as the men sprinted into the unknown night. Then, suddenly, a blank cliff face loomed out of the darkness before them that completely blocked their path.

"Dammit," swore Nestor. "We were being herded." The warrior drew Shadow Reaver, ready for battle, but Tyrell grabbed his arm.

"I can sense Kellen almost directly above us."

"Probably waiting to drop a rock on our heads, if the wolves don't get us first." Nestor strained to see into the swirling depths of the thick fog. "They're out there. I can see shapes running back and forth. They aren't coming in, but they aren't going to let us pass either."

"Well," said Galen, "then it would appear that up the wall is our only way out then. Let's get moving before they decide it's time to nip at our heels."

"Don't you think that is exactly what Kellen wants us to do?" growled the warrior. "Forget playing by his rules. Let's stab a few wolves and find a better way in."

"Galen's right, Nestor," said Tyrell. "Those wolves will come in too large a pack for us to fend off if we try to fight our way out." He sighed and shook his head. "Start climbing, big man." He turned and reached for a handhold along the cliff face. Galen, trained as he was for scaling walls, pulled himself up like a spider on a web, quickly passing the wizard. He called out hand and foot holds to his friends as he kept moving steadily upwards. Nestor gritted his teeth, sheathed Shadow Reaver, and pulled himself onto the rock wall. From below, the wolves howled, and Nestor watched a dozen mastiff sized brutes drift out of the fog to stand at the cliff's base.

Tyrell shortly found himself on a small ledge as Galen hauled him up. The wizard paused to wipe his brow and then reached down to grab

Nestor's outstretched hand. The three men rested under the cover of a small outcropping.

"Well, no rocks have fallen on our heads yet," said Tyrell.

"Kellen has probably figured that there are enough between our ears already," the barbarian snorted. "This is too easy. Kellen wants us up here. I've seen what an ordinary pack of wolves can do to a man, and I don't believe those below qualify as 'ordinary'. They were sent to hold us here on this rock."

"Full of good cheer tonight, aren't you?" muttered Galen.

"I'm just wondering how high up this cliff goes. Kellen's most likely standing up at the top, waiting for us to exhaust ourselves on this climb just so he can kick us off the wall one at a time."

"Well, try to land on a wolf when you hit bottom," snapped Galen.

"Galen, that's enough," said Tyrell. "We don't have any better options at the moment. The last thing we need is to turn against each other again." The mage glared at the young thief.

"My apologies, Nestor," said the younger man. "I just want this whole ordeal over with. Gods above, I just want my old life back."

Nestor put his hand on Galen's shoulder. "It ends tonight. One way or another. I swear, on my honor, that we finish it tonight."

Galen's face broke into a weary grin. "You know they say that there is no honor among thieves."

"We are so much more than thieves. We're brothers and close enough now to die for one another. There is no greater honor than that."

"Together, then," said Tyrell as he clapped his friends on their backs. "Let's finish the climb."

The three men gathered themselves and resumed their ascent. The fog not only made visibility terrible, but made the rock face slippery and wet. Tyrell's foot shot from his perch as he reached for a handhold, barely catching himself from plummeting into the open abyss below them. Galen moved easily up the stone face, while Nestor trailed behind, his focus on finding the next handhold that would bring him ever closer to burying Shadow Reaver in Kellen's breast.

The three men climbed on for what seemed an endless time, and eventually reached another ledge. Nestor looked to the moon. "We've only been climbing for about an hour. Does this damnable rock have no top? Much more of this and none of us shall have the strength to lift a sword, let alone run it through a squirming vampire."

"I'm more curious as to why Kellen hasn't thrown anything else at us," said Tyrell. "Wear us out on the cliff face, and let gravity finish us off," he said as he peered over the edge. The mage couldn't even see the ground through the thick curtain of fog.

"He wants to finish us off personally, I think," said Galen. "We've beaten his henchthings too many times now." The thief shrugged his shoulders. "If you want something done right, do it yourself."

"Or maybe his thirst for revenge is equal to ours," considered Tyrell. "We've thinned his ranks, wrecked his plans to conquer Tarnath, and chased him wounded back to this place. He's justifiably annoyed with us, don't you imagine?"

"Happy to be the thorn in his side," replied the thief.

"And the kick to his arse," said Nestor. The three men shared a quiet chuckle and moved again to the cliff wall. Above them, the cloud cover broke and the silver moonlight showed them the remaining 500 feet of the cliff face. At the top of the climb, the rocks grew even more jagged, like teeth gaping towards the heavens. Nestled in these crags, the trio saw their ultimate destination. Silvery stone walls of an ancient fortress loomed into the night sky above them. The heroes looked in awe upon Cliffside

Keep, a onetime refuge for elven kings in times of trouble.

It was now home to Kellen Ambrose.

Chapter Eighteen

"Quite a piece of work," said Nestor as he looked upon the keep. "It certainly looks like a hell of a difficult place to attack."

"Just as Drayton said it would be," whispered Galen. "Well, we are no army. Getting into places where I'm not wanted is my specialty." The thief began to reach for the next handhold when Tyrell grabbed his arm.

"Listen, Galen, Drayton also said that this place would be covered with traps and crawling with guards. We need to keep that in mind." Galen stared at the rock face before him, his brows knitted in quiet fury.

"It's only another obstacle to getting even with that son of a bitch."

"We know you're hurting, lad," added Nestor, "but we'd like to make certain that we all live long enough to grant justice where it's due." Galen nodded slowly, reaching again for the rock.

"I won't let you down," he replied. Nestor and Tyrell exchanged a quick worried glance and moved back to the cliff face.

The fog rolled back in like a white blanket, heavier than before. The three climbers did all they could to stay within sight of one another, but so dense was the cloud that each man was shrouded in his own isolated pocket. Every distorted echo sounded like the precursor to an ambush to catch the men at their most vulnerable. Tyrell waited for the impending roar of a rock fall crushing down from above. Nestor whipped his head back and forth expecting some new ghastly servant to materialize beside him and throw him off the mountain. He felt little reassurance from the elvensteel blade on his back, for how could he hope to draw it and fight while hanging from the side of the cliff?

Galen, however, silently welcomed any attack that might come. The young thief sought only to vent his boiling rage on something. If it lived and breathed, he would kill it. If it were already dead, then he would send it back to the grave. If Kellen dared show his face, then so much the better, he thought to himself with a grim smile.

Time again lost its meaning as the climb through the foggy haze continued. The top of the cliff had again become lost in the clouds, and they found no more ledges to take rests upon. The instead wedged themselves into crevices of rock when weariness demanded a pause.

"Galen, I don't suppose you can see how close we are now?" asked Tyrell during one such interlude.

The young thief strained to see above him, but only saw darkness and swirling fog. "Nothing yet. Surely, we have to be getting close by now though. Feels like we've been at this for ages."

The mage looked around him, surveying the rocky outcroppings that surrounded him. Cold, hard, and thoroughly uninviting was the quick assessment he reached. He sighed. *All I want is this nightmare to end,* he thought to himself. A wave of despair flowed over him. *What if we haven't got the strength or the ability, when we get there,* he wondered. *This whole adventure feels so hopeless.*

A dark shadow appeared from the corner of his vision, vanishing as he tried to focus on the shape, but reappearing as he looked away. "Come, dear one," whispered a sweet voice into Tyrell's mind. "Together we shall end your doubt and anguish." The wizard shook his head to clear the voice from his thoughts, but he found himself edging closer to the siren song of the shadowy form. He tried to call out to warn the others, but his voice caught in his throat. "Closer," beckoned the shadow, and Tyrell could do nothing but obey.

Nestor sensed Tyrell moving above him and resumed his climb, as rapidly as he dared. Loose stone from above rained down in his face, and he bit back a growl. Skillfully, he scaled the rock wall, until he saw the soles of boots just above him. "Have a care what you kick down the slope," he called up. He pulled himself up enough to see Galen looking down at him.

"Where's Tyrell?" asked the thief.

"I thought you were him. I didn't pass him on the way up."

"Well, you must have. He hasn't come past me either. Tyrell!" The thief's voice echoed into the night sky. "Gods above, he didn't fall, did he?"

"I imagine that he would have had the courtesy to at least scream if he were plummeting to his death." The warrior felt a shiver run down his spine. "Be ready, lad. I've got a feeling something is ab-." Nestor's words were cut off as the rock beside him exploded outward and a giant fanged head burst forth. The diamond-shaped head of a monstrous mountain serpent bucked into both men, grabbing Nestor from the wall and forcing Galen to scramble for a handhold to keep from falling to his death, as he slid down the rocky slope.

* * *

Tyrell crept around the rock spur, watching the shadow recede into the opening of a small cave. A terrible carrion stench assailed him as he edged closer to the opening. Go back for the others, he screamed to himself, but silently he continued on. "Come to me, dear one," called the soothing voice to him again. Helpless to resist, Tyrell entered the cave.

Although unable to resist the pull of the sweet voice, Tyrell had spent years disciplining his mind to attune to magic of all types. He found the tendrils of the beckoning call itself and could see the lines of magic that extended from the deeper shadows to himself. The mage stood his ground, reaching his focus out towards the call. The source of the dark magic felt his resistance and redoubled the effort sending waves of pulsing magic blasting away at the wizard's mental barriers. Tyrell gritted his teeth and reached out with his mind. A snarl crept over his face as he broke the magical bond through the sheer force of his will. The magical fingers retreated into the darkness once more, and Tyrell's will was his own once again. He started to turn and run back to the entrance when a cold, rotten breeze blew from behind him/

"Going so soon, darling?" It was the same honey-sweet voice that had called him to this place. Whispery and menacing, yet seductive and soothing, the feminine voice made him halt once again. He whirled and saw the coalescing figure of an ethereal elven woman step from the depths of the cave. "I so seldom get company. The tyrant of the keep likes to have his guest for dinner all too literally." She threw her head back and laughed a cruel twisted laugh. Her silvery gold hair floated around her pale face. Eyes of pure blackness bore into him with malice born of centuries of an unearthly hunger. Her pale lips parted to show rows of razor-sharp fangs. Though she was surely breathtaking in life, Tyrell stood in terrified awe of the deadly creature before him. Tyrell wondered if his friends would reach him in time even if he screamed for them.

"Oh, please, don't think for a moment that I serve the dark lord of Cliffside," the ghostly elf maiden purred. "I am but one of the lost souls that he has stolen from life. Gieralond was my name when I danced beneath the bright sun in the elven wood." Her eyes suddenly darkened. "It was that damnable brute that stole away with me as I frolicked in a midsummer festival. Beneath the stars, he lured me away with his rapturous gaze." Her voice snarled with malice. "And then he drank from me, and let me die. Our healers used all of their arts so that I would not become a creature as he was, but something went wrong. I rose again, wraithlike, a lost soul forever doomed to this plane, yet I still hunger as he does." As she looked at Tyrell, the wicked smile again found her face.

"My lady, truly I am sorry to hear how you too were wronged by Ambrose-." Tyrell's words were cut off as a backhanded blast threw him across the cave. He slammed against the rock wall, tumbling onto a pile of bones.

"Do not say that name," screamed Gieralond. Tyrell scrambled to narrowly avoid the jagged claws as the elven spirit lunged at him.

"My friends and I are here to face him," stammered the wizard. "Simply allow me to leave, and this night, I swear on my honor, that you and so many others shall have the justice that you deserve."

"Let you leave," the spirit said mockingly. "I think not, mortal. The dark lord would feast upon you and your pitiful friends, only to leave me dining on rats here in the dark. Oh, you shall find your doom tonight, my dear one, but you need not go so far to find it." Faster than Tyrell could follow, Gieralond grabbed the front of his shirt, hurling him deeper into the dark tunnel that led into the mountainside. Tyrell slid to a stop on the rough gravel floor.

"Now you will face me, mortal. I will drink your life force as I have not done in so many years, and I will add your bones to the piles around you." She threw back her head and cackled with glee.

*   *   *

Nestor fought through the piercing agony of the snake's fangs buried in his hip and pounded his fist against the side of the monster's head. The serpent was relentless in its grip though and held fast to the flailing warrior. Slowly, the rock serpent began to retreat back into its hole dragging Nestor along. Had the barbarian thought better of it, he would have let the beast do so, for Nestor dangled over the abyssal drop held aloft only by the huge snake's imprisoning jaws.

Instead, the warrior snarled and punched the serpent squarely in one if it's great glassy eyes. He pummeled on the creature's snout, but the snake merely tightened its hold. With a shake of its massive head, the serpent dashed Nestor against the surrounding rock in an effort to soften up its intended meal. Nestor took the blows without complaint, lashing out once again.

Galen caught a handhold about thirty feet below where Nestor and the snake thrashed around. The rock spur tore through his leather glove, and into the flesh of his hand, but the young thief's grip held. As he caught his breath and tried to calm his hammering heart, he looked above himself to see how his friend fared against the monstrous snake. As Nestor was beaten around on the rocks, Galen quickly resumed his climb, determined to get to Nestor before it was too late.

Nestor drew a dagger from his belt and plunged the blade deep into the serpent's face. The snake shook again in a wave of agony, again slamming the barbarian into the rock wall. The blade fell from Nestor's hand and was lost in the darkness below. This will not be the end, growled Nestor to himself, though the bruises and scrapes were beginning to mount up.

Galen drew his own dagger and hurled it at the snake's exposed throat with all of his might. The blade barely pierced the snake's scaly hide though, and if he had done any damage, the snake didn't show it. The serpent gave Nestor one last shake for good measure, and pulled back into the depths of the hole, dragging Nestor along with it.

The thief scrambled up the last few feet to the opening, only to see Nestor's feet dragged into inky darkness. "Nestor, I'm here," yelled Galen, as he reached out for his friend's foot. With a sudden rumble, however, the tunnel before him rumbled and groaned. With a deafening crash, the tunnel ceiling collapsed before him. As dust and rock billowed in a choking cloud around him, Galen realized that he was now on his own.

*   *   *

Tyrell barely rolled away as the elven ghost's fist cracked the rock wall he had leaned against just a moment before. He scrambled away on all fours, while his mind raced to figure a way out of this mess. Gieralond blocked him from reaching the cave opening, and the way behind him was unknown to him. It might lead deeper into the mountain or it might leave him in a dead end.

"You might as well stop running, dear one, and just accept your fate." The elven shade's fanged maw cracked wide in a terrifying grin.

"You'll not have me without a fight," growled Tyrell. He kicked a skull from the floor at the ghost, but she slapped it away and cackled that shrill menacing laugh again.

"So futile, but it does make your blood pump harder through your veins. Oh, you shall taste so sweet." She again grabbed the front of his shirt, lifting him effortlessly from the ground. As her hand touched him, a strange lethargy fell over the wizard.

She's right, he thought to himself. I can't beat her. Why do I continue to fight? Gieralond laughed again, the noise sounding distant. Tyrell's vision blurred as his strength ebbed away.

"No," he shouted. Tyrell's iron will dragged him to consciousness and forced his mind into the realm of magic. A sinewy black conduit snaked between himself, and the ghost drawing his energy away from. "An open pipe flows both ways," he snarled. Through sheer determination, Tyrell found the magical core of Gieralond's being and yanked back with all of his mental strength. A burst of revitalizing energy flooded him as he took the spirit by surprise. Magical warmth flooded through him, healing wounds and reinforcing his own magical defenses with every passing second.

Gieralond refocused her own determination and tried to draw back in a magical tug of war, but Tyrell had gained the advantage. He siphoned energy away from her, watching as her spectral form dimmed. In seconds she would be gone, changed into magical energy, and absorbed by the mentally dominant wizard.

The elven ghost realized what peril she was in, and shrieked in rage and frustration. "You cannot win, mortal!" She slammed her fist into the cavern ceiling. "The master's will shall prevail in the end!" Another smash of her fists into the ceiling brought loose rock down on Tyrell's head, giving Gieralond the moment she needed to sever the connection between her and the mage. Tyrell faced her as she glared with centuries-old hatred for the living.

"You have weakened me, nothing more."

"And yet you know how close I came to destroying you. Let me pass that I may rejoin my friends, and I will see you avenged."

"Destruction by you is only a possibility, fool. Destruction from my dark master is an absolute certainty." She lunged again at him, slower than before but still with inhuman speed. She hit Tyrell squarely in the chest knocking him backward into the deeper reaches of the tunnel. Gieralond again struck the cave ceiling, and this time her powerful strike brought down the tunnel in a hailstorm of rock and dust.

Tyrell choked for air, realizing that she had sealed him into the cave. A faint glow pierced the fallen rock as Gieralond stepped through the stone into the chamber. "And now it ends," she cackled.

"So it does," growled Tyrell. The mage lashed out with his magic and re-opened the conduit to the woman's ghost. Only a spark of magical essence remained compared to what she once possessed. Without hesitation, he grabbed hold of that final glimmer, ripping it from the otherworldly anchoring that held her to this plane. He was immediately hit with the force of all of Gieralond's emotions. Hatred for him, sorrow for the loss of the life she had been cheated from, and most strangely of all, he sensed pity.

In her final moment, before her eternal essence was scattered into nothingness, Gieralond felt pity for Kellen Ambrose. If this mage traveled with friends as powerful as he, then perhaps the dark lord was truly doomed.

The final spectral luminescence faded, and Tyrell found himself in complete blackness. Splendid, he thought to himself. Time to throw out a beacon, and draw every slithery, shadowy thing in Kellen's arsenal to me. He had no other alternative though. With a sigh, Tyrell called forth a magical globe of light to study his surroundings, but even that failed to help beyond an arm's reach.

The route that he had come through was gone, destroyed during Gieralond's fit of rage. There was no going back out that way. He had no choice but to follow the cramped tunnel deeper into the cave. Carefully he stepped forward, testing his footing. The slick rocks betrayed him with nearly every step though, and he stumbled several times. With shins and knees banged and scraped he paused a moment to lean against the wall and catch his breath.

As his shoulder touched the rock, however, the stone behind him gave way, and Tyrell tumbled backward into an old stone chimney. The mage crashed down through the old stone with rock spurs punching into him from all angles. He tasted blood after one particular blast to the ribs. He finally slammed onto a cold floor. Though barely conscious, his fingers felt the texture of worked stone. His globe of magical light was gone again, and he could see nothing.

I'm in the keep, he decided as he felt the brickwork under his hands. We're nearly there. Just need some rest and a light. A feeble glow enveloped his fingertips and gave him a momentary glimpse of the chamber before pain and exhaustion stole away his consciousness.

Two rows of stone sarcophagi stretched towards a grand stair at the far end of the room. Slowly the grating sound of stone against stone rumbled through the darkness as pale white hands began pushing away lids that had remained undisturbed for centuries.

*   *   *

Nestor went limp and allowed the giant snake to drag him as far as it wanted. It wasn't as if he had much say in the matter anyway. Without warning, the serpent's jaws suddenly released him, and the warrior sprang to his feet. Torchlight filled the chamber above him and lit up the great pit of worked stone that he now found himself in. A ledge ran along the top of the pit, ending in an archway that led off into a dark corridor.

"So, you're somebody's pet, eh?" Nestor looked over his wounds and gladly found them to be superficial. It seemed that being slammed against the cliff face repeatedly had hurt worse than the snake's bite. Nestor smiled at the great snake, now coiled up, with its massive head swaying gently back and forth. "Let's see how well you fare on even ground, you bastard."

As a boy, the warrior had played a game similar to his situation, except the snakes then were much smaller. He had learned that the key to avoiding the snake bite was to know the exact moment in which to sidestep the strike. With a flash of a knife, the game was over and the snake was dead. Over the years of his youth, Nestor had been the undisputed champion among the boys of his village. As he drew Shadow Reaver from the sheath on his back, the barbarian figured the principle here to be just like the contest of his childhood. Same game, bigger snake.

The great serpent slowed its rhythmic dance, then lashed forward suddenly with blinding speed. Its prey, however, rolled around the lunge, and the snake smashed its mighty snout into the solid stone wall of the pit. Shadow Reaver flashed down hard in Nestor's mighty hands and bit deeply into the creature's neck. Blood sprayed as the snake bucked wildly in pain.

Nestor deftly rolled himself onto the snake's back, clamping down tightly with his knees. The blood slicked scales made holding on difficult, but the barbarian only needed a moment. As soon as the serpent reared its head back, he'd slam the elvensteel sword into its skull and finish it off. To the warrior's surprise though, the snake rolled and twisted, crushing Nestor against the ground with the full weight of its thrashing body.

"Little worm doesn't play fair," he groaned as dragged himself back to his feet. The snake, wounded and in pain, slithered away from him, its slitted eyes watching the warrior's every move. Nestor scooped Shadow Reaver from the floor of the pit. "I won't be outdone by the likes of you," he called to the beast. "Shall we have another bout?"

The snake's eyes seemed to narrow in understanding and rage. Once again it lunged forth with astonishing speed. Nestor, still groggy from the repeated beatings he had taken, saw too late that he couldn't get out of the way. Instead, Shadow Reaver came up high, reversed in his grip, and plunged down point first. The snake's snout slammed into Nestor, plowing the barbarian against the pit wall behind him. The warrior's breath was blasted from his lungs by the force of the impact, and stars danced before his eyes. He fell to the ground with the coppery taste of blood in his mouth. Wearily, he lifted his head expecting great fangs to descend into his flesh at any second.

Before him, Shadow Reaver stood out from between the snake's eyes like some obscene horn. The legendary weapon had done its work just as the snake had slammed into him. Nestor chuckled as he slowly pulled himself to his feet. "Hope my luck holds," he muttered as he yanked the sword from the snake's skull.

The wall of the pit was pocked with rough stone handholds and he quickly made his way to the top of the hole. He took a quick pause to catch his breath, then he clenched Shadow Reaver's hilt once more as he plunged ahead into the dark corridor before him.

It was time to go after more dangerous prey.

*   *   *

Galen looked into the ruined tunnel that Nestor had been dragged into. The collapse was complete. There was simply no way to follow him through the debris. The young thief's thoughts moved quickly to Tyrell. Had the snake grabbed the mage as well?

"First Lorelei, then Tyrell, and now Nestor. No more, Ambrose," whispered the thief, his forehead resting against the cold rock wall. He threw his head back and screamed at the moon above. "No more! Do you hear me, Ambrose? NO MORE!!" His words echoed back to him. Somewhere far below, a wolf howled.

Galen turned his attention again to the ascent, deftly scrambling up the remaining fifty feet to the top of the cliff. He found himself in an overgrown courtyard. Crumbling stone columns loomed over the edge of the climb he had finished. Statues of ancient elven warriors stood their silent vigil as the cobbled stone led to a mighty pair of doors in the fortress wall. Tall spires reached into the darkened sky. As he studied the dark windows, one of the doors swung open silently in the light breeze, as if inviting him inside.

The thief grinned as he blended into the shadows near the fortress wall. He had made a career out of getting into places he wasn't wanted, and the first lesson he had ever been taught about burglary was to never use the front door. It was the most watched, the most heavily guarded, and possibly the most trapped. No, only a thief more arrogant than intelligent would walk right up and knock. The key to staying alive in his line of work was to go in where they least expected.

Like the turret balcony, he thought to himself. He'd have to be crazy to climb the tower after the long crawl up the cliff face. Or at least that's what he hoped the vampire lord would think. Quickly, as only a master thief could, Galen darted from shadow to shadow until he stood at the base of a tall tower spire. From his pack, he found a small grappling hook attached to a length of thin silk rope that was too fine for him to have used on the rough cliff face, but just perfect for scaling the fortress tower.

Galen thought back to the last time he made this sort of entrance. It had been the night that he had broken into the home of Lord Merkalan. The night this entire ordeal had started, and had brought him now to this moment, this place. This time, he swore to himself, I intend better results.

Though high above, Galen's grappling hook sailed true and caught hold on the first try to the stone railing of the balcony. "Here we go again," he muttered as he began to pull himself up the wall. He climbed like a spider on a silken thread, scaling the tower with ease. About halfway up, Galen paused to take a look at his surroundings. He froze when his eyes scanned the parapet that stretched along the wall of the keep proper. A torch flickered in the hands of a dark figure that leaned casually against the stone battlement. With a casual wave of acknowledgment, Kellen Ambrose walked from the battlements into the tower that Galen clung to the side of.

The young thief's rage spurred him on. He raced up the remaining length of the thin cord and swung onto the balcony. The lock on the doors was a mere inconvenience to him. With sword in hand, Galen Thale threw them open wide, entering the lair of the being who he hated above any other.

A long corridor led out of the turret and led to the castle proper. Dust and cobwebs filled the passage, but Galen was still surprised that the hallway wasn't swarming with Kellen's servants responding to the entrance of an unwelcome intruder. "Let them come," he whispered softly to himself. "I've lost too much to stop now." The young thief wasn't here for ancient treasure or glory.

It was payback time, and Galen Thale was ready to collect.

CHAPTER NINETEEN

A short stair led from the tower entrance where Galen stood to the hallway floor. Instinct buzzed within him that if Kellen hadn't sent a horde of guards and minions to intercept him by now, then something else protected this passageway.

The thief's carefully trained eyes scoured every inch of the hallway. Each footfall he made was carefully placed only after he was certain of its safety. Nothing seemed out of the ordinary, but this only made Galen that much more cautious. While he had indeed come on through the least likely entrance, he knew better than to underestimate Kellen's cunning. After all, he mused, *if I had centuries of sitting around with nothing else to do, wouldn't it seem appropriate to honeycomb your hideout with as many traps as I could devise?*

The thief's intuition and vigilance soon rewarded him. Just as he was about to take the final step, he spied the thin gossamer strand of a tripwire as fine as spider silk. A more brash intruder would have disregarded the line as nothing more than one more cobweb draping through the hallway, which was totally believable given the condition of the surroundings. The experienced thief, however, saw the filament disappear into a thin crack in the wall. With a small pair of razor sharp scissors that he had tucked into a pouch, Galen snipped the wire. He listened intently for the sound of any backup mechanisms tripping, but the corridor remained as still as it had been for centuries.

His painstakingly slow progress carried him past all manner of lethal devices tucked away to dispatch the unwary. Spray nozzles were nestled in between mortar joints. Darts, arrows, and spears were poised to strike from all different angles. Pressure plates were hidden among the stone floor ready to launch everything at anyone foolish enough to rush blindly into the hallway. Galen couldn't help but admire the extreme caution Kellen must have taken to protect this route into the heart of his home. Ambrose's efforts were far more commendable than those used by Tarnath's aristocracy.

Galen finally reached the far end of the corridor and passed through an archway. A new corridor branched away that marked that he was now in the main living area of the keep. Plush red carpeting covered the cold floor, and oak paneling lined the walls. Torches and candles flickered along the walls and tables of the elegant passageway.

The thief hugged the left wall of the passage as he padded softly forward. He remarked several ancient paintings that lined the walls of ancient elven kings and warriors, many of them slashed or marred as if someone in a rage had defaced them. One grand picture frame held tattered remains of an elven knight in resplendent armor. Galen gasped when he recognized the armor from the body of Gilgorad back in the tomb inside the cathedral in Khasharsta. The sight of the elven hero's portrait made the thief wonder again about the fate of his friends. He would give anything for Nestor beside him again with Shadow Reaver in hand, and Tyrell's growing magical powers blasting through Kellen and his guards.

"I never cared much for that particular likeness," said Kellen suddenly. Galen spun around to see a doorway across from the Gilgorad's portrait that hadn't been there a moment ago. Ambrose lounged in a great cushioned armchair before a roaring fire. "Come in, little thief, and let's chat. You and I have so much more in common than you might realize"

Galen entered the room, gripping the hilt of his sword more tightly. He was momentarily taken aback as he registered the lavish furnishings of Kellen's study. Ancient books from long gone empires filled bookshelves that had been artfully carved from the wood of a myriad of forests. He recognized opulent trappings and fabrics on the couches that he had only read about during his tutelage in the thieves' guildhall. Gold and crystal decanters sat on a tray between the fireplace and the vampire lord. Kellen swirled a ruby liquid in a crystalline glass that appeared so delicate that the thief feared even his feather-light touch might shatter it.

"You and I should not be enemies, Galen," said Kellen softly. "We are both creatures who thrive in the darkness. We have abilities when we are in the shadows that place us far above normal men." The vampire looked up at the thief. "Do you realize the empire that we could forge together? Were you and I to pool our resources, riches such as these," he said with a wave of his hand, "would be yours for the taking."

"And all I would have to do is serve a devil, condemn my soul, and forget the thousand injuries that you've inflicted on those close to me."

"Grudges are beneath men such as us, Galen. They show how foolishly we cling to mortal attachments."

"Then why did you destroy the portrait of Gilgorad out in the hallway? That seems very much like a grudge to me."

Kellen gave a snort of laughter, dismissing the notion with a wave of his hand. "A fleeting moment of temper from ages past. I have grown beyond such childish tantrums." The vampire lord leaned closer to Galen, and said in a conspiratorial whisper, "Join me, Galen, and all you desire can be yours. I can create for you an army of master thieves, an infantry of barbarian foot soldiers, and a council of wizards to advise you, if you wish." Kellen's lips curled back to bare his fangs in a wicked grin. "I can give you a thousand Lorelei's to pass away your idle hours, but do not deny that there is a blackness in your soul now that mirrors my own. You are a creature of darkness, regardless of what you believe, and such a burden will catch up to you, and drag you down unless you embrace it and bend it to your own purpose. Even if you manage to defeat me, would that make you whole again? Use that fury within you and make something for yourself."

The cold steel of Galen's sword hilt bit into his hand as he realized that he clenched it in a white-knuckled grip of hatred. The thief looked Ambrose directly in the eyes, his fury offering him immunity to the hypnotic fires that flickered within Kellen's dark gaze. "If there is darkness in my soul, it is only because you have placed it there." He pointed the tip of his blade at the vampire's chest. "I will use that anger for my own purposes, and right now, my only purpose is to avenge Lorelei, Tyrell, and Nestor." The thief brought the sword around in a fast overhand chop that cleaved through the back of the chair that Kellen barely managed to spring out of and cross the room to safety.

Galen and Kellen slowly circled each other. Ambrose snatched a small footstool from the floor and whipped it at Galen's head, but the young thief ducked under the makeshift missile while lunging forward with a thrust of his blade. Kellen batted the sword away from him with a quick slap of his bare hand.

With a snarl, Galen leaped forward, his sword humming through the air from the force of his swing. Kellen, anticipated the move, however, and caught the thief with a sharp backhand smack that rocketed Galen across the room. He crashed into a sculpture near the doorway, crumpling to the floor. Though he coughed from the dust of the smashed artwork, Galen's rage pulled him back to his feet and he charged in again against his foe.

Kellen nimbly danced away from each broad swipe of Galen's sword, but soon found himself out of room behind him. Galen grabbed the edge of a bookcase, and with a mighty heave pulled it over on Ambrose. He quickly leaped onto the back of the shelving and stabbed furiously through the wall of books to get to Kellen. The vampire roared after one such thrust, and Galen smiled grimly to himself knowing that he had scored a hit.

Suddenly, the bookcase bucked and Galen again felt himself thrown through the air. He crashed against the fireplace hearth as Kellen, fueled by his supernatural strength, hurled the bookcase against the wall demolishing it into kindling. The vampire turned with hatred burning in his eyes, and Galen felt the air tingle with magic. A gout of flame shot from the nearby fireplace, but the thief's lightning reflexes saved him as he rolled away with only a singed cheek.

"You should just lie down and die, Thale," snarled Kellen. The vampire lord bore no trace of humanity now as he faced the young thief with fangs bared and naked fury glowing within his blood red eyes. "Do you not realize that your doom awaits you? You are but delaying the inevitable."

"I'm not about to make this easy for you."

"You have no chance of defeating me alone!"

"And yet, I'm still standing." He gave his sword a deft twirl in his hand. "What else have you got?"

Kellen threw back his head and roared. With supernatural speed, he shot forward, grabbing Galen by the throat. Effortlessly, he lifted the thief from the floor and hurled him onto a couch across the room. So great was the force of Kellen's throw that the couch's back and side shattered, spilling Galen to the floor. Waves of agony screamed up the thief's back, but he saw Kellen coming forward. Using the cushions of the couch, the thief rebounded forward and answered the vampire's charge with a slash across Kellen's ribs.

"You fool," growled Kellen. "Your weapon cannot do any lasting damage to me!" He lifted his hand from the wound and tasted his own blood. Galen looked at the rapidly closing cut and realized that the vampire spoke the truth. "You can cut me a thousand times, and I will simply heal as fast as you can bring your blade to bear."

"Let's see if you can heal without a head," snarled the thief. Galen drove his knee up towards Kellen's stomach, but the vampire caught his leg and shoved him away. The rogue tripped over the broken remains of the couch but used his momentum to turn the fall into a backward somersault. Back on his feet, Galen slashed furiously as Kellen reached for him, his sword cutting deep into the vampire's outstretched hand.

Kellen jumped away, but Galen pressed his attack. Wild swings kept the vampire lord retreating step after step. Valuable decorations were smashed with reckless abandon as the two foes danced around the room. Galen feinted suddenly, forcing Kellen to realize that the thief's wild onslaught was not so wild after all. With a flashing backhand, Galen's blade sliced across Kellen's neck in a white-hot lance of pain.

Kellen fell against his desk, clutching the wound in his throat. Silently choking, he grabbed a marble paperweight, hurling it at the thief. The missile, though small, was backed by the fearsome strength of a master vampire, and slammed into Galen with enough force to knock the thief off of his feet.

Galen felt as though his side was aflame as agony shot through his ribs. He tasted blood, and drawing breath was suddenly a battle unto itself. Kellen dashed out the doorway, leaving a trail of black blood behind. The thief struggled to his feet. "Where are you going, you bastard?" he snarled after the retreating vampire. Leaning against the door jamb, Galen watched as Kellen ran down the hallway that he himself had entered by. "You won't get away that easily," he gasped as he stumbled down the hallway as fast as his battered body physically could.

Kellen held a hand to his bleeding throat, dazed and awed by the thief's audacity. Although he knew that his wound would heal, he had to keep Galen at bay long enough for his dark magic to do its work. Surely, the thief was close behind despite the grave injury that he had caused. Ambrose dared a glance over his shoulder to see Galen stumble out of the library. A cruel smile found the vampire's lips as he saw the thief's pallid face and the blood that stained the young man's lips. Kellen turned and dashed down his hall of traps, leaping easily to the few safe spots that carried him to the far end of the corridor.

Galen reached the entry to the hall. Ambrose stood at the top of the short stairway that led into the tower. He started to yell out to the vampire, but a coughing fit choked his words. He spat blood onto the stone floor.

"Save your strength, little thief," croaked Kellen through his still injured vocal cords. "What can you possibly hope for now? By the time you navigate the traps in the hallway, I'll have spirited myself away so that I can recover from this little scrap." He glared at Galen. "Your own wounds will not heal as quickly, I'm afraid." Hoarse evil laughter floated down the hallway to Galen's ears.

The thief's head pounded. His own heartbeat thudded in his ears. His ribs hurt worse than any pain he'd ever imagined possible. Though his vision danced and swam in front of him as he tried to hold steady, he could unmistakably make out the form of Kellen Ambrose, standing at the far end of this dangerous hallway mocking him. Dammit, he was too close to lose now.

As a wave of fury passed through him, Galen stood straight and tall. His eyes squarely met the vampire's own dark gaze. Kellen's taunting laughter faded as he regarded the thief curiously. The young thief gave a quick salute with his sword, and then suddenly sprinted forward into the very center of the lethal hallway. Keenly honed reflexes and pumping adrenaline carried the thief down the corridor as trap after trap fired after him. Jets of poison gas, flaming oil, and burning acid filled the spaces where the young man's feet had settled only a moment before. Crushing deadfalls, spears and arrowheads were all a footfall behind Galen Thale as he raced towards his foe. Pits, electricity, and even an old-fashioned bear trap sprang from secret mechanisms, but Galen ran on.

Kellen stood in shock as he watched the young man hurtling like a runaway comet on a collision course for him. When Galen reached the bottom of the short stairway, his leap carried him powerfully into Ambrose. He tackled the vampire, slamming them both onto the tower floor beyond. Kellen's head smacked painfully on the cold stone floor, and he struggled to focus his vision. Galen rolled off the vampire, and regained his feet, sparing a quick glance down the hallway.

The corridor looked like a battlefield. Scorch marks and acid burns lined the walls. Chunks of stone from the walls lay powdered to dust on the floor. The air itself was choked with poison gas and the dust of broken masonry. "That was one hell of a ride," he said with a chuckle as he stood over Kellen. "Did you really think I'd let you get away that easily?" he wheezed.

Kellen snarled and kicked the thief in the stomach. Galen's already injured side exploded once again in pain as he fell to the floor and retched blood. His sword clattered across the stone floor. As Galen pushed himself to his knees, the dark shadow of Kellen Ambrose fell over him.

"You have led an incredibly charmed existence," Kellen said as he loomed over the seriously injured man. "But you, Galen Thale, have caused me far more trouble than you are worth. It is past time for your good fortune to come to a smashing end." Kellen kicked Galen in the ribs again, sending the thief flying into the tower wall. The vampire grabbed the thief by the neck, hoisting him into the air. "No one has ever dared to attack me in my home," he snarled as he fired another thunderous punch into Galen's side. Galen spat blood into Kellen's face. "I am the lord and master of this fortress!" Another punishing blow snapped another rib. "I will suffer no one to injure me as you have tonight!" Kellen slammed the cutpurse against the wall.

Galen heard bones grinding against one another, and fought to keep conscious. He sensed rather than saw Kellen's face so close to his own. In desperation, Galen drove his knee into the vampire's groin, Ambrose's grip loosening slightly. The thief fired off a punch to Kellen's jaw, knocking him back. Lastly, Galen kicked out with all of his strength at the vampire's knees, sweeping Kellen's legs out from under him and dropping the fiend to the ground. Galen collapsed to the floor and dragged himself towards his sword.

The room swayed in Galen's vision. His breath came in slow ragged gasps. "Get up," he snarled to himself as he crawled across the dusty stone. His hand touched the cold steel hilt of his sword, and weakly he fumbled it into his grip. Painfully, Galen pushed himself to his hands and knees, when suddenly a boot heel stomped on his hands, shattering bones with a sickening crack. Too weak to even scream Galen looked up. Darkness loomed before him, like a specter of Death that the young thief knew he couldn't drive away. The shadow bent close to him as icy fingers clutched at the front of his shirt. The specter growled softly, like a wolf before it moved in for a final strike. Are those fangs, thought Galen? Are those glowing embers eyes? He tried to shake his vision clear, but the darkness would not lift.

Kellen looked at the dying thief in his hands. He knew that nature would do its own work should he choose to throw Galen to the floor. That, however, wouldn't begin to soothe the injury and insult that the young man had inflicted on him tonight. Ambrose slapped Galen across the face hoping that he might bring back some level of awareness to the rogue. Galen groaned weakly, and Kellen's wicked grin bared his fangs in their full glory. Ambrose threw back his head and howled a monstrous bestial sound that tore the night. With a mighty heave, Kellen threw Galen's limp form across the chamber again.

With a sickening thump, Galen slammed once more against the stone wall and then back to the stone floor. He knew his blood pooled around him. So close to death was he that he didn't even feel the pain anymore. He waited for the divine servants of Alhambra to arrive, and carry him to the fabled Halls of the Dead. As a curtain of darkness fell over him, he saw through the haze a vision of being wielding a sword of flame that raced down the hallway of traps towards him.

"How strange," came one fleeting final thought just before consciousness fled. "Who would have guessed Alhambra's minions had red beards?"

CHAPTER TWENTY

Nestor finished binding his cuts and scrapes, then peered down the dark corridor before him. The flickering torchlight revealed a narrow staircase that led up into darkness. He gripped Shadow Reaver's hilt and looked at the glittering blade. "I don't suppose you actually could do away with these shadows, could you?" he muttered. "Whatever's up there waiting for us is more likely to be at home in the dark than I am."

Shadow Reaver suddenly began to glow with a soft blue light that pierced the gloom.

"I'll be damned," whispered the surprised barbarian. "I don't suppose you've got any other tricks up your sheath, then? Can you lead me to Kellen?" No sooner had Nestor voiced his question when he felt a pull, an insistence in the back of his mind that he needed to go up the staircase. "All right then," he said as he began to climb the stairs. "I guess I'm taking direction from a sword now." Shadow Reaver's glow flickered a moment from peaceful blue to an angry red, then back again.

"Sorry, no offense intended."

The stairway opened up into a dusty corridor stretching off into the gloom in both directions. Nestor considered each path, seeing no difference between the two. He started to step to the right when Shadow Reaver's pull suddenly indicated the other direction. Smiling again to himself, the warrior went instead to the left. "We're going to make one hell of a team, sword." Shadow Reaver flashed briefly in a rainbow of color as if in appreciation of Nestor's words.

Ancient doors lined both walls of the passageway. Large rusted iron locks adorned them all. Nestor brought his eye close to a crack in one door but saw nothing but blackness beyond. He pulled hard on the handle and could feel the aged wood give under his strength. With a snarl, he pulled with all of his might, ripping the lock and handle away from the door in a shower of rotting wood.

Shadow Reaver's light played over the contents of the tiny room. Spider webs ran from corner to corner of the small cell. On the far wall across from the door, bones shrouded in tatter rags hung from chains fastened to the stone. A skull on the floor grinned up at him.

"That one was a foolish traveler who sought refuge for the night," wheezed a thin reedy voice from behind Nestor. The warrior spun around with Shadow Reaver at the ready to face the speaker. The barbarian saw a withered old man leaning on a crutch standing in the doorway behind him. "Master didn't much care for the lad's conversation though. Going on and on about making his fortune in the world, and what a difference he was going to make, and blah, blah, blah. Master grew bored and threw him in here. Sort of forgot about him after that. Of course, once the master started making plans to build his legions in the south, he stopped receiving visitors at all."

"And just who are you, old one?" Nestor asked. The barbarian was wary, for although the old man looked brittle enough to snap over his knee like kindling, Nestor knew that anyone serving Ambrose could not be taken lightly.

"Name's Falloran. I'm caretaker of the dungeons down here." He looked around the room. "Although there's not much care to take in this old place." He smiled a toothless grin at the warrior. "Main job nowadays is to feed the snake. Have you seen my pet, by chance? Raised him from a hatchling, I did. Slither, Guardian of the lower levels, I call him. It's actually feeding time anyway. Why don't you come along with me, and I'll show you. You've never seen the like, I promise." The old man started back down the corridor towards the stairway.

"Actually, friend," replied Nestor, "I did catch a glimpse of your pet already, and a fine beastie he is. However, I truly need to go and discuss some business matters with your master."

Falloran cackled. "And how did you plan to find him? You haven't got the key to the upper reaches. Come on, I'll show you to the master after we've fed Slither." He eyed the barbarian up and down. "Assuming, of course, that Slither doesn't take a liking to you first." A maniacal giggle shook the man's small frame. "Feeding time, feeding time," he sang. He grabbed Nestor wrist with a surprisingly strong hand.

Nestor jerked his arm away. "Your damn snake is already dead. Take me to Ambrose now, or you'll join him." Falloran's insane grin faded suddenly. His bushy brows furrowed.

"Slither…is dead?"

Nestor sighed. "I grow tired of your games, old man. Where is Kellen?"

Falloran's shoulders first sagged, then he began to tremble. Nestor took a step back as he brought Shadow Reaver between him and the deranged old man. Suddenly, Falloran shrieked and lunged at the barbarian's face with his long crusty fingernails.

Nestor slapped away the feeble old man's attack, shoving him against the stone wall. Falloran's frail body slammed against the stone, but he leaped forward again in his blind rage. A dagger appeared suddenly in his hand from some hidden sheath inside his sleeve. With a quick backhand slash, he cut a deep line across Nestor's shoulder.

The barbarian had reached his limit. He had been pummeled by zombies, kargs, vampires, and a giant snake. He was not going to put up with this any longer. Nestor's fist flashed out, crushing Falloran's jaw. The hallway echoed with a crunch of bone, and the aged servant of Kellen Ambrose crumpled to the ground.

The old man lay unmoving. Cautiously, Nestor rolled the man over with his foot. Sightless eyes stared up at the ceiling. Falloran's dagger jutted out from the old man's chest in a spreading crimson stain of blood. "Dammit," Nestor swore. "I only wanted you knocked out, you old fool." The barbarian spied a leather cord around the dead man's neck with a key on the end of it. Nestor snapped the cord and took it.

Nestor moved down the corridor, letting Shadow Reaver's urge's guide his steps through the dungeon. Abruptly, the hallway ended in yet another winding staircase that led up to a single door. A heavy iron padlock held the door shut. The lock looked brand new and well oiled in stark contrast to the rest of the dingy surroundings. As Nestor unlocked the stout lock with the dead man's key, he couldn't help but wonder what else Falloran might have kept locked away in the dungeon that wasn't meant to get into the castle proper.

A short corridor opened into a grand hallway that was lavishly decorated with gold and polished brass. A huge portrait of Kellen Ambrose hung on the wall opposite the great double doors that led out into the keep's courtyard. Massive stairs of polished marble climbed up the side of the hallway to an archway that led deeper into the fortress. Shadow Reaver sent him a gentle push towards the stairs, and Nestor obliged.

Through the archway, another extravagant hallway of plush carpeting and ancient paintings stretched out before him. Nestor moved softly to an open doorway and peeked into the room beyond. Smashed furniture littered the study. Great bookshelves lay overturned and smashed. The warrior's trained eyes could see the scars where sword blades had slashed not only the furnishings but the very walls themselves. On the floor near the doorway, Nestor spied an ornate paperweight stained with blood. He silently prayed that it hadn't come from his friends.

Shadow Reaver thrummed in his grip, as a wicked hiss from behind drew Nestor's attention away from the ruined library. Out of an adjoining corridor stalked two male and two female vampires. Dressed as elegantly as courtiers in a royal palace, they strode towards the barbarian. All were possessed of an unearthly beauty, but for the glistening fangs that betrayed their true nature. Their eyes gleamed with hatred as Nestor brought the elvensteel blade around to guard. Shadow Reaver pulsed with a power as if it was as eager to taste the vampire's blood as they were to taste Nestor's.

"The Dark Lord has already dealt with your friends, warrior," said the lead female. Her long auburn hair seemed to dance around her face as if caught in a summer breeze. "How sweet that you have been left for our own amusement," she purred.

"You'll not find easy prey here, bitch."

Her seductive smile fell away, into a ferocious snarl. "We smell your blood, mortal. We can hear the drumming of your heart. Share it with us willingly, and your death shall pass far easier."

"I haven't come this far to fall at the hands of the help," snarled Nestor. The barbarian warrior leaped forward swinging the elvensteel blade in a flashing arc. So fast and so unexpected was the warrior's attack that the vampires were caught flat-footed. Shadow Reaver cleaved the head from the shoulders of one of the males, and Nestor's backswing cut the other female from hip to shoulder. Shadow Reaver howled as it tore through vampire flesh, and the two fiends burst into flames as the blade drove them back to the grave.

The other male, a hulking fellow with sandy blond hair, grabbed Nestor's shoulders from behind and threw him to the floor. However, the soft carpet cushioned the warrior's fall. The lead female dove at him, but Nestor kicked out at her, his boot heel splattering the fanged woman's nose across her face in a spray of dark blood. A quick slash of Shadow Reaver found her arm, forcing her back.

Nestor jumped back to his feet and clubbed the male across the side of his face with the hilt of his blade. As the creature staggered, he grabbed the front of the vampire's fine tunic, and hurled him into a hallway table, smashing it to pieces. He followed in closely with Shadow Reaver, narrowly missing the scrambling monster's neck with the heavy swing. Nestor kicked out again, catching the male vampire squarely in the chest, and dropped him back to the floor. Nestor reversed Shadow Reaver in his grip, plunging the blade down through the fallen creature's chest. Another scream of victory from the sword as the big male burst into ashes. Nestor spun around to see the female vampire standing alone against him.

"The master will destroy you! His torment of you will last forever as he damns your soul," she snarled at him. Nestor stomped his foot on the shattered hallway table causing a splintered shaft of wood to leap into his hand. With practiced ease, he whipped the wooden stake into the vampire's chest, impaling her black heart. Before she could scream, she burst into ash.

"Damn you, too," Nestor growled. Shadow Reaver urged him on towards a ruined side hallway. Nestor realized that this corridor led away from the heart of the keep towards one of the corner turrets. The barbarian looked in bewilderment at the condition of the hallway as he carefully stepped past the burned and blasted rubble. Great holes in the once near impregnable walls now allowed the pale moonlight to bleed into the passage. Spent arrows, darts and spears littered the narrow walkway. The warrior's nose burned with the faint traces of harsh gases that had recently filled the hall.

Cautiously, Nestor pressed himself tightly against the side wall to get around an open pit in the stone floor. As he glanced ahead to the far end of the hallway, he spied a short rise of stairs that led into the turret. The barbarian's heart leaped when he heard the clang of steel and the sounds of battle coming from the chamber. With a howl of delight, Nestor quickly jumped over the remaining distance of the pit and bolted for the end of the corridor. It had to be Galen and Tyrell! They've got the bastard cornered! In his hand, Shadow Reaver buzzed with anticipation. Nestor's elation vanished as he then saw Galen's battered and bloody form fly across the room, slam into the wall, and fall to the floor, motionless. Then, Kellen Ambrose walked over to the young man's body and prodded him with his boot.

"No, no, no," screamed Nestor. "You bastard!" Nestor charged forward again.

Kellen stood over the fallen thief. He started to turn when he heard the furious roar of the enraged red-bearded barbarian behind him, but it was too late to react. Nestor exploded into the room, tackling Kellen from behind. His speed and power carried the two of them sailing over Galen's body into the wall beyond.

"You son of a bitch," roared Nestor as he hammered his fists into the side of Kellen's head in what could only be described as a berserker fury. Kellen, still shocked and surprised that Nestor was alive, lashed out blindly. He caught a glancing blow on the barbarian's chin with just enough force to knock the warrior away from him. The two men scrambled to their feet and faced off.

"Next time, lead with the blade, Canaith," spat Ambrose. "You might have stood a chance against me. Now you will only meet the same gruesome fate as your young friend."

"That remains to be seen, you bastard." Nestor lunged forward with the elvensteel blade, but Kellen's supernatural speed carried him out of the barbarian's reach. Nestor's intent, however, wasn't to injure, but rather to drive the master vampire back into the corner. The barbarian had played this game before with many other opponents. It was just a matter of patience.

Kellen's cruel smile told Nestor though that the vampire knew the tactic also. "We both know the rules to this little game, Canaith, but I am not some simple-witted mortal fool." Nestor lunged again with Shadow Reaver. He had to finish Kellen when the vampire had no room left to run.

Ambrose felt the stone wall against his back but the vampire lord was not without resources. His fingertips found the tiniest cracks in the masonry and as Shadow Reaver plunged forward, Kellen went straight up the wall and across the ceiling like an insect. He dropped to the floor behind Nestor, as Shadow Reaver dug a deep groove into the wall where the vampire had stood only an eye blink before.

Nestor whirled around as Kellen leaned casually against the balcony doorway. "You fools just don't know how to give up. All you shall accomplish here is dying. Painfully, and slowly. Had you left well enough alone, I might have let you and your friends live out the rest of your days in peace."

"Knowing that after we were dead and gone, you'd be free to return and try building your city of the dead again? You know damn well that we would never live with such cowardice."

"My but your sense of honor is touching," Kellen quipped. "I hadn't thought such a trait existed among thieves. You do still realize that you would have already been dead long before now, were it not for my own intervention?"

"Forgive me if I don't feel particularly grateful today. I hope you'll overlook my rudeness."

Kellen laughed. "I expect nothing less from a backwoods simpleton such as you. You should have remained with your people in your little mud huts in the foothills, covered in gaudy feathers and beads while plunging your hands into horse excrement to predict if this shall be a good year to go raiding."

Nestor's eyes narrowed. "You mock forces that you don't understand."

"No," shouted Kellen angrily. "I mock you, and these feeble attempts at defeating a veritable dark god!" Kellen darted forward with his inhuman speed and punched Nestor hard across the jaw. The barbarian staggered, but Kellen didn't pause to see the results of the blow. The vampire unleashed a furious barrage of fists, bashing Nestor from all angles. The barbarian tried to block and counter, but so fast were Kellen's attacks that he was never long in the space where Nestor anticipated him to be.

A ferocious backhand slap drove Nestor against the wall. Ambrose stood in the center of the room, crouched like a cat ready to spring as the warrior brought Shadow Reaver around in a defensive posture between him and the vampire. Kellen's eyes followed the tip of the blade back and forth as if mesmerized by the wickedly deadly blade.

"You shouldn't have let up," spat Nestor. "Never give an opponent a chance to get their second wind."

"Who said that I did?" snarled Kellen. The vampire lord lashed out, but Nestor proved the quicker this time and Shadow Reaver flashed across Kellen's brow in a blinding arc. Ambrose screamed in pain as smoke rose from the sword wound.

"There is nowhere that you can run that we won't hunt you down, Kellen."

"Your friends are dead, you fool. It is only a matter of time until you join them."

"Then I'll just have to finish the job before I go. If I go to Alhambra's halls tonight, I will not leave until you are dead first." The barbarian slowly advanced, Shadow Reaver's tip leveled at Kellen's chest. "There will be no vampire city. No more Dark Lord Ambrose. It all ends here. It ends tonight," Nestor thrust the blade at Kellen, but his heel slipped in a puddle of blood on the floor. The warrior caught himself before he fell, but the single moment cost him his advantage.

Kellen dashed forward and slapped Shadow Reaver out of Nestor's hand. The blade clattered to the stone floor next to Galen's still form. With one powerful punch, Kellen threw Nestor to the floor against the balcony railing.

"Yes, mighty warrior. It ends tonight." Kellen grabbed the warrior's shirt and hoisted him high into the air. "But not for me." With a mighty heave, Kellen Ambrose hurled Nestor over the balcony's edge into the cool, night sky.

CHAPTER TWENTY ONE

A young Tyrell Amalcheal smiled as pale blue light blossomed around his hand to illuminate the practice corner of the wizard's lab. His grin grew wider still as his mentor, Rialligen the Old, clapped his hands in approval.

"Well done, Tyrell! Your skills grow in leaps and bounds. Doubtlessly, one day you shall be one of the greatest of our brethren." The apprentice closed his hand, snuffing out the magical light. "Master Rialligen, you flatter me," replied the young apprentice. "My skills could never contest your own."

"Ah, Tyrell, the next lesson you need to master is one of self-confidence. A wizard must believe in his power if it is to serve him. Failure to do so can lead to disaster. If you fear that your power might be unleashed accidentally to the peril of innocent bystanders, then you will never learn to control the higher abilities to which you are entitled. Control your fears, or they shall control how far you are able to progress in our arts." The old wizard smiled kindly at the young man.

"I understand, master." Tyrell flashed a quick smile of his own. "But I still wouldn't dream of contesting you."

"Besides," called a sneering, nasally voice from across the lab, "I'll never let you surpass me." Tyrell turned to see Arimasthenes, the other apprentice under Rialligen's tutelage. Tall and lanky with greasy black hair, Arimasthenes looked as much like a dirty weasel as he portrayed himself.

The foul-tempered older boy had done everything he possibly could to steal away Tyrell's pleasure, tormenting the younger student with everything from embarrassing pranks to rough shoves whenever the master's back was turned. Several times Tyrell had found his dinner plate dropped on the dining hall floor. If Rialligen was a father figure with his kindness and encouragement, Arimasthenes was the jealous sibling who felt shunned after having squandered his share of the family fortune.

"Why do you hate me so much, Ari?" asked Tyrell bluntly. Rialligen settled back in his chair, his eyes pretending to inspect an ancient scroll, but the young boy knew his master wished to see how they settled their differences.

"I hate you because you come strolling in here, and are suddenly being held forth as the great and mighty Tyrell Amalcheal," Arimasthenes said mockingly. He poked Tyrell in the chest with a long skinny finger. "I am the rightful successor to Rialligen's power and station here. No swollen headed upstart is going to have me cast aside. All this knowledge and power are mine by right."

"Do you even listen to yourself? You speak of our master as though he has already passed along to Alhambra's Halls. He should disqualify you from further advancement simply on the grounds of the disrespect you show to him and his position."

"Disrespect? I have slaved for that man long before you ever showed your mismatched eyes around these grounds. I followed his every instruction and direction while you stood in the streets learning how to dance a coin across your knuckles to buy your bread."

"You mistake obedience for respect. You are nothing more than a trained dog, doing as you are told until someone throws you a scrap. You'll not become a wizard with that mindset. Do you even listen to Rialligen's instruction, for he teaches us more than just step by step drills on how to light a candle from across the room? A real wizard would learn from such a great man. You are no wizard, Arimasthenes. With your attitude, you'll never be worthy of more than dusting bottles of newt eyes and bat wings. You will never be as great as he is!" Tyrell stopped suddenly for he saw the look of pure hatred and rage that blazed in the older boy's eyes. Often times, Ari's rage preceded a beating. This time, however, his look was even more malevolent.

"And you won't live long enough to see greatness either, bastard," snarled the enraged apprentice. Arimasthenes' black eyes began to glow with magical power, and his lips began a dark chant that Tyrell recognized as a forbidden spell. The younger apprentice had seen his rival secretly using the same incantation to torture a rat in the cellar once.

Black tendrils of magical force lashed from Arimasthenes' fingertips and wrapped around Tyrell's limbs. Agonizing fire lanced through his body where the dark magic touched his flesh. A scream ripped from his throat as the magic tore through him like a thousand blades slashing at his skin. His knees buckled, and he crashed to the floor. From the corner of his eye, he saw Rialligen sitting in his chair, head bowed with a look of deep sadness creasing his face.

"Master, help me," cried Tyrell.

"No, Tyrell. I cannot. You must help yourself. The potential of a mighty wizard rests within you. You have the power to prevail if you choose to wield it."

Tyrell looked up at the evil leering grin on Arimasthenes' face. His evil laughter mingled ominously with the sizzle of raw magical power that stretched forth from his hands. Despite the searing agony coursing through him, Tyrell felt a sudden awareness flow through him. A siren song of magic sang to his senses unlike anything he had ever felt before, and certainly nothing that Rialligen had ever shown to him so early in his apprenticeship. With his teeth gritted, and a snarl on his lips, Tyrell fell into the stream of energy that flowed into him, as he stretched his hand out towards his tormentor.

A white-hot blast of lightning exploded from the young mage's hand, blasting Arimasthenes across the lab. The older boy smashed against the far wall, and his wicked laughter changed to shrieks of fright and pain as his robes burst into flame. Tyrell let out an exultant whoop as the lightning burned his foe, reveling in the seductive lure of the power that inundated him. As the destructive blasts rained from his fingers, though, Tyrell suddenly realized the true danger of the power he had unleashed.

He couldn't shut the magical fire off.

Fearfully, he tried to aim the destructive power away towards the emptiest corner of the cluttered room, but the lightning roared unchecked, destroying lab equipment, and setting ablaze scrolls and parchments that littered the chamber. Rialligen rushed to his apprentice's side.

"Tyrell, you must govern the magic lest it destroy you too! Will it to stop. Dominate it, not the other way around!" Though the old wizard screamed his words to him, Tyrell could barely hear him over the roaring waves of destruction that poured from his hands. The magic had begun to turn on him as well, for he felt the fire starting to burn his own skin as well now.

Rialligen grabbed hold of Tyrell's wrists, attempting to join the young mage's mind on the higher planes of magic. The lightning coursed over the old man's frail frame, but the elder wizard held fast. Tyrell watched in silent horror as Rialligen's skin blistered and peeled. The young man drew his focus to that plane of power that burned through him, and through sheer force of will closed the magical conduit. So abruptly did he cut himself off from the flow of magic that he was thrown back like a babe trying to hold a door against a charging dragon. Tyrell screamed as the backlash of magic ripped back through his hands and forearms. He watched as a network of crisscrossing scar tissue blossomed under his flesh. The lab was in ruins. Tyrell rushed to his fallen mentor, pushing aside flaming debris to reach his teacher. Feebly, Rialligen looked up and grasped at the boy's tunic.

"Do not let this deter you from using the power that is yours to command. Your heart is pure, Tyrell. One day, such magic under your control will be used to save the lives of those who cannot defend themselves. You have the ability to master such forces, but only if you do not shy away from them.

"Be the master, do not let the power master you." The old wizard's body tensed up, and then he sighed, breathing his last breath.

Tyrell Amalcheal sat up suddenly with a start and strained to see through the dimly lit room in which he found himself. The dream, no, the memory of that fateful day so many years ago slipped away into his mind's recesses as he studied his immediate surroundings.

The dim torchlight in the room showed two rows of stone sarcophagi that stretched back into the dark corners of the chamber. Slowly, the grating sound of stone on stone echoed through the cavernous room. Tyrell sensed, rather than saw, dark creatures rising from the stone biers in the gloom ahead.

"Stand down," he called out with more bravery than he truly felt. "My quarrel is with your dark lord, not yourselves."

"Ahh, but the master has sent us a plaything," purred a hissing voice from the shadows ahead. "Come to us willingly, mortal, and your death shall pass far sweeter than if you fight us."

Tyrell steadied himself with his back against the cold stone wall. He knew that he was in serious trouble. He flicked his hand upwards, creating a soft blue light that pierced the dark shadows to about ten paces around him. He found that he was in a small alcove that opened into the broader crypt. Half a dozen residents of those stone sarcophagi were slowly sauntering towards him. Their otherworldly beauty created a seductive pull that cried for him to join them in an embrace, but the wizard was experienced enough to know the allure of dark magic.

Though pale in general, the light that sprang from his hand did hurt the eyes of the approaching undead, so long accustomed to the lightless world of their tomb. A vampiress with long blond tresses waved her hand, and Tyrell felt the wave of magic that suddenly snuffed out his light spell.

"You'll have to do far better than that, little mage," called the lady with her velvety soft voice. "We've been around for far too long to be daunted by such feeble magic." Tyrell tensed as the undead host slowly closed around him. The smell of ancient decay and foul breath battered his senses. Worst of all though, was that he could sense centuries of hunger longing to be sated.

"Come, little mage," came a different voice in the darkness, male from the baritone. "Join us willingly and it shall prove far less painful than if you were to resist."

"Besides," said the lady again. "You have no power to stop us. Your feeble skills will not deter us from taking what we want of you."

The lady vampire's words inflamed Tyrell. His mind raced back to the memory of his dead teacher's words. He had the power to save himself if he only chose to wield it.

The vampires shuffled closer, as Tyrell's mind raced. If he drew upon the necessary magic, he faced the possibility of being ripped apart by forces that he might not be able to control. However, the vampires would certainly assure him of a similar fate.

A cold finger brushed against his cheek, and Tyrell saw the dimly lit red glow of vampiric eyes in the gloom. He felt the magical tug trying to draw him into that dark gaze and sweet magical embrace. An ominous chuckle pierced the darkness, but it was the long silenced laugh of Arimasthenes that had haunted his dreams over the years that found his ears.

Tyrell's mind flashed suddenly to thoughts of young Lorelei's body laid out on the table and the terrible destruction of the fires of Tarnath. He wondered again after the fate of his missing friends and cursed all the terror and destruction that had been caused by Kellen Ambrose.

It was time to end this.

Tyrell Amalcheal opened his mental focus up to the forces of magic that surrounded him, drawing them deep into the core of his being. He felt the power surge through him as it had those many years ago in Rialligen's lab. He reveled in the charging power as it built within him, but unlike the incident of his youth, Tyrell knew that this time he was in complete control.

He grabbed a male vampire that had crept closest to him by the throat as he released a devastating blast of fire that removed the creatures head from its body. With his other hand, a fanning jet of white-hot flame scattered the other undead away from him, cowering in terror and pain from the blistering light and heat. Another bolt of flame from Tyrell's hand bore a hole through the chest of another vampire, reducing the beast to ash.

The remaining vampires ran for the stairs at the back of the room, shrieking in terror. "The master said that this one's magic was weak," cried one. His protest was cut short as Tyrell's flames engulfed and consumed him.

Tyrell couldn't help but gape in awe of his own display. The hand that he had once nearly lost to a bolt of magic electricity now rained death upon these evil creatures. He felt the warmth of the magic flowing through him, holding him like a lover in a fierce embrace. His doubts over his capabilities had vanished now as blast after blast of deadly magic exploded forth.

Tyrell Amalcheal was a master wizard.

He had held the power within him all along. He realized that the call he had received from the Book of Torax'alamien would only have summoned him if he were worthy enough to control the incredible feats of magic that the tome contained within its pages.

Tyrell began to give chase to the retreating vampires, racing up the stairs that they had fled to. He paused a moment when he heard again the scrape of stone on stone, and he realized that more of the sarcophagi below were opening. Glowing eyes and razor-sharp fangs began to appear one after another. Tyrell knew that the vampires ahead of him moved with supernatural speed, but Tyrell couldn't leave this infested crypt at his back. He had to finish this quickly.

The wizard closed his eyes and dropped his consciousness into the whirling eddies of power that surrounded him. He barely heard the snarls and hisses of the approaching undead. He simply stood and delved into the arcane energies around him. Raw magic filled his every cell. The hisses below him began to turn into anguished and panicked cries for Tyrell blazed like a summer sun surrounded in a corona of fire. Finally, he opened his eyes and looked down at the vampire horde below.

"Find your peace now," he whispered, but the magic filling him made his voice boom across the stone chamber. Tyrell used his entire body as a conduit for the blast of fire. An inferno roared from his entire body directed into the space below. The vampires' screams could not be heard above the roar of Tyrell's mystic flames. So powerful was the bolt that the stone itself began to melt, and the brass torch sconces melted away. When the eruption finally subsided, the air before him shimmered from the ultra-intense heat. Of the vampire horde, no trace remained.

Tyrell's knees buckled, and he slumped against the wall. His vision clouded, and he could taste blood in his mouth. It would seem, he thought to himself, that even the mightiest wizards might have limits. He shook his head to clear his vision, then left the crypt in pursuit of the remaining three vampires.

He thought about the display he had just delivered. Given the time, he wondered just what sorts of feats he might be able to accomplish. A flitting fear dashed into his thoughts that he might accidentally tap into something that would seduce him to the point of corruption. With the kind of tremendous power that he had just used, he could level entire nations. He would have to make certain that he only used his powers for the right reasons.

Tyrell shook his head again, realizing that he had far more immediate concerns at the moment. Leveling continents would have to wait until later. He followed some short hallways, and after another small flight of stairs, he found himself in the castle's main hallway, dominated by a grand staircase. The three vampires stood at the top, their jaws wide open in complete shock of the rumbling display of power that they had heard even from here.

Tyrell held his arms out wide to the side. "I was afraid you wouldn't wait for me," he called up the stairs. He hoped his bravado was more convincing than he felt at the moment. He still hadn't gotten his second wind back quite yet. If these three took too much out of him, he might not have anything left to give when he faced off against Kellen. The vampires backed away down a hall forcing Tyrell to move quickly to keep up. As he reached the top of the stairs, what he saw made his heart leap.

An open doorway revealed a library in ruins. Books were strewn about, furniture was overturned and broken. In the hallway where he stood, a great battle had obviously taken place here with more broken furniture, and the telltale ash of destroyed vampires adorned the carpet. Tyrell felt that this had to be proof that his friends had at least made it this far. Perhaps they had already carried the battle to Ambrose. With a savage smile, Tyrell hoped that they hadn't already finished off the black-hearted bastard without him.

The three vampires spread out in the hallway before him. Their eyes were full of fear as they warily watched the mage's slow approach.

"Tell me where your master is. You need serve him no longer, and I can send you to your final peace with as little suffering as possible."

"The master said you had no real power. He said you were the weakest of the three," hissed the alpha female.

Tyrell sighed. "It appears your master was gravely misinformed." One of the two males leaped suddenly towards him, but the wizard's hand moved faster still and let forth a blast of fire that reduced the vampire to a heap of smoking ash. "I don't suppose either of you would prefer to be a bit more cooperative, now would you?"

The vampires snarled and charged.

Tyrell threw another jet of flame, but the shot went wide as his knees started to go out from under him. He needed a chance to rest, and these skirmishes weren't going to help with that.

"You are weak, little mage," said the female. "Your power is newly found, and you have stretched yourself thin. This shall be easier than we anticipated." With a howl, she jumped into the air and flew towards him. Afraid that he would be further weakened if he drew on any more magic, Tyrell tried something unexpected.

As the vampiress' clawed hands reached for him, Tyrell grabbed her wrist, twisted, and used her own momentum to hurl her across the hallway where she slammed face first into the hard stone. Tyrell's satisfaction was stolen quickly though as he was hit from behind by the remaining male vampire. In a tumble of limbs, they crashed to the carpeted floor.

"You die now, mage," growled the vampire into Tyrell's ear. "You, my friend, shall be mine to torment for all eternity."

"Like hell, I will," snarled Tyrell. He snapped his head back into the nose of the vampire and was satisfied with the resulting crunch of bone. He threw an elbow back that caught the creature in the jaw, and sent it rolling off of him. The lady vampire was suddenly back as well, though. With her supernatural strength, she lifted Tyrell from the floor, slamming him against the wall. Her long fingers closed tightly around his throat.

"Time to die, mortal"

Tyrell grabbed the fiend by her ears and jammed his thumbs into her eyes. She shrieked as Tyrell tore at her with a barbaric savagery that would have made his missing ally proud. As her fingers loosened around his neck, Tyrell punched and kicked, shoved and clawed, as he sacrificed finesse for brutal efficiency. The blind and flailing vampire whirled into a floor sconce, and the gossamer material of her dress lit up from the flame of the candles. Tyrell threw just enough magic power at the fire to boost the heat output, and the lady fell, ablaze and screaming, over the balcony railing. Tyrell saw her disappear in a puff of soot and ash.

The wizard whirled around to again face the lone male vampire that stood between himself and Kellen. "And then there was one," he said coldly. Tyrell's head throbbed from the brawl and the excessive use of magic. He had to catch his breath soon. The vampire fell to his knees with his hands outstretched in surrender.

"Mercy, I beg you. Your thief chased the master down the hall behind us," he said as he jerked his thumb in the direction of a side passage. "Your warrior friend followed behind shortly after. I swear that is all that I know. Please spare me!" The vampire looked pathetic as he waited for Tyrell's response.

Tyrell held his hands out to his sides. "I am a merciful soul," he said. The vampire's ferocity suddenly roared back into its visage, but Tyrell had expected an attack. As his hands swung back around to aim at the vampire, he grabbed hold of a broken leg of a destroyed hall table. As the vampire lunged back to its feet, Tyrell shoved the makeshift stake through the creature's chest. With a howl of agony, the vampire burst into flame and collapsed into ash. "But not today," he finished. Tyrell leaned heavily on the door frame beside him. He started to slide down the wall to have a quick seat, but his senses suddenly perked up as he became aware of a being of great magical power.

Kellen Ambrose was very close, and he wasn't happy.

With a groan, Tyrell ran for the hallway that the vampire had indicated to him earlier. As he passed through the opening into the long hallway, he stopped suddenly as he saw the battle damage laid out before him.

Scars of flame, blades, and sizzling acid scored the stone down the entire length of the hallway. Tyrell could only imagine all the insidious traps that had been triggered that were necessary to cause such damage. He said a quick silent prayer that his friends had safely navigated past this point.

Shouts from the far end of the hallway drew his attention, and the clash of battle renewed his vigor. He sprinted down the ruined hallway and leaped up the short stair that led to the tower guardroom. What he saw as he fell against the door jamb filled him with both hope and fear.

Galen lay slumped against the wall. Blood ran from the young thief's mouth, nose, and ears. Shadow Reaver skittered across the floor just as Tyrell slipped into the room. The wizard's eyes darted to where the blade had come from, and he saw Nestor and Kellen locked in mortal combat.

Then, to Tyrell's horror, he watched as the vampire lord lifted the barbarian from the floor, and hurled Nestor over the edge of the balcony railing.

CHAPTER TWENTY TWO

"NOOOO!" Tyrell fired a blast of magical force at Kellen as he watched his friend disappear into the night sky. The vampire staggered under the blow but whirled around with a snarl on his lips.

"So, the final thorn in my side appears at last," he growled. "Your friends are finished, and now only the weakling mage remains to face me." Kellen spat on the floor. "Do you still cling so dearly to that delusion, fool? Do you truly believe that you pose any threat to me alone?"

"Why don't we find out together?" said Tyrell with deadly malice in his voice. All of his fatigue and pain were forgotten as he glared at the master vampire before him. "I've learned a few tricks since we first met, you son of a bitch." Tyrell opened himself to the flow of magic, and his hands began to glow with growing power.

"Come and die, mage," growled Kellen. He raised his own hands into the night sky, dark power swirling around them as he drew upon his own villainous sorcery.

*   *   *

Nestor roared in anger as the wind rushed by him. He would not end like this. Too many things remained unfinished. Kellen had to be stopped, and he knew he had seen Tyrell just before being thrown off the balcony.

Nestor saw something against the wall fluttering in the breeze from the corner of his eye. Frantically, he reached out and caught hold of a silken rope that was tied to a grappling hook secured to the balcony he had just fallen from. Desperately, he clutched at the rope and held with all of his might. His descent stopped abruptly, and the barbarian screamed in pain as the sudden stop nearly pulled his shoulders from the sockets. He slammed face first into the stone wall of the tower, but his grip held. The warrior could feel the burns on his hands from where the rope had cut through his leather gloves, but he was alive.

The barbarian warrior looked down and saw that he was only about fifty feet from the courtyard below. It took him only a moment to deduce that this must have been how Galen had gained entrance to the keep. Gritting his teeth against the pain that screamed through his battered body, Nestor Canaith, with a strength denied most men, began to pull himself back up the rope.

"Hear me now, all you gods, above and below. I swear that if I survive this night I shall never again do anything that requires climbing so long as I live and breathe," he muttered.

*   *   *

"Do you believe that just because you found some moldy old book of spells that you are now a match for someone who has practiced magic for centuries? My very existence is one of necromancy!"

"You've done nothing but lie to us from the beginning, Ambrose," said Tyrell. "I can sense that your powers aren't as formidable as you claim." Tyrell kept his voice level despite the nervousness he felt. He had to stall for as long as possible to regain some of his strength back. He knew from his brief contact with Kellen's mind that the vampire lord truly did have wickedly powerful magic at his disposal. In a toe to toe fight, Kellen would prove to be a truly fearsome opponent.

"Does this seem as though I am lying, wizard?" Kellen hissed with sarcasm dripping from the last word. A bolt of inky black force lashed out towards Tyrell, but he threw up a shield that redirected the energy blast harmlessly into the stone wall. Tyrell quickly countered with a blast of fire, but Kellen threw up a shield of his own that sapped the flames of their heat, forcing them to wink out of existence.

"There is nothing you can hurl at me that I can't counter, Tyrell. Nothing you can do to affect me." Kellen and Tyrell slowly circled each other around the room. "Just lay down and die like your friends, and we can end this ridiculous charade." Kellen's eyes bore into Tyrell's own, and the vampire grinned to himself as the wizard's eyes began to go dull and glassy as Ambrose exerted his hypnotic gaze over the mage. Kellen chuckled to himself as he slowly advanced on his opponent. "I must confess that I am disappointed to defeat you so easily, Amalcheal." He grabbed Tyrell by the front of his shirt, still gazing into the wizard's blank stare. "You never struck me as foolish enough to fall for such a meager trick."

Suddenly, Tyrell grinned ear to ear and winked. A blast of fire slammed into Kellen's chest, hurling the undead fiend across the room. "I am no fool, Kellen. I am here for one reason only. I have come to see you die for all the injustice, injuries, and atrocities that you have caused. Tonight you meet your end."

"A bit melodramatic, don't you think?" Kellen waved his hands and a spray of black missiles burst forth from his fingertips. Tyrell again tried to throw up a shield, but so fast did the magical bolts strike that he only managed to deflect a few of them. The mage was slammed back against the wall, his chest burning as if venom coursed through his body. He summoned his magic, using the wall behind him to steady himself, as he purged the poison from his system. Too late, though he sensed another surge of power as Kellen cast again. The stone wall that Tyrell leaned against suddenly bubbled and flowed around his body, grasping him in an unyielding grip of granite.

"All too easy," said Kellen with a wicked grin as he stepped closer to the trapped mage. "Where is your bravado now, little mage? Have you yet realized that I am not so easily vanquished as my minions?"

"I've realized that you talk too damn much," growled Tyrell. Planes of power answered his call, and with a shattering crack, the stone imprisoning him exploded outward in a spray of granite shards. Kellen staggered back as a hundred tiny daggers of rock dotted his skin.

"So the devil bleeds after all," said Tyrell as stepped free of the debris. He dusted off his sleeves. "Very similar to what I did to that desk of yours in Tarnath." He smiled. "Much easier this time around, though."

"You will pay a thousand times over for every indignity that you inflict upon me, Amalcheal!"

Tyrell's anger surged. "As I intend to pay you for every innocent life that you have taken. Shall I start with Lorelei, Tessarin, or the nameless wretches of the streets who had nowhere to run from you?"

Kellen's lips pulled back in a wicked, fang-baring grin. "Perhaps you should start with your own friends," he hissed as we waved one hand towards Galen's broken form, and his other hand towards the open balcony.

Tyrell's gut wrenched in cold fury. "For them, you shall pay most dearly of all. You'll beg me to end your torment when I start taking vengeance for Galen and Nestor." Tyrell threw a bolt of lightning at Kellen, but the vampire's magic deflected it enough so that it was but a glancing blow. The vampire reeled back against the balcony rail, then threw his hand towards Tyrell. A billowing cloud of black mist roiled forth and enshrouded Tyrell. The mage immediately dropped to his knees as he felt his strength drained away by the devilish fog.

"A special enchantment of my own device," spat Kellen. "I've always called it simply a death shroud. Much like a vampire," he chuckled, "it drains your strength away little by little, but leaves you in a state of torment just shy of the release of death. It takes about a week to finally finish a man off, depending on how strong he is." He grabbed Tyrell by the hair and yanked his head back. "You are about to learn the true nature of begging to end one's torment. I suspect that you shall last somewhat longer than the average victim." Ambrose put his lips right against Tyrell's ear as he whispered, "And I shall enjoy every delicious second of your suffering." Tyrell clawed feebly at Kellen's wrist. "Save your strength, little mage. You are going to need it." Kellen threw his head back, bellowing a loud howling laugh.

"That wasn't very sportsmanlike to just toss a man from the balcony like that, Ambrose." Kellen whirled around in amazement to see Nestor standing on the balcony. Battered and bloody, the barbarian looked like something from a child's nightmare made flesh, but his stance spoke of raw strength, confident and powerful, and more than eager to continue the brawl.

"Will you three never die?" screamed Kellen. He jumped to his feet and squared off against Nestor who casually sauntered towards the vampire lord.

"Oh, it was sheer luck that saved me, for sure. But as you spoke of the night we met, the three of us together would be required to defeat the vampire. Had Galen chosen any other route into your keep, that circle would have broken, and I'd be a messy spot on the cobblestones below."

"And now you can become a messy spot in here with your friends."

"It's well past time that we settled up all accounts." Nestor held up his hands to show the torn leather gloves, and the bleeding palms beneath. "You owe me a new pair of gloves, Ambrose." Kellen rolled his eyes but realized too late that even that momentary distraction was enough for the warrior reflexes of the man before him.

"And I owe you this," snarled Nestor, as he launched a vicious punch at Kellen's jaw. The vampire felt a crunch of bone and spit blood and teeth under the punishing hammer-like blow of the enraged warrior. Kellen felt his feet lift from the floor as he twirled in the air under the ferocity of the strike. With a crash, he collapsed on the tower floor.

"Gods above, that felt good," said Nestor. His eyes quickly glanced over to Tyrell. He saw his friend spasming in painful convulsions under the effects of Kellen's dark magic. "Fight the bastard off, Tyrell. We've got him where we…"

Nestor's words were cut off as Kellen moved with the speed of a panther, and slammed his shoulder into the barbarian's stomach. Together they fell into a pile of tangled limbs on the floor, kicking and punching with furious abandon. Blood flew from each combatant as they thrashed around on the stone.

Tyrell was barely aware of the ferocious slugfest going on around him. The mage turned his full magical focus into his own body, placing himself into a magical coma. His awareness raced through his cells finding and destroying the dark tendrils of Kellen's magic that ate away at his flesh. A war of magic was being fought within his body, and Tyrell was determined to be the victor. Drawing in power from those highest planes of magic to which he had only recently become attuned, Tyrell drew a cleansing fire throughout his body. He screamed in agony as the flames coursed through his being, but slowly, Kellen's magic was driven out.

"Is that the best you've got, Ambrose," taunted Nestor as he splattered Kellen's nose across the vampire's face. Kellen didn't hear him though. So furious was the undead beast that he had shred all trace of humanity, attacking Nestor in his most feral, primal rage. He rained blows down across Nestor's head, neck, and shoulders.

Nestor knew that he couldn't keep this kind of fighting up for much longer. Ambrose healed from his blows far too quickly, whereas every blow the vampire landed felt like a sledgehammer pounding into his already battered body. Nestor knew he had to hold on though, and hope that either of his friends could join the fray, or, at the very least, find a way to get Shadow Reaver back into his hands.

Kellen hit Nestor with a hard backhand that rocked the warrior's head against the floor. Nestor felt the room start to spin, and his vision clouded. He knew his jaw was broken, and his mouth was full of blood. Never did the thought of surrender cross his mind. Rather, his thoughts filled with the dark and terrifying images of the city of Tarnath as it burned. Children and their mothers fled into the streets as cruel monsters bellowed out of the homes they came from. Nestor saw valiant men of the city watch mercilessly slaughtered as they tried to protect the citizens in their care. Nestor could feel the heat of the fires on his face and was deafened by the screams of the dying all around him. The terrors his mind brought before him fueled the barbarian's rage, and with a mighty heave, he threw Kellen to one side. Shakily he regained his footing, glaring at his adversary. "Whenever you're ready for another bout," slurred the barbarian through his broken jaw. "If you need a moment to catch your breath, say the word. Want to make this a sporting chance for you."

Kellen's eyes widened in complete shock. "What in Alhambra's Hell is holding you up, Canaith? Tenacity? Pride? Stupidity?"

"One or more of the above. You can be the judge." Hurry up Tyrell, he thought to himself. I can't finish this alone. Nestor's eyes darted momentarily over to Galen. The young thief was motionless in a pool of his own blood. His eyes stared blankly at the barbarian. Nestor quickly said a silent prayer for the boy's soul and squared off again against Kellen.

"You'd have been wiser to let the fall take you, Canaith, for now, you will die slowly and excruciatingly." Kellen moved towards Nestor with inhuman speed, his clawed hands reaching for the warrior's throat.

Suddenly, a searing blast of magical force slammed into Kellen from the side. As Nestor toppled over from the backlash of power, he saw Tyrell standing with his hand outstretched towards the downed vampire. Tyrell strode towards Nestor, offering his hand down to the warrior. So powerful was the magical curing that Tyrell had swept through his body, that not only had he purged his body of Kellen's poisonous mist, but he had reinvigorated himself so that he was as fresh for the fight as if he had just arrived.

"About time you showed up," growled Nestor.

"You look like hell," replied Tyrell.

"Been a rough night. I'll tell you about it later over an ale."

"First round's on me," quipped the mage.

Kellen regained his feet yet again, staring in awe at the two men. "You two are the two most unlikely allies that I've ever had the pleasure to kill."

"We're not dead yet," said Nestor. The barbarian's eyes quickly surveyed the tower floor for the elvensteel blade, Shadow Reaver, but saw no sign of it. Perhaps it had been kicked out of the room during the scuffle.

Kellen arrogantly stretched up to his full height. "For all your struggle and sacrifice, I hope that you find it somewhat frustrating at least that your attacks have done so little damage. It won't take long for all of the minor stings that I've suffered at your hands tonight to heal and be gone."

"The fun is just beginning," said Tyrell. The wizard's mismatched eyes suddenly blazed with magical energy. He held Nestor back with his hand as a noxious green raincloud suddenly materialized above Kellen's head. Ambrose dove forward just as a deluge of sizzling acid burst from the cloud.

Ambrose drew a great wind from the depths of the gorge outside and directed the elemental fury towards the two men. Tyrell, however, was no longer the fledgling wizard who had arrived at Cliffside Keep. The man before Kellen Ambrose now commanded the forces of a master spell thrower. As the gale blew in, Tyrell grabbed the air currents with his own magic, ripping them apart.

"You can't win, Ambrose. I've beaten everything that you have thrown against me. Your reign of darkness is over." Nestor clapped his friend on the shoulder and circled around the vampire. Kellen crouched like a caged animal, looking for somewhere to retreat, but he was given no exit. He knew that he had to fight or die, for there was no prayer for escape.

"To the end, then, gentlemen," the vampire lord hissed. Nestor charged in, knocking Kellen's head back with a ferocious punch. Tyrell loosed a bolt of white-hot fire that struck Kellen squarely in the center of his chest. Ambrose screamed in agony as he was hammered by both flame and fist. He drew upon his magic to boost his own regenerative powers so that the terrible punishment he suffered was at least held to a stalemate. He would not fall so easily.

"For all the innocent people you've hurt...," growled Nestor.

"For all the suffering and misery you have left in your path...," yelled Tyrell.

"We sentence you to death." Shadow Reaver suddenly punched through Kellen's breast. Tyrell and Nestor looked on in surprise to see Galen standing behind the vampire lord. The young thief was broken and bloody, but his eyes burned with the determination to stand here for the end of the task that the three men had set out upon together. Galen collapsed back to the floor as Kellen thrashed around, screaming in mortal agony.

The vampire's defenses were completely shattered as the elvensteel blade burned through his very core. The sword itself began to shriek in triumph as it tore Kellen's life force from his body. As Kellen's magical shields fell, Tyrell's column of fire engulfed Ambrose as well, exploiting with ruthless efficiency the weakness of vampires to flame.

Ambrose collapsed to the floor, ablaze and with the mighty weapon piercing his body. The companions watched as Kellen's skin turned papery like parchment and burned away. Ash filled the room as the vampire's flesh peeled away. Kellen's charred skeleton thrashed weakly on the floor until soon only a fanged skull, obscenely grinning at the three men remained. With a loud clatter, Shadow Reaver fell to the floor, and Kellen Ambrose's ashes scattered into the night air.

Warrior and wizard dashed over to the fallen thief. Tyrell quickly assessed Galen's injuries, but what he found was not comforting. Galen suffered terribly from the wounds he had sustained during his solo battle with Kellen. Truly it was a miracle that the thief wasn't already dead, thought Tyrell. The wizard tried to direct his magic into healing his friend but found the boy's life force spilling out faster than any magic could try to contain it. No matter what he tried, Tyrell knew that there was no way to save Galen's life. Sadly, he looked up at Nestor and shook his head.

"We did it, lad," said the warrior, his voice choked and husky. "You, me, and Tyrell pulled it off. Just like the bastard said we could do. It truly took the three of us to bring the vampire down."

Galen looked first at the warrior then at Tyrell with glassy eyes. "You two look terrible," he gasped. The other men couldn't help but laugh, while tears streamed down their cheeks.

"It's been one of those days, my young friend," said Tyrell. The mage wiped away some of the blood spilling from Galen's mouth away with the edge of his cloak. Galen coughed, and a fresh gout simply restained the space which Tyrell had just cleaned.

"I guess I'm breaking up our little circle," wheezed the thief. "Gods alone know what kind of trouble you two will get into without me around." The thief smiled. "I'm proud to say though that you two, my two dearest friends, are here by my side at the end." Galen grabbed each man by the hand and gave the weakest of squeezes.

Nestor tried to speak, but his words failed him. The big warrior who had faced terrifying horrors, and suffered incredible beatings looked up at Tyrell for help. The wizard simply smiled sadly and put his hand on Galen's shoulder.

"One day our roads will meet again, Galen. For now, the time has come for you to go join your lady again, my friend," said Tyrell. He gave the thief's hand one more gentle squeeze.

Neither man felt the least bit of shame from the hot tears that rolled down their faces as Galen Thale smiled, shuddered, and died.

Tyrell Amalcheal stood before the burned ruins of Kellen Ambrose's townhouse in Tarnath. Fallen timbers thrust into the still smoky air like the ribs of some long dead ancient beast. The wizard took small satisfaction that Kellen's home had not escaped the ravages of the Night of Terror.

Children searched through the rubble of other nearby structures, searching for any trinket or treasure that they might be able to barter for food. So much suffering, thought Tyrell sadly. And for what? The effects of this horror would be felt for some time to come.

The crunching of boots in the ashes turned Tyrell's attention around. Nestor came up and gripped Tyrell's hand in a firm shake. The wizard smiled at the red sash with gold trim that now adorned the warrior's waist and marked him as an officer in the Shadow Lords. "Thought I might find you here."

"I guess I've come full circle." He shifted nervously as Nestor eyed the stuffed knapsack at the wizard's feet.

"So where are you off to next?"

"Anywhere else. Away from here. I need to have a place where I can safely explore these newly found talents I have discovered. Better to find a place of solitude in the event that something runs wild." He looked around again at the hungry children, now chasing after a larger boy who had discovered a burnt apple. "This place has enough to deal with for now without adding the risk of miscast magic." Tyrell looked back at his friend.

"I'm for staying," Nestor answered to the wizard's questioning gaze. "Believe it or not, Lord Commander Knarya has offered me a commission, and the town does need all the help that it can get. I heard that Drayton is organizing a force to lead down into the sewers again just to make sure that all the vampires are cleaned out. You should stay. Go along and help him."

"He has Shadow Reaver. He'll need no other edge than that. Besides, there's nothing left to find. All of Kellen's created minions turned to dust when he died. Drayton will find nothing but piles of ash." The two men stood in silence looking at the townhouse.

"Tyrell, the boy knew the dangers we all faced, and he stood right along beside us to the end. Not all the magic in the world could save him. With his lady gone, the lad's only remaining purpose was for vengeance. He got that and found his peace. He died a true hero, not a common thief."

Tyrell nodded. "Which is precisely why my grief for his death feels all the more proper."

Nestor stared at the wizard then nodded his head. "I suppose that's true," the barbarian said softly. "Swear something to me then, my friend. Swear that this time a year from now, you'll return here so you and I can toast the lad's heroism. He deserves no less a salute than that from us."

"I swear it." The wizard smiled again at his friend, and then hoisted the knapsack over his shoulder. Nestor grabbed the mage in a fierce bear hug, let go after a moment, and then turned towards a group of men who were attempting to pull down a fire damaged wall.

"Nestor," Tyrell called out. The big warrior stopped and turned his head. "Did we manage to prove anything?"

Nestor scratched his beard for a moment in quiet contemplation. "We proved that there truly is honor among thieves." Nestor waved farewell, turning away as he began shouting orders to the work detail.

"I suppose we did," Tyrell said softly. The mage took one last fleeting glance at the ruined townhouse and turned away. As he walked down the soot-filled street, he lifted his face and enjoyed the warmth of the bright sun on his face.